Surfing The Tsunami

SURFING THE TSUNAMI

Phil Woods

Aureus

First Published 2012
©2012 Phil Woods

Phil Woods has asserted the Author's right under the Copyright, Designs and Patents Act 1988 to be identified as Author of this Work.

This publication is printed on paper derived from sustainable forests. The cover is made from recycled material.

ISBN 978-1-899750-44-3

Printed in Great Britain.

A catalogue record for this book is available from the British Library.

Aureus Publishing Limited
Castle Court
Castle-upon-Alun
St. Bride's Major
Vale of Glamorgan
CF32 0TN

Tel: (01656) 880033 Fax: (01656) 880033
Int. tel: +44 1656 880033 Int. fax: +44 1656 880033

E-mail: sales@aureus.co.uk
www.aureus.co.uk

Before I was five years old,
my Mother always told me
that happiness was the key to life.

When I went to school,
they asked me what I wanted to be when I grew up -
I wrote down "Happy".

They told me I didn't understand the assignment.
I told them they didn't understand life.

John Lennon

1

I knew it was going to be a big accident long before I hit the wall. I'd ridden past it on that crumbling coast road so many times, assuming it was just a grassy bank, but on impact, it turned out to be weed strewn stone. I thought this wasn't the ideal way to find that out as my shoulder was punched out of its socket by the rock, and that drowning immediately after a motorcycle crash was a pretty unusual way to go too. Looking back, the crash probably saved my life.

The size of the giant black wave barrelling across the bay - where there should have been a sapphire blue ocean - had drawn my eyes from the road and stunned, held them long enough for the Honda to just drift off line. The sandy verge sucked and clawed at the front wheel and the bike yawed sideways, and into deeper trouble. I cracked open the throttle, leant right back and pulled on the bars, trying to lighten the front end enough to get some steering back, and somehow managed to pull the old girl back onto the hot, pockmarked tarmac.

A mile or so back down this coast road, the giant tsunami had hit the fishing port first, and being Poya (full moon) day, a public holiday, all but two of the town's one hundred and fifty three fishing trawlers were at anchor. As the wall of stinking black water overwhelmed the coast, it ripped the entire fleet out of the harbour, scattering them like toys in a toddler's tantrum. Two of them had made it this far north, spinning around the top of the massive, towering waters as they hit the reef just off-shore. The unseen mass of coral tugged at the giant swell from below, turning it into more of a wave, slowing it down a bit too, but not enough to stop the water consuming the stretch of brilliant white sand to my left, and it just kept coming, about forty feet high and ashen black, quickly engulfing the narrow coast road just ahead of me.

Getting the bike back under control left me with a big, heart hammering adrenalin rush and even less room for manoeuvre than there could have been. There was only thick Sri Lankan jungle on my right, and a wall of black water ahead, cascading across what should have been a thirty foot drop to the beach on my left. Up ahead I spotted a small track heading inland that maybe I could reach, but even with the wire tight I lost that little race, the ocean outran the sprinting bike, and I just ran out of room. The Honda fired me out of the saddle like a rodeo rider when we hit the stone bank, and I ricocheted off the top of the wall up into the air as the water engulfed the road, spinning me round high up inside the maelstrom of its ashen blackness. It tasted bitter and as bad as it looked, and felt harder than the wall when it hit me, but a cubic yard of seawater weighs a ton, and contains enough deuterium to make a bicycle, an utterly useless statistic that just popped into my head and really hacked me off, because I didn't want to die thinking about useless crap like that.

The gigantic wave tore inland, and dragged me deeper as it consumed everything in its path, more powerful than anything nature had produced for centuries. I traded my futile struggle for a few more seconds of holding my breath then suddenly, I was lifted up from below, free of the grasp of the water and numbed, back in sunlight for surreal seconds, surfing the tsunami somehow, belly boarding on a big section of corrugated metal roof beneath me, looking down on the jungle canopy being engulfed just ahead, and the calm emerald green of the mountains' tea plantations in the distance.

I sucked in air, as part of the wreckage of one of the fishing trawlers somersaulted past in a cloud of billowing orange nets, clipped the section of roof I was clinging to and pitched me straight off. Something heavy hit me back under the water, knocking the big breath I'd taken straight out of me, and my mouth snapped open in a silent scream of pain as my left leg was ripped sideways, dislocating the hip. Thick black ashen foetid water inflated my lungs like balloons, and my terror fuelled fight for survival became detached withdrawal from conscious life.

And in that moment I knew she was lost to me forever, knew I'd never watch her gently scoop her hair behind her ears again, knew I'd never need to find the courage to say the three words that I'd wanted to, since the day we'd met. I'd known immediately, with absolute certainty, before we'd even spoken. And I saw her smiling face in the deep blackness that beckoned me as I said a little prayer; please keep her heart beating, somewhere, safe.

2

Mongoose had become quite a friend over the months I'd been living at the Ranasinghes' guest house, set in shady tropical gardens at the top of a hill, on the coastal road which wound past it, and on down to the busy little town and fishing harbour below.

He was shy and so reclusive it took me a few weeks to even work out what actually lived in the sandy burrow tucked behind one of the big brick posts. Their patchy remnants of render revealed the faded sunburnt ochre of handmade bricks, that held in place the squealing rusty old hinges of the tall, white iron entrance gates.

The hinges never got oiled, as they announced arrivals and departures equally effectively between dawn and ten at night, when the gates they supported were unlocked, the hours all decent members of society were abroad. Well, I was abroad, rather indecent and enjoyed the very late and the very early hours. Mongoose however, turned out to be even more a creature of the night than I, although it has to be said, for entirely different reasons. Patrolling the dense undergrowth of the fertile guesthouse gardens in a nocturnal quest for snakes wasn't something I was desperately keen to try. And I was sure Mongoose wouldn't have been enthralled with the prospect of spending time with the Arrack-swilling ne'er-do-wells of the town's crumbling, nefarious, mens' drinking club.

On the night we met, I was locked out as usual, and, not for the first time either, had lost my footing clambering down the inside of the ninety year old wrought ironwork, before falling in a heap on the long grass at the side of the stony drive with enough of a thump to momentarily silence even the busily chattering cicadas. The moon was only a quarter or so away from fulfilling itself yet again and its cold, blue light illuminated the sleek and silken trot of a mongoose, which my fall had stopped dead in its tracks. It dropped a very poorly, slim and deadly Banana snake from its mouth and looked me over, without fear, wondering, I guess, what its neighbour was doing sitting on its front door.

I woke gently in the soft light of a cool moist dawn breaking and entering, stealing the night from my little first floor flat overlooking beautiful verdant gardens, wild in places, tamed in others. The strident and melodic morning calls of creatures of the day began to mute the more cacophonous tropical nightlife that had sent me to sleep, in the sticky humid warmth of another night at this travellers' rest. I spent a while in that place between sleep and waking, clinging on to a dream about my journey here, that was evaporating with the night.

I'd kept going south until I'd reached the ocean and just couldn't go any further. Unless on a boat. I'd peeled the back of my damp cotton shirt off a plastic seat, and, hunched and stiff, stepped off the battered old red bus at its last stand. I hadn't even asked where the end of the line was, when I'd paid for the ticket a long way back; the driver had disappeared along with all the other passengers, so I guessed that was that, and got off.

Stretching myself back upright after the long cramped journey, I walked past a small mosque, a childrens' playground next to a tiny cottage hospital, overlooking a lake, covered in the green pads and big, fat, vibrant pink waxy blooms of water lilies. Bright green dragonflies were busy in staccato hunting. The narrow tarmac lane became a track, climbing past a dusty oval cricket pitch, where two goats were busy shaving the wicket, the bare sandy outfield boundaried by a girls' high school on one side, a grey prison wall, topped with razor wire on another, before it finally reached a small cliff top naval station, perched high on the southernmost tip of this beautiful island.

The ocean below me was the colour of a kingfisher's wing under the lighter blue sky of its egg, the white surf scurrying up creamy sand beaches on deserted crescent bays, fading hazily from sight into sea spray and far distance. Below me, a dozen or so incongruous brown cows nuzzled at a trail of high tide flotsam, two black crows hopped from back to back, searching for insects hidden in hair and hide. How now? Five degrees north of the equator, there was only ocean from here, all the way south to

Antarctica, more than half a planet away. The thought of all that water, and all the miles I'd covered let my tiredness loose and I worked my way down to the beach, propping myself up against a row of grey plaster elephants' heads, embedded in the low, whitewashed balustrades of a neat, open air, triangular Buddhist shrine.

One of the big blue-black birds perched on a bovine backbone removed a juicy fat white warble fly larva from beneath the hide, which wriggled in a vain attempt to escape the wicked pointed black beak. One deft flick sealed its fate. An enormous royal blue butterfly with a long yellow tail, bounced towards me, riding the gentle sea breeze and settled on some sea grape blossom, scratching a living at the top of the beach where I sat. My head nodded forward until a little while later, under the brim of my hat, two cheap blue plastic flip-flops containing thin brown feet connected to skinny legs appeared. Looking up, I was confronted by the flapping orange robes, furled black umbrella and matching briefcase of a Buddhist monk, peering through two thick, bottle bottom lenses of ancient spectacles, which enlarged his intelligent myopic eyes to absurd proportions. White stubble on his head suggested he must have been in his seventies, maybe more.

"How do you do?" he asked in that unusual tone of voice that suggested he really wanted to know. In an effort to reciprocate this kindness, I didn't tell him.

"What are you doing here? Are you Buddhist?"

"No, Just resting a while. Thinking of staying here for a bit; it's a beautiful place."

"I am Buddhist clergy. And if you give me a present you can walk with me. I will meet you with Mr. Ranasinghe. He is a good fellow, with a quiet place you can stay."

He was right, the monk. I took a shine to Mr. Ranasinghe the moment we met, cut a rental deal and installed myself in the flat, which was flooding with light as the sun scythed its way through the cloudy mist of the dawn, completing its job, chasing the shadows of the night from the gardens below me. I pursued several dozy mosquitoes, bloated on the dinner I'd provided, around the inside of my night time net, trapping two inside an old pineapple jam jar, kept next to my pillow for this very purpose.

A vivid scarlet crested woodpecker appeared on a teak tree trunk outside, and clamping itself to the bark with scaly claws, beat out a funky rhythm, scattering the grubs and insects in the bark. It picked them off one by one with an amazingly long, darting tongue, while the sunshine brightened the colours of the plants enough to dazzle my wakening eyes. Every tint, shade and hue of green in this variegation, provided the background for rainbow blooms limbering open for the day.

A grey-green, muscular monitor lizard swaggered past below, joints arthritis-stiff, body still cold. It settled itself serenely in a strategic pool of sunlight, just a few feet away below the little balcony at the top of my stairs, blinking and angling its head towards the warming rays. Unseen on early morning patrol, Mr. Ranasinghe disturbed the birds, clapping his hands to frighten off a final few fruit bats malingering from their midnight feast in his breadfruit tree, and they joined dozens of birds of all shapes and hues, including the woodpecker, scattering to different perches, calling their warnings. Somewhere, a big, overripe coconut crashed to earth from high above, splintering leaves and branches en route, chased by a bushy stripe-tailed squirrel scampering down the trunk, pursuing a breakfast nut bonanza.

And the monk had rifled through my bag like a child at a tombola, relieving me of a Dutch murder mystery paperback, the price for his guidance, which he added to five other books tucked under his arm, neatly tied together with thin coir string. I was sorry to see it go, the characters inside the pages were old friends. As we walked along a grassy path overlooking the ocean in the bright evening sunshine, he told me of a young Englishman he'd met recently, the favoured son of very wealthy Londoners. He'd left his family distraught, renouncing and disposing of all his worldly goods, including an annual six-figure trust fund income, before he'd joined a Buddhist monastery only a few miles away from us; wooden bowl, umbrella, robe and sandals now his only possessions. His father was mortified that his business footsteps would never be followed. He couldn't come to terms with the boy's decision and they had argued, without resolve, before he'd left. But two years into the young man's training, quite by chance and to his delight, his father had discovered, carefully stored in a lock up garage in north London, his son's blue and gold Subaru Impreza. Some things are so difficult to give up. I had a secret little stash myself.

And I thought about smoking a cigarette, a long, black, sweet Russian Sobraine as a darting, furry flash of brown through the bushes was Mongoose, unusually late back from its nightly duties, our serpent sentry patrolling through the night. We became good friends.

I sang Lennon's curse to Sir Walter Raleigh in my little kitchen - he really was such a stupid git. But he did make good bikes. The whitewashed walls were criss-crossed with a road network I'd drawn in pencil, which fol-

lowed the regular routes of the big brown ants that had colonised one corner of the bright white room. Roundabouts, motorways, junctions of all
types were inscribed on the walls. At various points of interest - more often
than not, the mountain section of the Isle of Man TT race course, which
climbed over the hotplate, skirting a handy shelf - I placed the jam jar
upside down on a match, leaving just enough room for an inquisitive ant
to enter, but not enough for a less intellectually endowed mosquito to
escape. This turned the flying foes I feared, Anopheles Gambiae, the size
of a grape pip and the world's biggest killer, into road kill, small reward for
the ants' diligent scavenging duties, which reduced my housework substantially. I'd watched the colony with growing respect, once through a
magnifying glass, *a la* Dr. Mengele, as they took on a scorpion on the
veranda floor and won, dismantling what they could; gruesomely, some
parts were even removed pre-death, before the carapace was transported,
coffin bearers at a funeral, to its darkened grave beneath the floorboards of
this first storey, via London's pencilled, orbital M25.

Throughout nature, ants have the biggest brain in relation to bodyweight; these guys were such courageous fighters, independent, but worked
hard for the good of their society for which they would, unhesitatingly, lay
down their lives. They were great trackers and brilliant hunters, dedicated
and careful parents, inquisitive and fearless. And they drove on the left.

The kettle was ready for the dark fermented leaves of Broken Orange
Pekoe, steam from the kettle authentically replicating the swirling mist that
shrouds the mountain section of the world's greatest race circuit, that
courses its way around Snaefell's peak, overlooking six kingdoms. The
early happy sounds of immaculate, white uniformed, red beribboned plait-
ed schoolgirls passed by on the road outside, lifting my spirits as the full
daytime jungle orchestra swung into tropical mood. I opened the door to
a kitchen cupboard where I kept a loaf of bread, to find myself eyeball to
antennae with a big brown cockroach, who had apparently spent the night
tunnelling through the centre of my breakfast. I grabbed the loaf, knocked
the cockroach scuttling into a saucepan, and gave it a flying lesson off the
balcony. With the snap accuracy one often achieves without calculated
aim, it arced through the air, rolling and tumbling as it fell to earth, landing helplessly upside down, as it happened, just a few inches in front of the
monitor lizard. Apart from revolving its articulated eyeballs into focus, the
lizard remained unflapped by this unexpected arrival from above and, with
flicking tongue, scooped the beast into its waiting jaws.

The victim's wiggling antennae protruded briefly between grey scaly lips, but, like the arms of a drowning man appearing above the surface, soon disappeared below without trace. The lizard blinked, finally, it seemed, in surprise, gave a final munch, a flick of the tongue, a lick of the lips, then resumed its reverie, with a brand new mystery to contemplate, in the rising heat.

With everything else scoffing, I was starting to feel left out, so salvaged a couple of untunnelled slices and one crust from the loaf, toasting them on the disc of aluminium that sat atop the little single electric cooking ring, turning them after only a few seconds, nicely browned. Meanwhile, my flatmates, the ants, performed amazing feats of strength, hoisting crust crumbs twice their size or more, carting them off around the gyratory, temporarily jam-jar jam free, back to HQ, between twin-scythed jaws. I exercised mine rather less strenuously on the toast, buttered with ginger-spiced lime marmalade, sinking molars through the crunchy exterior into the fluffy white warmth inside. Hoping it was cockroach-shit-free, I pondered the mystery of bread's popularity in a climate that can't grow wheat, yet where free food falls off trees and hits you on the head - occasionally fatally in the case of coconuts - every time you take a walk through the jungle. Still, this is a country that only recently stopped blowing up its coral reefs to extract lime for the cement industry, where a twenty five year old civil war had destroyed so much and achieved nothing. Tourism still born, still further, with every bomb reported in the Western press. The LTTE - the Liberation Tamil Tigers of Eelam – fighting for 'freedom' for over a quarter of a century. Tens of thousands of adults and generations of children had only ever lived in a war zone on this tear shaped island off the southern coast of India. On a map it looks like the subcontinent is weeping a vast salty teardrop back into the Indian Ocean. Which it has every right to do.

I did come across one holidaymaker further back up the coast, who'd left Seattle many years before and worked his way around the globe, finally settling in Kyoto. He made a living, and ends meet, teaching English and collecting up the two year old consumer goods his Japanese neighbours left out on garbage days, because they were out of date. He recounted a recent Christmas visit home, where the prodigal son was introduced to new additions to his family, and his old peer group and he told me,

"After fifteen years away, I was surprised how easy it was to fit back into my life there. But I wondered how many of them would fit into mine?"

And I'd felt my journey was finally over when I'd settled into a lazy routine here, not believing for one moment that it had, in fact, only just begun.

The accelerating grating sound of another suicidal tile sliding off the roof of our neighbouring house, was followed by doodlebug silence before its shattering crash when it hit the ground, termites turning the rafters of the huge, deserted, ramshackle old colonial building into gruyere cheese. To one side, in a barely habitable outhouse, lived the lonely old survivor of a once rich family, now fallen on hard times. She was fed and cared for in her dotage by a nearby Christian convent, through a legacy bequest from a distant relative. My favourite nun, immaculately dressed in cavernous black and white habit, was gliding her way there with effortless grace, carrying a morning meal, wrapped in white muslin.

She looked up at my greeting as usual, and the light of inner peace, joy and happiness danced in her brown eyes as they met mine, before propriety stole the moment and gaze was curtailed to glance. She slipped through a gap in the wall and the big silver cross suspended from her neck by a thick chain caught the sunlight. And I wondered, if she ever spoke; and if Jesus Christ had been hanged, whether Christians would have worn a scaffold around their necks, or a noose, and if Judas Iscariot had actually been on their side all along.

An ancient, creaking wooden cart appeared, pulled up the hill and around the corner by two enormous water buffalo, each pair of black horns spanning over six feet. The driver swung his beasts of burden across the mounting traffic of passers-by. They parted the conga crocodile of shimmering white uniformed schoolgirls, snaking under black umbrellas next to trishaws, bicycles, tuk-tuks, buses, lorries, cars ranging from old to ancient, goats, and a mottled cow that had decided the middle of the road was the best place to lie down and clean out its nostrils, with its big black damp tongue; quite a trick.

A plump, bare-chested, bespectacled and slightly cross-eyed Mr. Ranasinghe, resplendent in striped sarong, swung open his screeching gates in a bit of a hurry, as the buffalo didn't seem too worried about plodding straight through them and on up the drive. They came to rest under the shade of the vast, tall mango tree, its dark green foliage heaving with hundreds of fruits, most not yet quite ripe, but ready for harvest. The monitor lizard, disturbed, waddled off into the undergrowth with a more fluid gait than when it had arrived, whilst Mongoose kept a keen, beady eye on all the action from the safety of his burrow.

Mr. Ranasinghe, arms crossed and contemplative, rocked gently from one sandaled foot to the other, as he surveyed the fruit-picking task ahead with the cart driver and I joined them, picking up a few bruised drops from beneath the tree and made friends with the buffalo. I bent towards them, sniffing and exhaling loudly through my nose, arms and mangoes out of sight behind my back in regulation bovine greeting manner. Steamy dank ruminative breath came back and I wondered if they smelt limes on mine, as open-palmed, I offered the fruit to these huge beasts, one black, one brown, both good healthy specimens, who crunched up the light green fruit, syrupy orange goo drooling from their lips. I scratched them behind the little bony lump between their horns, while they happily munched away. For a while, they took a back seat to the flood of cheap reconditioned tractors from Europe which started to appear in the island a few years ago, until it was realised that the rice paddies were compacting under the weight of the heavy machines, they didn't provide a free fertilising service either and the timeless image of men steering ploughs pulled by water buffalo was restored to the rural landscape.

"Want a hand Mr. Ranasinghe?" I asked, just as several more tiles dropped from the roof of the Dutch house, this time disturbed by the commotion of a troupe of twenty or so monkeys arriving to perch on the few remaining ridge tiles. Several known local offenders leered at us from their vantage point.

"Look at them up there, the blasted fellows are back to steal my mangoes." the proprietor said, jabbing an accusatory finger at the roof, where various unsavoury toilet duties were now being performed, along with other, even more distasteful and unmentionable personal activities.

"Look's like they've been recruiting." I said, nodding towards the rooftop, where numbers of the mangy, brown scavenging miscreants were steadily increasing - usually a very bad sign.

"It's time to try out the new weapon then is it?" I asked.

"But it is not quite finished, and it needs proper testing." said Mr. Ranasinghe, who appeared to have entered into a staring contest with the gang's ringleader, a big, tough brutish male, with an insouciant, disdainful manner, who was easily identifiable by his size and a rather nasty case of piles. Too much forbidden fruit.

"This looks bad to me Mr. Ranansinghe." I said, "I'd better nip down to the town and get that ammo we ordered, it should be in by now - if they're going to attack we'll just have to run with what we've got."

The wonderful sounds of childrens' laughter brimmed over the walls of the primary school at the top of the hill as I toddled down past the corrugated iron cinema, which was featuring an early James Bond movie when I took shelter there one night, during a heavy rainstorm. I shouldn't have bothered because the roof leaked so badly it didn't make much difference to how wet I got, and the seats were infested with every bloodsucking, biting and itch-generating insect known to mankind, as my buttocks found out to their cost. It was as hot as a rent boys' Femidom in there too, as the whole place was sealed tight - apart from the gaping holes in the roof - doors locked to prevent the army of interlopers outside from seeing one iota of 007.

It must have been over a hundred and ten degrees in there by the intermission and I failed to attend the second reel, having repaired to the bar round the back, which had a refrigerator full of the necessary amber coolant.

Even this early in the day, there was already a queue of nervous, thin men with hunted faces who had let the local coconut whisky get-the better of them, all waiting for the cinema bar to open and a chance to stop the early morning shakes. Along with producing some of the worst whiskey, Sri Lanka has the highest level of alcoholism in the world, a fact that somehow doesn't add up. Shouldn't it be the Scottish Highlands, or Cognac?

Next door, the tyre repair shop was hard at work inside, on a wheel from a big yellow bus outside, rows of resigned brown faces of packed passengers still on board watched me pass, all tilted to one side, supported by an industrial-size trolley jack. The Betel nut seller sat behind her little wooden rack which contained a neat row of ready made green-leaved parcels for her morning trade, each customers' particular mix of nut, spice and lime paste prepared with practised ease. She stopped her own chewing, and beckoned me over, entreating me with a welcoming grin of bright red-stained tongue and blackened gums, sporting rotten brown teeth. She held out a free sample of the gruesome mixture, proffered in an upturned, soap dodging hand, hoping I'd finally sample the dubious pleasure of her narcotic product. I declined for the umpteenth time, with a nod of the head (the local 'no' [undulate your head from side to side for 'yes']) and a tip of the hat. The last thing I needed was yet another vice.

Shoe repair man, puerile umbrella specialist and a nut and pulse seller completed the row of street traders before the communal water standpipe, where a very young girl was filling earthenware pots, while a puppy, its mother, two crows and another cow took advantage of the overflow, overseen by a smartly brown uniformed guard, leaning at the same angle as his shotgun against the wall of the Peoples' Bank, nervously pulling on a cigarette. An insecure security guard. Good time for a bank raid.

There were shouts and cries ahead of me as the hill turned and flattened out into the main street proper, where the giant banyan tree drooped its roots to earth from high branches above, giving cool shade to a big circular crowd, crying high with the unmistakeable sounds of bloodlust. I was tall enough to see the serious fight going on in the dust and grit of a makeshift roadside ring. The protagonist with the gold satin shorts moved in close to deliver a vicious uppercut to the jaw, just as his opponent ducked and swayed sinuously sideways, the punch finding only thin air, throwing its owner off balance. Seizing its chance with lightning speed, the dark hooded fighter struck, clamping its victim's arm between mottled brown, killer's jaws. The big King Cobra held its grip long enough to deliver its poison to seal the little Macaque monkey's fate, before rearing back, tongue flicking, cold skin glistening, black eyes glittering. There was a big, simultaneous intake of breath from the crowd at this fatal blow and believing it was all over, a dozen or so commuters hurried away in the direction of the bus station. But the Macaque, teeth bared, mounted a new attack, and charged forward, crouched on all fours, then stood upright, popped the serpent's head back with a dexterous short left jab, before throwing a perfect right cross to the snake's lower jaw, snapping its mouth shut with a loud crack.

I jumped onto a low-slung branch of the Banyan to get a better view. The Cobra, now hurt, swayed back, hissing loudly and opened its hood wider. The monkey, unperturbed by the threat, was growing in confidence and with the crowd now roaring its support, moved in closer, swinging a wild left hook that missed again, but with fancy footwork, threw caution to the wind and lunged, grabbing at the Cobra's throat, which weaved and struck back, frenziedly trying to lock its jaws into the Macaque's armpit, with two or three savage bites with what was becoming rapidly apparent, were toothless gums. With the snake grimly hanging on, the monkey calmly picked up a length of the cold black body and with its own set of vicious, sharp yellow teeth, just what the Cobra seemed to be missing, executed a nasty looking bite of its own. The Cobra thrashed around in pain, knocking the lid from a big wicker basket as the animals' owner, the snake charmer, whose travelling show had got completely out of hand, waded in with a long stick to break up the fight, just as it was getting interesting. The cheers of the crowd had turned to boos at this party-pooping, then screams, as a dozen or so assorted snakes slithered out of the basket and writhed towards them in a massed escape attempt. The snake charmer abandoned his peacekeeping efforts to round up the escapees, and the fight broke out once more to even greater cheers from the section of the

13

crowd which wasn't beating a hasty retreat from the advancing snakes.

The Cobra, looking perplexed as to why his colleague wasn't writhing on the ground in ready-meal death throes, lunged again at its panting foe who was ready this time, and, redolent of Cassius Clay's despatch of Brian London, landed a rapid combination of punches to the snake's head, sending the crowd into delirious rapture. Cascades of coins rained into the ring as the unarmed Cobra, which had sensed this was not going to be his day, snaked back into the basket to fight again, another. The snake charmer closed the lid behind him and on the rest of his recaptured staff, all now present and correct, if rather battle scarred. The Macaque, having taken one last bite out of the Cobra's retreating tail, like a boxer celebrating an easy win, raised its arms aloft, and chattering away, paraded around the ring, soaking up the crowds' adulation. They became even more generous, cascading additional coins into a little wooden collection box the snake charmer had quickly thrust into the monkey's hands, sensing a profit opportunity from this brand new, barnstorming act his performers had accidentally put on for the crowd.

The Macaque jumped from shoulder to shoulder, the little wooden box filling up with money. As he moved through my part of the dispersing crowd, he took a flying leap onto the top of a red backpack on the shoulders of a tall, slim white girl I hadn't noticed, standing in the middle of the crowd. She turned in surprise, laughter playing across slim lips, neat white teeth; she had a bit of trouble getting a fat brass five-rupee coin into the brimming box. The Macaque snatched it, and scampered off to its master who swapped the takings bonanza for a small sweet banana. Everybody was happy. Except the Cobra. And I thought what a shame it was that Mongoose wasn't there to play the winner.

The crowd had quickly dispersed into the bustle of the town and hanging on to one of the liana like roots, I watched from the shadow of my low perch as the girl took off a straw hat, put her back pack on the ground and shook loose thick auburn hair, cut short for the heat, with coppered highlights that sparkled in the bright shafts of dappled light shining through the banyan's vast canopy. She wore a raw matt black cotton vest, cut off at a bare midriff, sari style, above baggy silk trousers of blue, soft pink and gold. High cheekbones and a pretty, pert ski slope nose were dusted with freckles, softened by a light golden tan. Strong chin below a full mouth. Long, delicate neck.

Her neat black Ray-Bans swung towards me as I jumped down from the tree.

She took a pace backwards, startled, and said in English, with a gentle Dutch accent,

"Who the Hell are you, Tarzan?"

"Er, no, sorry to surprise you like that." I said, and introduced myself, holding out a hand which she took in hers, cool, soft, feminine strength and firm.

"I just got in on the bus. My name's Marian." she said. "Is that how you say it? In, then on?"

"Yes. In on. Strange but true. Not many people make it this far South."

She took off her glasses and warm, friendly humanity shone from deep, grey-green eyes and I felt a little lurch inside me.

"I'm looking for a room, I tried a couple of places down on the beach but they're full, where are you staying?"

"It's a little guesthouse at the top of the hill as you go out of town. You'd have passed it on the bus. It's good, clean and cheap and they're sort of little flats, so you can shop and cook if you want to, but I eat with the family mostly. Great curries, lots of fish, vegetables from the garden and the best dhal and poppadoms you'll ever taste."

"Well, that sounds great, lead me to it." she said with another wide smile, wiping delicate beads of sweat above her upper lip with a slim strong forearm, dusted with little blond hairs, a tiny lone mole on paler, porcelain skin on the side of a wrist. I imagined, stunned at myself, what it would be like to kiss it. I tried to pull my slack-jawed self together and said,

"I've got a little errand to run at the hardware store over there." nodding across the road. "Then I'll take you up there; you'll like it, I'm sure."

And we walked back up the hill together, hot sun already making the tarmac sticky underfoot and as we talked, I stole more glances at this lovely girl. The betel nut seller ignored her throng of customers to give us a long twice over as we passed, the brown parcel of Chinese fireworks from the hardware store tucked under my arm, and I realised how different I felt going up the hill, to how I'd felt going down it. A bit like Janet and John. Nothing like a boxing match, no matter how bizarre, to liven one up a bit and somehow, inside, I had a feeling I already knew this stranger beside me.

The thought was stillborn though, because as we turned the corner at the top of the hill, primal screams pierced the air above the sound of the passing traffic. This morning of violence was about to escalate into war.

3

Sunburn dragged me back to consciousness, automated self-preservation overriding my battered body's shutdown. But it was the searing pain in my hip, and from the shoulder that had hit the wall, combined with convulsive vomiting and burning lungs that quickly diverted my attention from the scorching skin. Vision from one eye was blurred, from the other, nearly closed and swollen, minimal. In fact, there didn't seem to be a part of me that didn't hurt, except my left leg, which was numb and lifeless, hanging in mid-air from the dislocated hip, like a side of pork from a butcher's hook. The taste in my mouth and throat from the vomit and the water I'd ingested was of acid, foetid bile and salty ash.

I was wedged in a big Frangipani tree, where it split into three at the top of the main trunk. It had been stripped of every leaf and flower to my level, maybe thirty feet up, and I'd been strained out of the water rushing through it, like plankton in a whale's baleen. My head was thumping and spinning with the whirling pits; like I'd drunk far too much and been mixing my drinks, but with a simultaneous major hangover too. I could move my left arm, but it was pretty weak from my shoulder-charging the wall during my ejection from the Honda. I remembered feeling the shoulder relocate during my pitifully hopeless, frenzied attempt at swimming under the water.

Both of my right limbs were wrapped tight in a piece of bright orange fishing net and I started to wriggle, trying to disentangle myself. There was a big piece of masonry suspended in a knot of netting below me, which was pulling it tight, pinning me down on the branch, and I spent quite a while trying to untangle the nylon mess and dislodge it, without success. I was weak and faint, but aware enough to know I had to get out of the sun, out of the tree and inland onto higher ground, away from the ocean, as quickly as possible. The effort made me dizzy and sick on nothing but bile and blackened, watery sand again, but each purge was helping, and the image of a pendulum popped into my head. I swung the net below me until its arc was big enough, and a couple of small tugs steered the lump of rendered brick into the trunk of the tree. The impact broke it clean in half, snapped some of the netting and suddenly it tore free, dropping into what looked like a large plate of brown cod's roe in a hollow dip in the ground below me. Apart from some pins and needles as they caught up with my circulation, with the netting looser, I wiggled my toes and drummed on the smooth bark with my fingers and both my right leg and arm seemed OK.

I gingerly touched a lump on the back of my skull bigger than a duck's egg, thickly caked in dried blood and I was bleeding freely from a gash on my cheek, onto the bark of the hefty branch. The blood was coagulating on top of a layer of stinking, brown-black, ashy slime. What felt like a broken nose had been clicking and moving around with each retch. My throat, lungs, mouth, nostrils and exposed skin were all on fire, and I was struggling to find any reason to remain conscious. The painless comfort of blackness beckoned, and I wavered in its twilight for quite a while, with only *déjà vu* for company.

Even with the dried slime caking my skin I was still burning up, and knew I had to get into some shade. With both arms free, I managed to get most of the netting off me, and had started to focus better with the one eye that was open. As I looked around, warm syrupy water trickled out of my right ear and I realised I'd been deafened too, ears clogged up with the same sticky paste that covered everything around and below me. The sludge must have been putting pressure on my inner ear too, affecting my balance and causing the dizziness, because my head began to clear quite quickly. I'd been looking at the cod's roe again and with improving faculties, managed to make out what the odd shapes were below me. This was all the confirmation I needed that I had, in fact, died in the water after all, and wasn't surprised that my first choice destination under such circumstances had been declined. My heart tried to beat its way out of my head with a hammer, and a big new wave of nausea ran right through me. I retched, violently this time, my stomach empty, but rapidly filling up with a tightening knot of dread. Just a little thin bile and enough sand for me to chew on trickled out of the corner of my mouth, as I swallowed a despairing sob.

The physical effort of the convulsion had tensed my body, arching my back like a hissing cat, and with a sound like a 't' bone torn out of a steak, the top of my left femur sprang back into its socket with an agonising rip. The pain was immense, hot and fiery, and as the sciatic nerve snapped back into its rightful place, every muscle in the leg went out of control with cramp, the limb twisted like a corkscrew and my foot, for thankfully, only a few excruciating seconds, pointed backwards. I screamed with the pain like a stuck pig and my nose began bleeding so heavily, I choked on the blood.

The big temple flower tree that had survived the onslaught grew on rising ground that had slowed the tsunami's all consuming advance. I was around five hundred yards inland from the malevolent threat of an iridescent and placid sea that sparkled innocently away to the western horizon. I didn't want to be here, and I wished I could follow the sun on its slow descent; two thirds high in the sky made it two-ish in the afternoon. It seemed the huge lump of ocean that had Hoovered up the Honda and I, had deposited me about three quarters of the way through its journey tearing inland, flattening and uprooting everything in its path, save for really mature trees like this one used to the coastal monsoon storms, strong and pliable enough to withstand its anger. The pins and needles were fading, feeling was teasing back into my left leg and the blood from my nose and cheek was slowing to a trickle.

My left ear popped, which also cleared more of the sludge out of my nostrils, along with the clots. The first clear sounds I'd heard since early morning were human voices in terrible distress drifting towards me, along with the smell of black smoke from a column rising in the centre of the remnants of the shattered village that surrounded me. The vision from my open eye was improving rapidly now, along with my cognitive function. The old crash helmet I'd been wearing must have been torn off at some point; how much protection it gave me I'll never know, but either way, I realised my head must have taken several heavy blows.

Half a dozen houses stood at the highest point I could see, but elsewhere only sections of the strongest built walls of houses remained standing. Most had been reduced to ground level. A couple of hundred yards to my right, a woman in a rich dark red dress, torn at the shoulder, sat amongst rubble. The rusty, twisted reinforcing rods of a once flat roof grew at crazy angles around her, stripped of the concrete casing that had entombed them. Plumbing hung from some of the masonry remains, dribbling thick brown fluid into the twisting rivulets and remaining eddies of black salt water below, still retreating from its inland invasion. Her head was bowed and held in her hands as she rocked, in shock, gently from side to side. A middle aged man, naked, except for a ragged vest, wild eyes streaming tears, walked through the destruction on what must have once been a path, his lips moving rapidly with silent words, arms wide, downward pointing in supplication. In one hand, was a child's white school shoe. Half of a jagged solid concrete gatepost, wrought iron gate crumpled and askew, said Hotel, part of the 'H' absent, the premises it advertised, completely missing.

A row of telephone poles lay at crazy angles further up towards the higher ground, where a weakening dog was struggling vainly to escape from wires trapping its hind legs. Sparks and smoke crackled from a mains transformer on the top of a wooden pole, which was lying in a pool of water and everywhere there was debris; of all shapes and sizes, natural and man-made. Taller palms, upright and untouched topped the ridge, but the lush tropical vegetation that normally surrounded everything here was entirely absent, apart from a smattering of uprooted trees, and a few bushes lying on their sides, like forgotten teaspoons in an emptied sink. A large, six-man outrigger canoe pierced the side of what must have been a substantial house, overlooking the bulk of the village below it. Here, lay only a patchwork of foundations, the standing shards of walls, large slabs of concrete reinforcing and big barnacled boulders dredged from the deep of the seabed. They were all too heavy for the water's slow retreat, that had eventually followed the ocean's headlong rush inland, to have carried them back.

I'd been swept inland from the road, along with the rest of the traffic on the arterial route that follows the coastline and most of it was intact, although big sections were missing in places where the water had got underneath it. What must have been a bridge over a small river outlet was missing. Wrecked, overturned vehicles littered the area, cars like upturned beetles, and a dozen or so tuk-tuks, one upright, seemingly undamaged, apart from a smashed windscreen, was neatly parked, but on the concrete first floor of a building's skeletal remains. The only truly recognisable building left was a small Buddhist temple just a hundred yards or so away, the tree I was in must have supplied the temple with its garland flowers. A red fifty-seater bus was beached up against the temple, one side of it had opened up like a sardine tin. It had come to rest on a big, solid stone image of Buddha, whose head and shoulders were visible, neat black hair, pink skin and orange robe, and it looked like he was sitting inside the bus, introspectively gazing past me towards the ocean, through one of the cracked windows. It was a fine piece of work, the sculptor had found the right balance between aloof enlightenment and gentle humour. But it was wasted amongst the bodies of the thirty or more drowned passengers surrounding the effigy.

I turned my head away from the appalling scene and followed his gaze far away to the horizon and wondered when the ocean's Mr Hyde was going to make another appearance, an action I was to repeat countless numbers of times over the coming days, with the catatonic repetition of the deeply disturbed. I could make out part of a bright yellow painted wooden sign, pinned under a big sheet of broken plate glass and started to orientate myself, seeing a pattern in the foundations and remains of the buildings, making out the shape of the village and what must have been the main street leading up the hill. A few blue hand painted letters on the part of the sign I could make out, said '*stores*' and quite a large corner section of the building remained standing, probably surviving because it pointed directly towards what was left of the beach, and must have acted like the prow of a ship, giving the building a bit of protection. Two young men in sarongs emerged from the part of the building still standing, picking their way through the debris strewn all about them. A twisted fish-seller's bicycle with a large, untouched wooden box bolted to a luggage rack behind the saddle, '*supersonic*' stencilled above a blue painted fish; a small red flip-flop, an upturned baby walker, buckets, plates, clothing and broken masonry everywhere.

They walked down a new looking, wide set of cast concrete steps, that must have once led up from street level to the front of the shop, each holding two bottles of Coca-Cola. I called out to them but managed only a croak past a swollen tongue that I must have bitten at some point. They didn't hear me and continued to thread their way uphill. Thirst and painful prickling from the worsening sunburn drove me to finally confront what lay below me. There was nothing else for it, I secured the net to the big branch and slithered down it towards the trunk. The net was an illegal mesh size, too small for deep-sea fishing or footholds, but fine for fingers, and I used it a bit like a rope ladder, but with only really half of my body working. I had little strength in my left leg and arm, plus my sense of balance still wasn't perfect, and although the slime was drying, the sun was only forming a crust on it and I lost my grip and fell into the pool of corpses, around twenty or so, in the hot and slimy, stinking mud that lay in the hollow beneath the tree that had saved me. I made the mistake of scrambling too hard to try and get out and panicked, revolted, as the dead body of an elderly, very fat lady disturbed by my struggle, rolled over and wrapped a stiff, bent, outstretched arm around my waist, as if she was trying to haul me deeper into this foetid, macabre mire.

There were fish too, mostly dead, but some still alive, gills useless, mouths gaping for oxygen on the surface of the thin mud and suddenly, out of nowhere, Marley's *Three Little Birds* just appeared in my head, and I began singing along inside myself, even though I knew everything was definitely not going to be alright. It was very slippery, not that deep, just a gouge in the ground where countless feet had trodden over decades, people coming to harvest the blooms. The corpses weren't really floating, just massed together like dumplings in a thick stew, but densely packed, heavy and difficult to move, and I was pinned down by the fat lady, immersed up to chest level, heart pumping so hard I could feel every beat thumping through me. *'Every little thing's gonna' be alright. Rise up this morning, smile at the rising sun....'* and I lay there in a total funk, closing my eyes in cowardice to the horror all around me, the simple chorus revolving around my head like a mantra, a displacement activity for a traumatised mind. Tears rolled down my cheeks, stinging the open wounds, and I heard myself whimpering like a child, in fear, desperation and self pity, as continuing panic washed through me, and I knew this had to be my nadir, nothing could possibly, surely, ever be worse than this?

Relieved of my weight, the branch I'd been on had sprung upward, shedding dozens of its creamy, yellow centred flowers from its upper reaches. They had slowly caught me up, falling all around, like big flakes of snow, gently floating to earth in a windless winter's fall. Their sweet, cloying perfume mixed with the smell of ashen seawater and death. More flowers and petals were coming down and I realised that my tears were silent; it hadn't been me whimpering. The sound was coming from above me, higher up the tree than I'd been lodged, where a little girl was perched, maybe eight or nine years old, in a simple pink dress, arms wrapped around a vertical branch of the tree, standing on a horizontal side branch. She was surrounded by blooming, open Frangipani flowers, lit up by the backdrop of a crystal clear blue sky. In any other circumstances, I would have reached for a camera to try and capture such a perfect image, but it gave me focus instead, and an immediate purpose, spurring me on to escape from the clutches of my deceased neighbour and I got it together, managed to haul myself out of the terrible quagmire and limp unsteadily through the black and brown mush, to the remains of the hotel. Some feeling was coming back into my left leg, but it was about fifty percent down on power; it would have to do.

I used the surviving entrance gate as a ladder, propped sideways up against the trunk of the tree in the shallow edge of the dreadful pool, and with difficulty, I managed to get back up to where I'd been only a few minutes before, calling out to the girl,

"It's OK, I'm coming to help you. It's OK, it's OK.", as I climbed towards her through the thick perfume of the dense flowers. She was shivering with fear, soaked in sweat, and her hand was icy cold in the vicious heat of the tropical afternoon when I stroked the back of it. I kept talking to her, but she didn't understand anything apart from "OK". She must have heard reassurance in the tone of my voice though, and let me prise one small, bony hand away from the branch of the tree, and I held it in mine for a minute or so to gain her trust.

Her hair was cut short, crudely, her dress cheap and ill fitting. She appeared unhurt, but had obviously been crying for a long time. Only one cheek was wet with tears, the eye above the other was missing, the lid sealed and sunken into the socket, the iris of her open eye, pure white. It was surreal, a little girl, completely blind, and me, in this beautiful tree, in the midst of so much horror. It took a long time to convince her to trust me with my few words of basic Singhgala, touch, and a hundred more "It's OK's" until finally, she wrapped her arms tightly around my neck, clambered onto my piggy back and we descended from the Heaven-scented branches to the Hell that awaited us below.

The party of blind children had been excited on their hundred-mile school bus trip up the western coast, an annual visit to an eye specialist in Colombo. Their usual driver was sick, the one on this fateful day, just filling in. The happy singing of the children had stopped abruptly along with the minibus, when the driver had hit the brakes as an initial, small swell preceding the main tsunami, broke across the road ahead of them. They couldn't have been far behind me. Instead of simply turning right on any of the roads and tracks that led inland to this village, he panicked, slammed the gears into reverse, but only managed to slew across the road and into the line of traffic he'd created behind. Then, for reasons known only to himself, he switched off the ignition, and removed the key, immobilising the minibus and trapping all the other vehicles. He ran off down the track he'd also blocked, which had offered tantalising escape to all the travellers on this part of the road.

The two female teachers accompanying the blind children, specialists in their field, fought for their pupils' lives before their own, but neither survived. They got two children out, carrying them inland along the same track, running with them to safety, but they managed only the initial trip with a blind child each to the base of the Frangipani tree, the easiest one to climb, wrapping the childrens' arms around the trunk, telling them to get as high as they could. The main tsunami engulfed the two teachers on their way back to the minibus, along with the driver. The little girl on my back, who'd loved climbing trees before she'd begun losing the sight in her one good eye, was the only survivor from the seventeen souls who had set out with excitement and hope in their hearts that morning. I tried to picture, and still do so to this day, how those little children met their deaths - was it better they couldn't see the terrible black waters coming, or worse? With sight, they would have had a chance; a few other drivers and passengers had escaped by running inland and uphill, but the handicap of blindness that had blighted their lives, sealed their eventual fate.

With effectively two limbs at full power, I really wasn't physically capable of doing this; even though she was tiny, the girl's weight made the descent much harder, but we made it back to the final rungs of the gate with the amazing power of adrenalin. I gently pulled the little girl's hands, still shaking, apart, and lowered her onto sticky terra firma. She groped for me, and a small, cold hand squeezed inside mine. I was pleased for her, pleased she couldn't see the terrible things that surrounded us. Limping badly, I led her up the gentle slope, skirting the pools and streams of water still trickling into what had once been a busy little fishing village, guiding her up the concrete steps and into the remains of the little general store. Part of the shop's stock room had indeed, survived, which gave us respite from the sun, and I banged the caps off a couple of warm bottles of Coca-Cola on the edge of a broken wall, which I knew would help get rid of the foul taste in my mouth, quench our thirsts and give us some energy. I found a carton of plastic wrapped ginger biscuits floating in water too, opened them up, and sitting her down on a slab of fallen wall, put them in the little girl's hand. She'd stopped shaking now and had begun to eat. I stared at sodden cartons of cigarettes, thousands of Gold Leaf, floating in pools of water behind the counter.

My hip was in a very bad way, sitting down wasn't an option, so I drank standing up, murmuring and gently touching the back of the girl's hand to let her know I was still there with her. A few minutes later we were back-tracking through the debris and found the wrecked house of the lady with the dark red dress. She was still there, sitting amongst the wreckage.

She was startled when she saw us, still in deep shock, but she had a small smattering of English and was instantly protective of my little companion. In Singhala she quietly explained what had happened to the blind girl and where she was. I'd spotted some aloe vera cacti that had survived in what must have been a small garden and snapped the pale green pointed stems in half, to get at the cooling, healing jelly inside, as Mr. Ranasinghe had taught me.

"Like snot!" he'd said, squeezing it like toothpaste into my hand, nature's natural cure for sunburn and many other ailments of the skin and body. One whole side of a building nearby remained intact, rooms within visible and exposed like a dolls' house, furniture smashed, clothes and possessions strewn around, but a mirror on a wall had somehow survived and a one eyed stranger stared back at me from it. I surveyed his damage and cleaned the wounds up as best as I could, with a half bottle of Arrack on loan from the grocery store. I couldn't bring myself to meet his gaze for long. The cheap firewater coconut whisky took the last of the foul taste out of my mouth and helped me a little, to face what lay ahead.

Word had spread inland and a few people were arriving in vehicles and on foot, some in desperation, or hope, some to help, some to search, some even, to steal whatever they could find. A relative of the woman in the red dress arrived by bicycle and I left her and the child together, along with a few damp rupees and began doing what I could to help people, which frankly, wasn't much. I lasted as long as I could, stiff, cramping up and sore, drained, and out of adrenalin.

The little blind girl was desperate to find her friends – a bus, with twenty seats, she'd said. Of course, she didn't know the colour, but just about every vehicle in the tropics is white for obvious reasons, and I promised to look for it and return with any news. Walking seemed the only way to stop my hip seizing up, and I'd found one big flip-flop and a sneaker that was only just too small. Footwear helped me pick my way between the ruins and the debris.

The cream painted bus had the name of the Blind School in black letters across the rear doors. It had been crushed like an egg box in the giant mincing machine the tsunami became as it picked everything up on its path inland, rolling and tumbling, churning its accumulating contents like washing in a machine which in turn, had battered and smashed everything the waters reached. I pulled the little bodies that I could get to out of the wreckage and slowly carried them, one by one, up the slope, to an open market building just high enough to have escaped the waters, where other survivors were bringing the dead, and looking for the missing. I lay each of the seven children in a row, together, on the concrete floor. It seemed pointless closing their eyelids; it was difficult for me to bend too, so I didn't bother, thinking it might make them easier to identify.

On my way back to face the little girl from the Frangipani tree, I found a red public phone box lying on its side. The handset was still there, waterlogged but undamaged enough to work, but all the lines were down and without electricity, no mobile phone transmitters were operational either, even if I had one, and I wondered how long it would be before serious help arrived from somewhere. It was to be a long time coming.

So, around a dozen of us began with the Frangipani tree, then worked our way through the village, from what had been house to house. It was overwhelming, but the three people we found trapped, managing to get them out of the buildings alive, kept us going. As the light began to fade so did my resolve, along with the last reserves of strength and I needed to lie down desperately. I was too scared to rest anywhere near the beach, we were all terrified more tsunamis were coming. So I limped up towards the houses that had survived on the higher ground, hoping to find somewhere safe to rest. Halfway up, squeezed between what was left of a row of squatters' shanty houses, glinting in the light of the low golden sunset, were the incongruous remains of a pale blue fishing trawler. It had beached upright, its keel and half its hull missing, but its wheelhouse was intact, and I got some rest on some old sacking I found inside.

Marian had been due to travel on the early morning southbound train from Colombo, and I'd been riding north to meet her at the end of the line, just a little further up the coast. The tracks ran next to the beach, or just inland for most of the long journey south. I had no way of knowing how far north the tsunami had reached and surrounded by total devastation, feared the worst. I broke down then, completely lost it in fact, praying for her soul, weeping for what had happened to this beautiful island and for all of its innocent dead. But mostly though, I'm ashamed to say, I wept for myself.

4

We could hear smashing pottery, primal screams and shouted Singhalese invective from Mr. Ranasinghe's garden before we were even halfway up the hill from town. The monkey troupe had decided to conduct their own mango harvest while I'd been watching one of their pugilist cousins downtown, and bumping into this lovely girl walking beside me.

"I think Mr. Ranasinghe may be having a bit of a problem with some monkeys." I said to Marian, filling her in on the conflict's history as we hurried the last quarter of a mile. We scampered through the open gates under the surveillance of a quizzical Mongoose, paws, shoulders and head cocked to one side, out of the burrow, listening to Mr. Ranasinghe's voice, outside, outsized and out of character. The early morning's monkey detente was over, and full-scale war had broken out. The hairy army's surprise offensive now saw them entrenched in two strategic positions, in the canopy of the huge mango tree at the centre of this fruity primate dispute, and the roof of the main house. Mr. Ranasinghe was fighting a lone, Rorke's Driftesque battle from a defensive catapult emplacement amongst some thick shrubbery, just in front of the long, wide veranda that ran the length of the house. The buffalo cart driver was also under sporadic attack, ducking behind his big wooden cartwheels and steadfast animals, both wholly unperturbed by the surrounding furore, steadfastly munching their way through the serendipitous hail of fruit from above. A magnificent, well drilled team effort was being orchestrated from the monkeys' elevated tree positions, via a front line of a dozen or so troops, giving covering fire of small, unripe, and underdeveloped bullet hard mangoes. Other troupe members, chattering gleefully, carted off fatter, healthy and riper fruits across the roof of the main house and with acrobatic leaps, onto the safety of the roof of the neighbouring, decrepit old Dutch house.

Mr. Ranasinghe, popping up from the bushes, loosed off a couple of ineffectual pebble pot shots, which fizzed harmlessly past two members of the opposition above. His firepower had diminished rapidly once he'd used up the bowl of aerodynamically shaped small stones kept next to the catapult by the front door, ready for the regular monkey garden robberies. Usually there were only seven or eight raiders at any one time who had been relatively easy to intimidate and frighten off, but due to the current fruit bonanza on offer, the latest recruitment drive had obviously been successful; dozens of mangoes had already been plucked from the massive tree. Whole branches were being systematically denuded and Mr. Ranasinghe, having exhausted his supply of pre-emptive ammunition was now reduced to digging around in the topsoil for more, less flight worthy stones.

As he reared up through the bushes again, pulling the tubular elastic taught, firing a vicious looking small piece of jagged rock that narrowly missed a forward monkey emplacement, he spotted me.

"Thank goodness, you're back at last - did you get them?"

At that very moment, distracted by the arrival of reinforcements and hope, he suffered a direct hit on the forehead from a huge, bruised and yellow mango, discarded by quality control from the frenzied harvest aloft, and allocated to the front line troops for ordnance. It exploded upon impact, showering him with its overripe gooey, carrot coloured interior, big lumps of spattered flesh covering his head, slimy juice dripping off the thick lenses of his glasses; one large slice of mushy yellow skin, glued itself to his forehead. Marian started to laugh, my jaws quickly lost their grip on the inside of my cheeks, and I joined in.

"Don't just stand there laughing you bloody fools, help me!" he shouted, launching another catapult shot at a large female leering at him, as she bounded along a lower bough steadying herself with only one hirsute arm, making off with five plump mangoes tucked under the other. She saw the shot coming, swayed languidly backwards as the stone fizzed harmlessly past, then danced a derisory little jig, culminating in a couple of coquettish, athletic spins, and a distasteful display of her bright pink, distended genitals. A further escalation ensued, as a pincer movement closed in on

Mr. Ranasinghe's position. A second monkey battalion now began to strafe the gardens with roof tiles, plucked with incredible finger strength from the roof of the main house, then hurled like Frisbees. More than a dozen monkeys were involved in this new, scattergun attack; one lucky shot, utilising heavy back spin, landed in a pile of empty Arrack and soda bottles stashed at the side of the house, awaiting return to the liquor store, each one carrying a valuable pecuniary deposit.

The sound of the breaking glass increased the shrieks of delight from above and a heavy fusillade of shots smashed with renewed energy into the same area. Each direct hit was followed by a celebratory display of yellow teeth gnashing, shrieking and now, hairy chest thumping. Marian, still giggling, dashed for cover under the veranda as I raised an arm and the big brown paper package of Chinese firework rockets I'd just collected from the hardware store.

"Where's the weapon Mr. Ranasinghe?" I said, as another barrage of fruit cascaded towards him from above.

"Quick, in the garage, hurry before these dirty rotters wreck my whole house." he shouted above the sound of shattering bottles, cowering as glass and mango shrapnel burst all around him, peel firmly fixed to his forehead from the last direct hit, still unnoticed in the heat of battle. I pinched my nose and mimicked field radio static.

"Message received red leader, understood, wilco, over." just as a king coconut hit me square between the shoulder blades, knocking the wind right out of me and pitching me forward a couple of paces. I only just kept my balance, I was winded, it really hurt, and signalled the opening up of another new front. I looked up at the grinning miscreant in the towering palm tree behind me, clinging onto the trunk just below several big clusters of coconuts. Now it was personal. I doubled up like any self-respecting infantryman in no monkeys' land, dumped the sandals and ran bare foot, as fast as my flapping sarong would allow, zigzagging my way to the garage, drawing intensified fire and three or four near misses from the new king coconut heavy artillery.

I dived unscathed into shadow through the open garage doors, where Mr. Ranasinghe kept his pride and joy, a maroon 1955 Humber, along with a massed accumulation of assorted junk behind it, stretching back several yards and untold years. And, good heavens, a pair of motorcycle handlebars poked up through the rubbish, right at the back. Vincent? Scott? Brough Superior? With mounting excitement I pulled away some rotting timber, boxes of yellowing brittle newspapers, fossilised paint pots, piles of old tyres and heaps of ragged rice sacks to finally reveal the corroded silver wing of a Honda badge, on a rusting blue petrol tank.

The tearing sound of rending wood outside and what sounded like a palm frond crashing to earth brought me back to my mission. I spotted the wooden box containing eight three foot lengths of old copper tubing, crudely strung together with thin coconut rope, Gatling style. I tore open the package of fireworks, and stuffed the bright red waxed paper bodies and wooden sticks down each tube, like loading shot in an old musket barrel, and pulled the wooden sticks through until the blue paper fuses emerged from the bottom of each tube. The mayhem, barrage of fruit and oversized nuts was continuing apace as I emerged outside, clutching the secret weapon Mr. Ranasinghe and I had plotted one alcohol fuelled evening together. Word had got out; a gaggle of small, gawping boys clung to the entrance gates to watch the fun and games, and quite a crowd had gathered on the veranda, including Marian, barefoot, freckled, beautiful and grinning.

Carrying the much vaunted secret weapon, I dashed back across a field of fire now littered with smashed tiles, squashed fruit, broken glass and coconut shrapnel as the buffaloes, still masticating and drooling orange goo, reluctantly pulled their empty cart and driver in the opposite direction and full retreat away from the war zone, with not one mango on board. The rooftop squad had paused in their tile assault for a bit of celebratory po-going along the heavily cemented ridge tiles, their tenacious grip so far defeating all attempts at removal. Like an idiot, the heavy thud of another king coconut into the soil just behind me, prompted a theatrical vault and dive into Mr. Ranasinghe's shrubbery dugout, playing to the enraptured crowd.

We shouted for a light and Jonah, one half of a recently arrived American couple, threw us a lighter and, vacating the twig bare surroundings of Mr. Ranasinghe's defensive emplacement, we attacked in classic, outnumbered SAS style, kneeling down in the direct line of fire, in front of the house, under the fascinated gaze of this swelling audience of family, guests and passers-by. Bazooka style, using my shoulder for a launch pad, Mr. Ranasinghe lit three fuses, unleashing the first salvo from the secret weapon upon the unsuspecting animal kingdom. The rockets launched with a lurch, raced roof ward, spraying orange tail sparks over the two of us. There followed a disturbing smell of gunpowder and burnt hair, which turned out to be mine. One rocket had scorched between two mesmerised monkeys, exploding behind them with a loud bang and a starry burst of

29

crimson colour, regretfully rather diluted in the bright morning sunshine.

The second fizzed straight into one of the newly gaping holes in the roof and disappeared, apparently a dud, the third ricocheted off some of the few remaining roof tiles, exploding instantly into a thousand fizzing white stars, normally designed to cascade to earth from high in the night sky. A moment of awed silence from audience and protagonists on both sides followed this initial attack. The shock over, monkeys uprooted from their spots and scattered, and with the hair fire on the side of my head thankfully extinguished, we moved the weapon further back on my shoulder, adjusted the angle slightly, turned ominously like the gun turret on the prow of a battleship and loosed off salvo number two, with a touch more elevation. The powerful Chinese missiles scudded through a freshly denuded section of mango tree and scored a direct hit, straight into the foremost line of the front line troops aloft there. Green and blue explosions this time produced enthusiastic "oohs!" and "aahs!" and an empathetic "ouch!" from the human onlookers, as the monkeys bounded away in screaming retreat, two or three with mangy dun fur singed and smoking. I knew how they felt.

We fired the final rockets over the heads of shocked monkeys scattering in all directions, now a ragged, rapidly retreating troupe. They dropped much of the illicit fruit in their rush to escape the pyrotechnics of our high technology riposte, to the beaming delight of Mr. Ranasinghe, who bowed at the enthusiastic applause from the small, international crowd.

"Superb shooting Mr. Ranasinghe, congratulations." I said. Flushed with victory, he clapped me on the back and smiled, fleetingly however, as he surveyed the carnage surrounding us. Everyone was trying hard to be serious.

"At least they didn't reach the custard fruit......." his voice trailed off as he looked across at another of his prized trees which only the day before had sported several dozen of the delicious, spherical green fruit. Only one or two heavily chewed carcasses remained, suspended from what were obviously inedible stalks, the remnants of a fruit bats' raid during the night and the morning's monkey avarice.

"Look at that, all gone! Buggar all the bloody rotters!" he said, stamping up the steps and across the veranda past a silent crowd, collectively trying to decide between laughter, silence, commiseration or support. He yanked at the front door, which flew open, crashing into the wall behind him as he stamped into the house. The resulting tremor was sufficient to dislodge three more roof tiles, which dropped straight onto the only remaining stack of bottles at the side of the house, smashing a dozen or so more valuable empties.

I'd thought the wisps of smoke drifting from one of the holes in the roof was just the aftermath of battle, but as I'd looked up to see if any more tiles were set to come off, with smoke beginning to billow out of several holes, it was now apparent the rocket that had disappeared through one, had set the roof on fire.

Twenty minutes of frenzied fire fighting now began. I clambered up a carved wooden column supporting the top of the veranda, onto the main roof of the house and, not trusting the ancient rafters, much of which were now revealed by numerous missing tiles, spread my weight on my stomach, commando style, working my way up to the ridge line, the same offensive position our hairy, vanquished aggressors had held only minutes before. The town's very low pressure mains water system was a sporadic supply at the best of times, and only just dribbled its way to the top of the hill and into the elevated concrete cistern on legs next to the house, which was quickly emptied by the buckets of water swung across the roof to me, efficiently filled by Lars the Swede. I was throwing the water into the hole where most of the smoke was escaping, while one half of a gay male Italian couple manned the pump at the borehole, filling saucepans and cooking pots from the kitchen. His partner and Marian ferried them to the first floor and on up through the hatch into the roof space, where Mrs. Ranasinghe wielded an old carpet beater at the flames, while Mr. Ranasinghe and Jonah's girlfriend Dixie, emptied the saucepans at the numerous fires our incendiary device had begun.

As their room was right at the top of the house, partly in the roof and filling up with smoke, Jonah started throwing their bags and belongings out of the window. The final item to emerge was an enormous marijuana plant, still in flower and sporting its root ball; its owner appeared outside a few seconds later, picked it up and brandished it, shouting up to me,

"Can I leave this in your place?"

The fire extinguished, a lively debrief was held over elevenses of papaya, with all of us sat around the big kitchen table of the damaged, but no longer burning house. I removed the glistening, spherical black seeds in the central hollow of the orange slice of fruit, slashed the succulent soft flesh with the edge of a spoon, squeezing the juice from half a small green lime into my neat incisions. Dust motes and small pieces of fine ash floated in the shafts of sunlight streaming into the room. They frolicked with coils of steam rising from the china cups of fragrant tea that Marian had poured, her slim golden arms, delicately proportioned, scaphoid and tendons tensing in sculptured wrists, when she placed the heavy green teapot back on its wooden rest. Tiny pink scars crisscrossed a freckled forearm. Mrs. Ranasinghe, quiet, reserved, eyes veiled, long black ringlets neatly tied at the nape of her neck, ground coconuts and shredded fallen mangoes for chutney and jam - the despoils of war - and served small, warm, freshly baked coconut cakes to our little gathering of travellers and their tales.

Newly arrived Dixie, a high energy, willowy twenty year old, told us of Jonah's and her trip across the Yucatan peninsula, and a flight from the high mountain airstrip of San Cristobal de Las Casas. They'd boarded a flight, en route to Palenque for the peyote cactus harvest, and were belting themselves into their seats when an official ordered them off the plane – there'd been a problem processing their card payment. They'd gone back to the little tin roofed airport building with the pilot holding the flight, engines running, at the beginning of the runway. Five minutes later, the official still counting their dollar bills, the captain's patience ran out, along as it happened, with his luck. Dixie and Jonah dashed outside when they'd heard the props' revs rise, waving furiously at the cockpit in vain, and watched the plane carrying all their possessions, backpacked into its hold, scurry down the runway and into the air. It climbed to around four hundred feet and exploded, with a full fuel load, in a huge ball of flame. There were no survivors.

I'd noticed the new bags on their fall to earth earlier. There was a *South American Handbook* * in the collection traded and left behind in the little library Mr. Ranasinghe kept for guests. Later on, I looked up the route under 'Air Services' in the small, fat hardback : *No major aircraft can land here. San Cristobal-Tuxtla Gutierrez Tues Thurs Sat at 13.45. 84km. Regular daily flights to Palenque 07.15 (some crashes), booking only at airport.*

Mr. Ranasinghe strode in with a new, calmer countenance, a clean shirt and a forehead devoid of mango skin. He swung open the door to the huge old American fridge and cleared his throat, demanding attention.

"Who would like some of my sister's buffalo curd?" he asked, flourishing one of the big circular earthenware pots plucked from within.

"Yes please, I'd love to try some." volunteered Marian, with a smile.

Mr. Ranasinghe was delighted to perform for an unsuspecting newcomer.

"You know the market, down in the town?"

"No."

* South American Handbook ISBN 0 900751 26 6

"Well, you can buy curd there, but you should always have my sister's, just help yourself from the fridge here. I will put it on your bill. But it is very popular and sometimes we run out. That means we have to get it from the market and if you are going to buy curd there, you must first throw it at the wall like this."

Mr. Ranasinghe hurled the full pot of boiled water buffalo milk through the air, and it crashed into the far wall of the kitchen, where the smoke blackened earthenware pot shattered, leaving a perfectly intact, whole curd adhering to the yellowing plaster.

"Now, you can see this is a good curd because it is sticking to the wall. If it falls to the floor without sticking like that, then don't buy it; if it just droops and slides down slowly, do not pay the asking price. You can save yourself a lot of trouble and buy it from here though. My sister's is the best in town."

A fresh pot, without shards of stucco, was liberated from the cool fridge and we dutifully shared it under the avuncular gaze of our host. I removed the thick, sickly skin and revealed the creamy white yoghurt underneath. I knocked several tiny forager ants, tirelessly searching for a point of entry off the neck of an old Arrack bottle, their energetic attention drawn by the tiny trickle of dark brown, nearly black treacle oozing down its neck. The bountiful coconut tree provides everything you need on a tropical island and a lot of other places too. The wood for housing, flooring, furniture, cooking. The rootball for kindling. Coconuts for food, drink, lighting oil, shells for cups, bowls, even ornaments. Coir for stuffing, rope, big trunks for outrigger canoes, palm fronds for roofing and matting. Treacle tapped from flowers high in the crown of the tree. Dark and sweet and delicious with buffalo curd. Ferment it for palm wine or toddy. Distil the toddy for arrack. Use the empty bottle for treacle. Perfect.

Later, Mr. Ranasinghe took the old Humber out to buy new roof tiles and sunshine fingered through the open garage doors sagging on their hinges, probing the darker recesses at the back of the rickety building. Musty, mouldy sacking and rotten wood filled the dank, warm air with dust as I cleared away all the junk that surrounded the Honda. An enormous variety of insect wildlife scuttled away in fear and protest at being disturbed. I freed a beautiful, tawny mottled moth trapped in a thick, deserted and bedraggled old spider's web, then dragged the old bike outside on flat tyres, propped it up on a rusted centre stand, springs protesting at long forgotten exercise and stepped back to see everything present but a long way from correct. Rust, age and the tropics were fast devouring this old twin cylinder, down whose bores I dribbled some oil, after removing the plugs. I took off the seat and back peddled rapidly out of range of a big brown mother scorpion, tail up and pointing menacingly in my direction, aggressively defending a brood of young, all of which inhabited a nest in the recesses of a box containing an ancient, bloated battery. The neighbouring paper air filter had been neatly chopped into comfy bedding.

Under the shade and amongst the scattered debris of the denuded mango tree, I sat on a small cast concrete garden seat contemplating the metallic blue bike and my next move. Surrounded by flowers and plants of breathtaking beauty, I listened to the birds above me returning to the former war zone, probably wondering what had happened to all the fruit. Two spiders of different size, appearance and breed were constructing webs on a bush next to the seat, and I watched with fascination as the ephemeral strands emanating from their bottoms became entangled and firmly glued together. Both stood stock still, sensing a catch for which they weren't quite ready.

The smaller one tried to pull its snared main supporting strand taut, and the movement gave away its position to its neighbour. What looked like a retreat on its part, was the reverse. It followed its tramways to the centre of the half built web and out on another spar towards confrontation; the spiders squared up to each other on territorial borders and a scrap ensued, front legs whipping and mandibles chomping, both grappling for position and leverage. Mongoose came sidling up the garden towards me and sat patiently on his haunches next to the bench, sniffing, waiting for the hard-boiled egg he could smell in my pocket.

"Life's tough here, isn't it?" I said to both of us, and Mongoose seemed to agree with a little nod of the head. His small, neat brown fingers brushed his whiskers, then grabbed the egg I rolled along the ground towards him and began picking at the brown speckled shell.

"More tea Dr. Doolittle?" came words from behind me, and I turned to see Marian carrying a tray, with the same teapot she'd wielded before, two cups and a bowl of sugar. Mongoose padded away with the appearance of a stranger, and sat watching us both from a few feet away, nibbling at the white top of his snack.

"Lovely, thank you."

"How's the bike looking?" she said, sitting down next to me, picking up the teapot.

"Mind your legs sitting there, there's a few mosquitoes hanging around.

Not to mention these guys." I pointed out the scorpions, who had thankfully decided to vacate the under seat area of the bike, and we watched them clambering down the frame, led by mum, marshalling them into a semblance of order towards nearby undergrowth, displaced refugees on the move.

"The bike, as you can see, is looking a trifle bleak." I continued. "I was wondering if it would fire up, or if it's too far gone."

I pointed at the fight. The larger of the two spiders had a strength advantage, the smaller, greater mobility and their fight had continued until the smaller one got a good grip on a side leg of its enemy, who lost it trying to wriggle free and retreated hurriedly, with a lopsided gate. The victor carried its trophy, still jerking, back to its nest site and thinking it was still in a fight, began to wrap it in silken threads.

"This is such a beautiful place, thank you for introducing me." Marian said.

"It wasn't entirely selfless," I replied, "and Mr. Ranasinghe needs the money now he's lost most of his roof. How long are you going to stay?"

"I haven't decided yet, I want to go up to the mountains soon."

The tea tray sat between us and we talked and talked, sipping the tangy amber liquid, among the vibrant serenity of our surroundings, and her eyes sparkled with fun and intelligence and life, and the dappled sunlight of the afternoon.

Later, I swam and snorkelled from a little crescent shaped beach near the naval station and dived with a mask into another world of beauty. Swimming is always a place for contemplation for me, and I thought of her, then slept on the powdery sand in the shade of a big rock, waking up suddenly from a deep sleep. The sun had chased its afternoon arc and a couple of scorched knees told me I'd been here a little too long. A teenage boy was squatting on his haunches next to me, using the hem of his sarong to polish the same seashell he'd been trying to sell me for weeks. He held his head to one side and squinted at me quizzically through the dazzling light bouncing off the white sand. A fat black crow scavenged the water's edge. The boy's English was improving as he practised his sales pitch, which had become refreshingly honest.

"For you, the price today is one thousand five hundred rupees. For German peoples, three thousand; see, a good deal, you should buy for your wife."

"You know I'm not married Samanda." I said.

"But you will be one day, and then the shells will all be gone, or much more money, and you'll be sorry you not buy today."

"Did not or didn't, Samanda, that's short for did not. You can't just say not."

"OK. Did not. You'll be sorry you did not."

I took the beautiful irridescent silver shell from him, so light and delicate and as always, I wondered what its former resident looked like.

"It's a wonderful shell Samanda, stunning, but fragile, it'll break too easily, and I travel light and I don't have a girlfriend either."

"Yes, but if you buy the shell, you can give to a girl and she will be your girlfriend. Or you can give to a girl you like enough to marry."

"You're getting too good at this Samanda, I think I've taught you all I know."

On the way home I'd strolled back past the town's single pump station and back up the hill with the Honda's petrol tank under one arm, a litre of the bright red liquid inside, under a sky filling with billowing black clouds. Marian looked up from a paperback and waved from the shade of the veranda. The Honda's spark plugs were scrubbed and replaced, battery terminals and connections cleaned and the petrol trickled like blood down the fuel pipe, disappearing into two thirsty carbs. I carried out a quick under seat scorpion check, the presence of which so close to one's testicular region I felt best avoided, then straddled the bike, fiddled the ignition switch to 'on' with a thin penknife blade, swung the kick start and amazingly, the engine coughed on the third and fired into cacophonic, blue smoking life on the fourth. The old Honda began clearing its throat and started to run sweetly as it quickly warmed up in the close weather. Big fat rain dropped into the dust around me as the storm clouds got serious above, and began to shed their watery load onto the thirsty waiting jungle below. I killed the engine and saw Marian trotting down the slope towards me, grinning broadly behind a victory sign, just as the rain began sheeting down in earnest and we dashed for the open door of my flat.

Shaking the water from our hair we stood in my little living room, laughing like children as the rain hammered on the roof above, gurgled along the gutters, poured onto the brick patio from the deep valleys of the banana tree leaves, and chuckled out of sight into the rudimentary drains.

"What a lovely old gramaphone." Marian said, spotting the ancient wooden machine I'd found in the local market, "Does it work?"

Standing close, I showed her how to wind it up and play a record. She smelt wonderful, and it was a struggle not to touch her as she flicked through a dozen or so old 78's that came in the job lot, before deciding

36

Marlene Dietrich should tell us how she was falling in love again.

"Fancy an Arrack, with some proper coffee, Dutch - Douwe Egberts - personal import?" I asked from the door to the kitchen, waving the crimson packet at her.

"Sure, thanks, that would be a real treat." she said, walking towards me as the band struck up, her gaze drawn immediately to the action going on around the kitchen walls.

"Wow. Do you train these ants or something?"

The whitewashed walls and pencilled road network were carrying exceptionally heavy two-way ant traffic. Large serrated edged sections of bright green leaves, several times larger than each of the hundreds of insects on the road, were being transported towards the nest, while a busy stream of workers hurried along the same route in the opposite direction, to collect another load. Marian followed their brand new off road route around the corner and along the wall facing the front door, down to the skirting board and through a gap between the door and the frame, into my bedroom.

I filled the kettle with water, fitted its whistling cap and followed Marian through the bedroom door to find her, hands on hips, staring at the vast marijuana plant being systematically stripped by my friends from the colony in the corner of the kitchen.

Must have been quite a party at the end of the A3.

5

The beach was dotted with lumps of buildings, the occasional vehicle, big sections of coral, rocks, pieces of furniture, clothing, electrical goods, rotting fish and vegetation, and the dead bodies of the old, the young and the unidentifiable. With each incoming tide, the ocean returned the corpses of those it had carried off to sea, retreating from its terrible foray inland.

Survivors giving up looking for loved ones in the wasteland onshore, were switching their search to the water's edge. I was a long way from able and desperate to get further up the coast to find out if Marian's train had made it through, but I helped where I could, lifting and carrying bodies. There were no boats left, at least none that were intact and Sri Lankans generally don't swim, so they just had to wait. Some didn't want the help of a foreigner or were beyond it, inconsolable to the point of losing their reason, watching the black shapes bobbing out at sea, slowly making their way towards the beach. When they eventually washed into the shallows, they became a person and yet another life lost among the 58,000 Sri Lankans and foreign nationals who perished that day. So many more survived, but lost their reason to live.

I'd found a bicycle, but my hip really wasn't up to the job of pedalling and there were only parts of the road remaining anyway, depending on how hard the ocean had struck each part of the coastline. The tectonic fault line on the seabed off the coast of Indonesia a thousand miles away had fractured upwards, punching the ocean above into a vast ripple. Boats out at sea rode the long, unremarkable high swell it caused with relative ease, but struggled to navigate home because what should have been familiar coastlines, were unrecognisable. Sailors were staggered at the devastation on land, not able to understand why they hadn't been swept away at sea themselves by the giant waves. But it was only once the vast, swollen body had reached the shallows of the coast that the sloping topography of the seabed accelerated the water in many areas to over five hundred miles an hour. Spits of land, reefs, rocky outcrops and the angle of particular stretches of coastline where they met the sea, all made a difference to the force and height of incoming tsunamis. As this process happened, the ocean swelled its deformation, drawing water back from the shoreline, revealing seabed never seen before.

Off the southern Indian coast near Mahabalipuram, half a mile or so from the beach, to great excitement, onlookers saw conical buildings and what appeared to be an ancient temple jutting from the seabed. The prospect of seeing newly exposed coral reefs without getting wet, or walking around a suddenly exposed headland to the next bay was an understandable temptation. Many people were caught out in this way. Tourists in resorts with time on their hands were the first to perish, swept up by an ocean out of control, blackened by volcanic ash in its vortex that stained their white skin. It took a while for me to work out that lengthy exposure in water lightens black skins too. It all added to the confusion.

As with all islands, so much of the population lived off the sea and was concentrated on the coast. More often than not towns develop where there is easy access to the ocean, good mooring, an estuary providing river transport and fresh water - often all three. By late morning, limping badly with the effort, I'd reached one of these, a small town, or rather, what had once been a small town. Only a well-built mosque and a bigger Buddhist temple that had been turned into another temporary morgue had survived the devastating impact. The rest of the town had simply been obliterated, the very presence of human beings, erased, apart from the twenty or so survivors and four or five villagers from further inland who'd brought food and basic medical supplies, doing what they could for the injured and the dispossessed. I was lucky enough to be given some dried fish and dahl by one of them, and crucially, there was fresh water from a mobile tanker that had been driven to the edge of the remains of the town, a vehicle usually used to fill up storage tanks in the dry season of the Southern Province, with sweet drinking water transported down from the mountains. It was warm, bordering on hot, but I filled and refilled a plastic water bottle I'd found and drank until I was bloated, reading handwritten notices on the walls inside the mosque - now everyone's communal accommodation - with messages for the missing – 'Have you seen.......?' 'Chandra, I am OK, looking for you.' A few had photographs of the missing attached, all but one, stained and water damaged.

I retraced my steps back towards the beach, where what turned out to be two brothers I'd passed were still sitting outside the remains of their family home, which had imploded. Why and how they had come through it, without injury, I shall never know. The clothes they wore were ragged and filthy, so I guessed they must have been caught up by the water and like me, by chance, had somehow survived. They seemed to have made it back to what was once their home but I had no language I could share with them, so I never found out. We divided the food onto broken clay roof tiles, squatting on pieces of fallen masonry, and ate in silence. Afterwards, I helped them pull out a stinking dead pariah dog that had got stuck fast as it bloated in a drainage ditch full of rubble at the side of house, and dug a shallow grave for it, more to give them a constructive displacement activity than anything else. We used some sharp scooped debris that I only realised after a while was smashed, painted corrugated asbestos sheeting, still in widespread use for lining roofs on the island. * Even though burying the dog was a pretty futile gesture, I'd hoped it would get rid of the terrible smell, but the odour of decay remained. Things rot quickly in the tropics, flesh particularly; you learn to treat cuts without delay, and with respect until they're fully healed. It wasn't hard to work out that the smell was coming from inside the remains of the little brick house. Survivors with nowhere else to go, camping outside the wreckage of a home exuding the hideous smell of their decomposing family, was a dreadful scene I was to experience over and over again.

I led the boys the mile or so back to the mosque, which was the only shelter left for the community, where an elderly gentleman, neighbour, family, or a friend of their family I didn't know, thanked me in Singhalese, wrapped his arms around the boys' shoulders and led them off, picking their way through the rubble, heading inland. They seemed to know him, one of them had smiled briefly, but they were so distressed and troubled it was hard to ascertain the relationship exactly, or whether I'd done the right

---

* The full impact on survivors from the consequences of breathing asbestos fibres, and for those who went to help amongst the broken buildings, will not be known for many years. An expert study though, commissioned in the immediate aftermath was entitled The Silent Tsunami, and concluded that the water will eventually take twice as many lives with this part of its legacy, than it did during its terrible advance on that fateful day.

thing. I couldn't find anyone who spoke enough English to find out if the boys did in fact, know him, and I had second thoughts and started to follow them to see where he was taking them, but gave it up quite quickly, mainly because, still carrying injuries, I just couldn't keep up on the debris strewn terrain.

Looking back, I was still in shock myself, numbed by what I'd been through, just adrenalin keeping me going. The destruction was so all encompassing, and on such a huge scale, that it was impossible to do anything other than find food and water, try to survive, help those still alive and less fortunate than I'd been to remain so, rest when I could, and keep heading north. I didn't think it was possible to be shocked by anything any more. The looting that quickly began was understandable; in the midst of all the devastation the thin veneer of civilisation was quickly replaced with feral survival instinct. Combing the remains of a shopping street for food was acceptable to me, and in the first couple of days it was the only way we could survive. The men I came across concentrating their efforts on getting inside the vaults, safes and tills of a wrecked bank building, showed appalling disregard for human life when there were people still trapped in neighbouring properties, and should be thoroughly ashamed of themselves.

Stories abounded of LTTE raiding parties snatching orphaned, or lost youngsters to train as child soldiers in their stronghold in the Northeast. This was never officially confirmed to the best of my knowledge and was of course, a heaven sent propaganda opportunity for Colombo's Government. The tsunami had reached as far north as the heavily populated coastline in areas controlled by the Tigers, and with no Government support, hospitals or emergency aid forthcoming, the people in that part of the island must have suffered the most if not at the time, then in the disaster's aftermath. Organising and despatching child snatch squads to other affected areas seemed like a convenient fantasy to me, but human depravity can sink to levels below belief.

What must be the lowest possible depths were reached when orphaned children were snatched by organised paedophiles offering food, shelter and hope to those most vulnerable, and incapable of defending themselves. I know this happened. I met and even briefly came to trust an American man, posing as a childcare specialist, who was orchestrating the kidnap, sale and trafficking of children as domestic servants (slaves) and 'workers' (child prostitutes) in the brothels of the Middle East. By lucky chance he was exposed, regretfully just managing to escape the country before he

41

could be arrested; the trail of human misery he left behind him remains to this day.

In the early afternoon a Police officer from Hatton, many miles distant arrived on foot, followed by a couple of dozen walking wounded and a serious, nervous young third year student between terms at Galle's well respected Medical School. He was carrying quite a lot of medical and other supplies and began a triage process on the wounded, more of whom continued to straggle in from outlying areas in search of food, water and help, in what was once an important town. I helped rig up an awning on the side of the mosque to shelter the injured, using rope and a sail salvaged from a yacht buried deep into the side of the broken shell of a three story house, some of the contents of which, including a perfectly made double bed on the third floor, had been untouched by the water. We pulled the bed to earth off the edge of the broken floor using a crude grappling iron made from reinforcing rods, along with a portable radio which was increasing the staggering scale of the disaster that had overcome Indonesia, India and Sri Lanka with each bulletin. News about our area of the southwest coast was limited, with no real hard facts beyond the obvious one, that both local emergency services and medical facilities had either been destroyed or overwhelmed, and that accessing the area was proving very difficult, as all the transport links ran down the very coast that had been affected.

There were joyous moments occasionally during that day. Incredibly, an infant had been found hungry and thirsty, but alive and safe after thirty-two hours, wrapped in a fishing net, suspended from the branches of a tree over a mile inland from the town. But the cries of joy from his mother when they were reunited, were drowned by the inconsolable tears of the bereaved, the lost and the lonely. A father found his own dead child in the same lake where he fished every day and carried him to the bank where he sat, cradling the fragile little body in his arms, mute with grief, stroking his son's hair with catatonic repetition. Crabs had eaten the little boy's eyes and ears, the spectre of which, of course, would never ever leave his father's memory.

As with every town of substance, it had a market, and a particularly large one, once a month on Poya days, when farmers, artisans, traders and craftsmen from many miles around, and far inland would bring produce and goods to sell, buying and bartering for the things they needed. Typically, as was the case on this fateful holiday, their wives would bring their youngest children too, along with their own harvests to trade and sell. For the tsunami to hit the island on the morning of a Poya was the cruellest hand of fate, and probably doubled the loss of life. Countless farming couples and their young children never returned to their inland communities from what should have been a normal and uneventful monthly trip to market. In many villages, whole generations of adults and children lost their lives, leaving communities consisting only of the very young and the very old. The reeking black water only wreaked its havoc at most, just over a mile inland, but it reached the very centre of the island in so many ways.

The Policeman brought some order and led by example, rolled up his shirtsleeves and began to dig the first urgently needed grave himself, in a clear piece of ground at the edge of the town the survivors agreed was their only choice. Beginning with the bodies that had been identified, we used more heavy cream sailcloth for shrouds and worked late into the night, bathed in the light of a huge, low moon, burying fifty-three people in graves recorded by the Policeman. It was a pragmatic process not least because of the health threat, but many graves were subsequently reopened and internments reversed in the search for missing people, particularly holidaying foreigners. Exhausted, after a few mouthfuls of tuna some women had baked in sand on the beach, I climbed up onto a small bunk I'd discovered while looking for tools in the stern of the yacht.

The final news bulletin we'd listened to on the radio at midnight reported the cold, bare fact that the early morning Colombo train had not arrived at its destination, its whereabouts was unknown and that a search was under way to locate it. I froze in the heat of the night, and my stomach turned into a cold, hard knot. I wrapped my arms around myself, curled up into a foetal position, which reduced the pain from my hip and gently rocked myself into an exhausted sleep, hoping against hope that another wave would come in the night and this time the cruel sea would save me from a crueller world.

6

Jasmine blossoms floated on the surface of a wooden bowl of water at the centre of the table, their scent mingling with the spicy fragrance drifting from the food dishes surrounding it. Central was a small mountain of white, fluffy fat rice, harvested from Mr. Ranasinghe's paddy fields further along the coast road. Fish had arrived just before twilight, and Mrs. Ranasinghe had peppered thick steaks cut from the carefully iced sear fish she'd chosen from the light blue painted wooden box, bolted to the luggage rack of the fish-seller's heavy black and pinstriped, Kolkata built Hero Royal bicycle.

Side dishes of ladies' fingers in a delicate coconut sauce, devilled aubergine, Mrs. Ranasinghe's fabulous snake gourd dhal and a big pile of crispy triangular poppadum pieces. Glasses of ice-cold lassi for the fiery aubergine, liberated from the fridge, poured by Mr. Ranasinghe. A golden foaming beer arrived too, the big brown bottle sweating with condensation as it emerged into the night from its magic repository. The huge, ancient, cream coloured Frigidaire had taken on mystical legend amongst the guests. None of us could work out how everything we took from it, at all hours of the day and night - eggs, butter, curd, sodas, fruit - with the kitchen and house seemingly deserted, invariably and accurately appeared on the neatly handwritten bills at the end of each week, correctly apportioned to each guest.

I'd tested the system every way I could, mounting early morning raids in the smallest hours, long before dawn, when I knew the household

would be asleep, surreptitiously removing one egg, before stealthily creep-
ing back to my rooms for what I thought was an illicit dawn breakfast. But
there, without fail on the weekly bill it would appear, *1 egg Rs. 7/-* .

I had broken the news to Dixie regarding the skeletal remains of the
marijuana plant, and tried to comfort her with an assertion that its dona-
tion had made the ant colony very happy. We'd discussed the magic fridge
too, and Mr. Ranansinghe's billing system. Pulling her own weekly account
from a shirt pocket, she pointed, with a wry smile, to the final entry, *Ganga
Rs 175/-*.

I balanced a little coconut sambol on a triangle of poppadum, prompt-
ing me to plunge my upper lip into the frothy blond beer, easing some of
the cool fluid past two fiery tonsils. No cutlery, just mix each dish with a
little rice into a glutinous ball, and pop it in one's mouth, with sticky fingers. When in Rome.

Dixie and Marian were hitting it off. Their discussion about elephants
turned to turtles and I joined in.

"There was a turtle laying eggs on the Resthouse beach last night. The
moon's still big enough and I was thinking of going again tonight. Do you
want to come?"

A nod and a beam from Marian breathed on the little flame inside me
I'd thought long dead. Pilot light must have been flickering. Mr. Ranasinghe produced a bottle of Special Reserve Arrack, we drank a toast to
mama turtles and as dinner ended, the evening began.

Crusty crimson stains of betel juice splashed the powdery plastered
walls in the bar of the town's crumbling mens' drinking club. It was in a
permanent state of social disgrace, tucked out of sight and harm's way in a
shady side road off the main street. The clientele when we arrived consist-
ed of the usual combination of professional drunks, riff-raff, ne'r-do-wells,
misfits, failures, outcasts and pariahs, amongst whom I felt very much at
home. It was particularly packed that evening as the sale of alcohol had
been banned the day before because it was a Poya day, the monthly full
moon holiday. There was a full moon the day Bhuddha was born, the day
he achieved spiritual enlightenment, and the day he died. Since then,
nothing much appeared to have changed at the club, the only apparent
additions, a mid-twentieth century refrigerator, an awful neon strip light
festooned with cobwebs, and a flyblown poster of a half naked Japanese
girl, hanging above our drinking companions' heads.

Marian and Dixies' entrance had stunned the exclusively male clientele
into silence, which made the gigantic eruscation Marian produced after her

first gulp of the nutty Nurawa Eliya brewery's Lion lager, as shocking as a pistol shot. A couple of hundred wide white eyes watched her wipe the white froth from a lightly freckled, tanned upper lip with the back of her hand, and the ice was broken in the heat of the night. She winked at me with green-grey eyes that flickered with depth and mischief and the stuttering flame that danced on the end of a crude wick, burning coconut oil from a rusty old tobacco tin, in the midst of the bottles that covered our table. We traded more information and found that a country girl had met a city boy.

Jonah, Lars the Swede and in particular, the novelty of girls on the premises had drawn an additional crowd to my usual line up of cricket anorak boozing partners, and the drinks had been coming thick and fast. 'Old' Arrack - guaranteed at least six weeks old - and soda was freely flowing in an overt attempt to see how long the women could last.

The waiter, Muttiah Muralitharan's doppelganger, was busy retrieving empties, bringing replacements and helping homeward bound drunks, (who'd put in big efforts early on), to find the exit and navigate the rotting old wooden steps outside. By the time we'd all lost count of how many drinks we'd had and whose turn it was to buy more, three hours had slipped by. Lars was introducing the novelty of Arrack and soda slammers, and it was always going to be downhill from that point. Thirty minutes later, male egos to the fore, slammers were very much in vogue and the learning curve only just begun. The effects of the first few had begun to snowball with the last couple and I slipped out to the beach, leaving Renuka the chef, Bandula the builder, Winston the apothecary's assistant, an off duty policeman called Newton, (who'd called in for a drink on the way home and who should have known better), leading several other barflies and a couple of ominously frisky, fresh looking newcomers. All were in tacit agreement to drink us international interlopers under the rickety woodworm ridden table, groaning under the weight of elbows and drinks. It was a good time to slide away into the late evening.

A row of sleepy houses lining the narrow sandy street leading to the harbour and the Resthouse beach beyond, were gently quiet, at the end of the day. Faint singing drifted from somewhere, a gently burbling radio. An old man squatted in the doorway of his humble timber home, smoking a cheroot. Each inhalation illuminated his creased, sun dried face in the darkness. We nodded amiably at each other, murmured our greetings and I glanced behind him as I passed by, at three generations of his family at peace together, in the small sparsely furnished single room, warmly lit by

an oil lamp. I skirted a sleeping pariah dog and compared my barren lone-
liness and material wealth to the riches of that lucky old man. And I wondered what was to become of me. And I dared to hope.

I turned off the road and began picking my way around the giant snails
traversing the twisting narrow footpath which dropped to the sea, as they
conducted their glutinous night time rendezvous amongst the succulent
sea grape. A slight breeze caressed the rippling skin of the vast sleeping
ocean, and broke the moon free from its cloudy prison. Beams of white
and blue splendour leapt from the Sea of Tranquility and its thirty six year
old footsteps and danced across the water, igniting the phosphorescence,
coaxing the tide back to its high mark. South to the horizon, the bobbing
lights of unseen shrimp boats lured their prey up from the depths to the
inky surface, into their shallow nets and an airy grave.

I'd checked the site of last night's turtle nest and with no surprise, the
eggs had been robbed, still a stolen delicacy, despite the education and
laws designed to stop the stupidity. Some habits are hard to break, especially ten thousand year old ones. Thinking about a cigarette, I trudged
further along the beach, where I'd buried a stash of fifteen of the sticky
pearlescent spheres myself – no egg thief had followed my human foot-
prints and they were undisturbed and safe. I sat, pleased, back propped up
against a big warm rock, still radiating heat from the day, eyes wide, scan-
ning the scimitar beach for twenty minutes or so, sobering up, then, suddenly, lumbering out of the shallow surf, came the dark, low shape of a
Leatherback's shell. She was immense, probably a hundred years old, so
still young on the turtle scale of things, two hundred and fifty years being
more of a ripe old age. I stayed still in the shadows, watching her, painful-
ly slowly, like a wounded soldier, drag herself up the steep slope of the
beach and as she came closer, I could hear her pant with the physical
effort, the rasping, wheezing gasps of a heavy smoker, at the top of a long
flight of stairs.

I hurried back to the club where the only thing supporting the police
officer was one of the upright teak posts supporting the veranda, to which
he clung, eyes closed, blind drunk, as another customer swayed unsteadily
behind him, helping himself to a bundle of rupee notes from the shiny
leather wallet he put back in the officer's back pocket. With an absent-
minded, friendly pat on the officer's backside, he zig zagged back to the
bar and the mayhem inside. Two more unconscious drunks were slumped
across our table, cheeks resting on the sticky surface, one, arm outstretched, still clasping his unfinished drink. Lars, beneath his feet on the

floor, was snoring soundly. Glasses were breaking, tables crashing, fists shaking, arguments breaking, dinners regurgitating; Dixie and Jonah were nowhere to be seen but there, in the middle of the carnage staggering a shuffled waltz, was Renuka the chef, clinging onto Marian's shoulders for support, who was sporting a wide smile and the policeman's hat, garlanded with a white bougainvillea cutting. I bought another drink for everyone still standing and we slipped out of a side door, back into the warm night towards the beach, and Marian into local legend.

The deep gouges of flipper tracks led us to the top of the beach where she was laying eggs in a shallow sandy burrow, next to a carpet of creeper flowers where we sat, in the gentle moonshadow of a palm tree. The glowing trail of a shooting star fizzed an arc across an indigo velvet sky, scattered with a million diamonds, confusing the fireflies that danced among the eddies of a warm breeze at the top of the beach. I'd made a small fire earlier from broken coconut shells and pieces of driftwood, heating up some fat stones which I'd buried in the sand with the cashews I'd bought from the market. We sat in silence with mama turtle, liberating the warm roasted nuts from their charcoaled green shells, listening to her laboured breathing through tiny nostrils at the top of her beak, loud, even above the sound of the receding surf. This was one tired lady, no midwife at hand, no doting father to hold one either, no medical team, no relatives waiting to help, just a journey of thousands of miles back to the beach where she herself had hatched over a century before.

And she'd survived the human pillaging, our so-called intelligence not even extending to limiting the plunder, if only to ensure a continuity of harvest and dodged the predators waiting for her in the air during the frantic, fateful scamper down the beach with her brothers and sisters and those lurking in the salty shallows at the edge of the ocean.

Now, a century later, having carefully, clumsily covered the eggs with her back flippers, with a long deep sigh, she began the journey down to the ocean yet again, and for some reason I felt moved to speak to her, congratulate her on a job well done and it was only then I realised how privileged we were to have witnessed the event.

Pushing backwards with all four flippers down the slope of the beach, her progress was still slow, hauling her vast bulk a few inches forward at a time. After the efforts of the last couple of hours, it took her another half, with what appeared to be the last of her strength. Pausing, panting, tantalisingly close to the water, one big wave rushed just far enough to splash her nose with flotsam to rejuvenate her and with a final, huge effort, the front of her torso at last became buoyant as a second wave washed underneath her. She savoured the moment of transition between ungainly, lumbering, defenceless lump and effortless, swooping, soaring mistress of the oceans. We followed her graceful progress seaward through the shallows with my torch until she dived out of sight and into our memories, without a care in the vast blue depths of her world.

We swam after mama turtle, Marian with the grace and strength of a dolphin, sliding sideways, up and under the surface, the skin of her torso glistening and lithe in the moonlight, disappeared, and unseen, grabbed my ankles and surfaced, laughing as I toppled backwards into the water. Then small, strong fingers pushed between mine as she helped me up from the sandy shallows, the breeze cool enough now to stiffen the nipples on her perfect breasts. Bathed in bright moonlight, her skin was covered in water droplets, and fine down, turning to soft blond hairs on her arms, legs and thighs. Her body was a delight, slim hips framing a strong flat stomach that palpitated with her laughter as mine ached for her. Our eyes met and in that moment's silence before she kissed me, everything was said. And her wet, salty lips were the sweetest thing I'd ever tasted.

We walked home hand in hand through the quiet, and the moonlight, and the heady night perfumes of jasmine and orchids. My heart was beating so much faster than the climb up the hill past the little post office required, and I couldn't look at her, I couldn't speak. I felt detached from the real world, the painful world, the hateful trial of life, and I just floated along as if I'd never left the ocean and immersing myself in the depths of emotion.

Inside the gates, she turned and pulled me towards her, and as I gently kissed the freckles on her shoulder, she breathed into my ear,

"Tread softly in your sleep, you'll be walking in my dreams." and she dissolved into the shadows, and was gone.

I lay awake, listening to the nightlife, drifting into sleep in late early hours and I was standing on a low, frosty, night time river bridge, over a fast moving weir, watching an adolescent swan on the moonlit water, upstretched under the stars, gently beating her wings, testing her growing strength, not to fly, but just to lift her weight and dance across the rushing current, only the tips of her webbed feet touching the water. Such poise and grace and exuberance of a nature's youth so beautiful, it brought tears to my dreaming eyes and I woke to the sound of rain, shivering in the blessedly cool dawn that came with it, and pulled the sheet over the novelty of a chilly shoulder. And I had been so cold inside and so lonely, for so long. And the image of the snow-white bird stayed with me in half sleep, as the tears slowly rolled onto the damp pillow beneath my head.

"Father, Oh Father! What do we here in this land of unbelief and fear?
The land of dreams is better, far above the light of the morning star."
William Blake

7

I lost count of the number of shrines and temples I passed, untouched by the water. I say untouched, but of course they'd been submerged. I was hugging the coast on that long walk north, plodding mostly across brightly moonlit sand, scattering fiddler crabs to scuttle back into their burrows from macabre meals. There was nothing I could do other than walk on by the majority of the corpses still being washed up by the sea, as I wasn't physically capable of moving an adult body on my own. The forced exercise was lessening the combination of numbness and pain in my hip, though I was still having to protect the shoulder that had hit the wall. The part that I could see had turned a deep blue black, the grave digging hadn't helped it either, it had been on the edge of dislocating again several times with the effort.

Four or five children's bodies I did move, taking them above high tide mark, allowing them some dignity where I could. I was hoping their remains would be cared for at first light when I knew survivors in the area with no alternative, would come down to the beach to perform toilet and washing functions. I also felt an overwhelming sense of guilt that I had survived and they had not. Bizarrely, I even apologised to them for it, before leaving them alone with an inappropriate Christian funeral prayer I remembered I'd forgotten I'd learnt as a choirboy in England.

I only turned inland where I had no choice, or if the ground was too high for the water to reach, where the coast road would be untouched. On those unblemished stretches of tarmac I made good progress, passing through silent small roadside settlements, where the lack of damage to the buildings seemed incongruous, the pristine vegetation out of place. The downside away from the onshore breeze on the beach was the mosquitoes. Without any citronella they were avenging the swathe I'd been cutting through their numbers ever since I'd arrived on the island. I had to keep slapping at every area of exposed skin, swiping awkwardly at their favourite, (and itchiest) area around the elbow, where they sneaked up from behind. I filled my empty bottle from a well next to a deserted house, but the water was salty, the aquifers contaminated by the ocean's intrusion. Occasionally the road would just stop, fractured in mid-air, with a drop to the desolation below so large, I had to retrace my steps and find another way.

At the top of one or two beaches, I rested inside the shells of buildings the water had ripped through, more often than not with just one or two walls remaining. The remnants of houses close to the beach were usually the only structures where large parts remained standing. The massive force of the ocean shattered everything that stood in its path, collecting and accumulating churning debris, paradoxically thereby, becoming more destructive, the further inland it progressed. Amidst these wastelands away from the shore, the shrines remained. Buddha's expression was usually neutral and impassive, sometimes though he surveyed the destruction surrounding him with the half smile of someone lost in contented thought. Mostly, the shrines were of solid cast concrete built for longevity of course, rather than tsunami proof strength, but even so, I cannot remember seeing one of his effigies broken or even chipped. It was truly incredible.

The terrible, continuing traumas all survivors were experiencing, and desolating news about the train, had prevented any sleep on the broken yacht. I had been reeling under the successive shocks with this latest blow triggering mounting desperation. Lying down for a few hours had helped me physically though, and I found a couple of tins of fruit in a stowage locker in the yacht's little low stern section where I'd been resting. I opened one of the salt corroded cans using a broken piece of reinforcing plate on the wheel, and ate the sweet pineapple rings inside before resuming my journey north with a sense of purpose, and hardening resolve, in the very early hours of December 28th. I guessed I'd covered at least seven difficult miles as the crow flies by first light, the moon's disappearance over the horizon darkening the skies enough for an enforced rest, just before dawn. The rising sun silhouetted a water tower jutting above some coconut trees and its hidden promise within, which turned out to serve quite a big cluster of school buildings. Half of them were on higher ground and were now home to around two hundred people, including a few foreigners from a local tourist resort that had been completely wiped out by the surging water. With the water system wrecked and no electricity to automatically pump salt polluted water out of the aquifers and into the big concrete tower, it was holding hundreds of gallons of fresh, sweet drinking water.

The other half of the classrooms had been flattened, while the ocean had picked the administration block back to its steel bones. The roof, and all the walls of the three-storey building were gone. Most of the reinforced concrete floors remained in place, as did an undamaged golden statue of Buddha, sitting, legs crossed, on a ledge at the top of a doorframe that must have supported two large entrance doors. The wall immediately behind it was completely missing and I could see no means of support for the whole structure, nor any reason for it to have remained in place. This was no crude, mass produced casting, but a sculpture of quality and sensitivity, Buddha's expression one of contemplative serenity; something in his posture suggested he was on the brink of imparting wisdom to the institution he oversaw, whose function was to do the same.

He didn't have to. The ruins surrounding us, being slowly illuminated as a wind and flawless day dawned, were the most graphic portrayal possible of the impermanence of the things we touch. Stripped of even my few remaining possessions, I had been given no option other than to let go of them completely, but a chance to possess what is truly real. The circumstances however, were very far from ideal.

The school was on the outskirts of my destination, large areas of which had escaped undamaged. This included a processing plant selling sacks of rice. Some of the tourists taking refuge in the school had gladly paid the exorbitant prices being demanded, for what was rapidly becoming a priceless commodity. A rudimentary kitchen had been set up in a science classroom, which was producing two basic meals a day using the rice, augmented with vegetables, begged, borrowed, bartered or pillaged, with fruits and nuts foraged from the surrounding area. Locals in fear of further tsunamis - as were we all - had begun, with great trepidation, the task of salvaging what they could find from the wreckage of their homes. I was generously invited to eat by a Swedish family in the middle of the worst holiday they will ever have, and, sitting at a school desk for the first time in decades, breakfasted on jack fruit, rice, and small, sweet seeds I couldn't identify, served in half a coconut shell, with a ration of the precious fresh water that had towered above the waves.

Leaving them with thanks, a full water bottle and good luck wishes, I cut inland, following a path across a headland, a well-trodden track through dense sub-tropical forest used by generations of schoolchildren. It eventually dropped gently down towards the coast again, suddenly widening into a single-track road and suburban houses at the edge of town. The buildings were tightly packed, many in terraces. The cast, reinforced concrete structures seemed to have fared better than the brick built buildings.

Life was going on; a plump, middle aged woman with long, unkempt hair and dirty clothes, picked through a pile of rubble and debris that must have once been her house, with what looked like an upturned piece of road machinery at its centre. She turned when she heard the sound of my footsteps clambering over strewn rubble, stood up and stared at me, clasping a handful of salvaged cutlery. I must have looked a very sorry sight and probably threatening too, so I smiled and nodded trying to reassure her, and walked on by. I followed the sound of a diesel engine thumping down the street where a mother and two sons stood in a wide, internal opening in a wall that used to divide two pale green downstairs rooms. The jagged opening was now the entrance to the remaining half of their house. She was dressed in a rainbow-coloured smock, printed with pink and blue orchids and was leaning against one wall. Next to her stood a bespectacled, studious looking teenage boy who was taking a break from sweeping plaster and dust outside, joining his shirtless younger brother. Like everyone else I'd encountered since the disaster struck, even some of the dead, the expression on the faces of all three was still one of dazed shock, as they watched a large bulldozer shove the remains of half their house into a pile. The masked driver of the big yellow machine was clearing a dusty path through the main street and I walked through a cloud of dust in its clanking caterpillar tracks, past the neighbouring house, which was just a series of concrete floors and low, broken, whitewashed walls. Two men with sledge hammers were knocking down the remnants, while a boy and a slim young woman, in a blue checked dress, chipped the plaster off the fallen bricks, adding them to an orderly stack of several hundred, salvaged in readiness for rebuilding. Hope sprung eternal and so did a pariah dog as it leapt over the bricks trailing something edible from its jaws, chased by a loping, hungry pack that disappeared into yet another broken building, where out of sight, a scrap over the food broke out. Along with us humans, the dogs that had stayed behind were getting hungry too, hunting in ever-larger packs, getting bolder, and dangerous.

The sounds of the fight had excited a young dog, maybe six months old, that was chained to the railings of a first floor balustrade in a modern, expensive house a bit further down the street. A black and white outrigger canoe without much damage was jammed underneath the overhanging balcony in the rear courtyard of the deserted house, floating on a sea of broken masonry. The wide, cooling, open plan arches of the ground floor had allowed the water to flow through the property, leaving the floor above untouched. I climbed carefully up a cast concrete staircase which had lost its handrail but seemed structurally sound, leading from the court-yard to the open balcony, walking past a row of untouched terracotta pots holding small cerise bougainvillea plants and released the dog's chain as soon as it wagged its tail at me. It padded inside and emptied the water from the pan of a western style toilet in a sparkling bathroom with a pol-ished concrete floor. I lifted the lid off the cistern and we quenched our thirst together.

There was more clean water from a tank on the roof and a piece of nat-ural sponge on the edge of the bath, and I wasted a few pints cleaning the accumulated filth of the last three days off my skin, hoping the owners wouldn't mind too much, while getting used to the gaunt, cut, bruised, troubled stranger looking at me from the full length mirror.

The screaming outside started while I was still washing, and I looked out of the window to see a massed exodus of everybody in the street running over debris the bulldozer hadn't reached, towards the higher ground I'd walked down earlier. I threw on my shorts along with the remnants of my odd footwear, hurried back down the concrete stairs and outside onto the road. The bulldozer driver was clambering down from his perch, yelling that another tsunami was coming and I completely froze, in a total funk. It's difficult for me to recount exactly how I felt. I couldn't see the ocean because of the higher buildings nearer the coast, but knew I couldn't be more that a quarter of a mile from the water and that my chances of sur-viving another tsunami hitting that street were somewhere between slim and none. And slim was currently out of town. I seemed to be rooted to the spot, way beyond panic. The feeling of visceral terror was so immense, it overwhelmed my normal decision-making process, and paralysed me. The multiple smells pervading the stricken town were joined by a new, sub-tle fragrance. With reflexes conditioned to such environmental stimuli, I recognised the deceptive, astringent and sweet musky smell that hung in the air. Fear.

It was the strident sound of a bicycle bell behind me that broke the spell. An ancient black machine was being ridden, one handed, up the street by a wiry woman, wearing what looked like a tablecloth wrapped around a wide pair of hips, on one of which was balanced a toddler in matching yellow striped shorts and singlet. A pretty little girl around seven or eight years of age in floods of tears straddled a red painted luggage rack behind the woman, hanging onto the same wide hips over the bumps and ruts the teeth of the bulldozer bucket had gouged into the soft hot tarmac. They'd reached the back of the bulldozer itself, but the road in front was impassable for a bicycle and slow going for two young children and a panting mother, wild eyed with fear. The sight of me didn't help.

My brain suddenly got into gear and bump started the thought that there were less intact buildings between here and the coast to break up and slow down a tsunami, but if the bougainvillea in the house behind us had been above the water line last time, then even if what was coming was higher than before, we'd still have a chance, assuming the weakened building could stand another battering. Getting onto the flat roof would give us an even better chance and I pointed up at it. The woman's gaze followed my finger and she gave me another disparaging once over, but she must have known it was her best chance too, as she didn't hesitate getting off the bike, when I beckoned to them to follow me back to the courtyard and up the stairs to the balcony. There were metal grab rails built into the wall at the end of one of the balconies giving access to the roof and I climbed them, lifting the children from the woman's up-stretched arms below before she joined us, smoothing her ruffled hair and clothes once she'd reached the top, determined to protect her dignity in the company of a battered, odd looking, refugee tourist.

Up on the roof we were high enough to stare at a calm and picture-perfect blue ocean, an oil tanker in the shipping lanes just short of the horizon, sailed serenely through sapphire waters sparkling in the morning sunlight, with no sign of a wave bigger than two feet high. The dog was still on the first floor below us and wouldn't stop whimpering, so I went down and brought him up too, much to the woman's disgust. I appeased her a bit by producing the water bottle I'd left in the bathroom and we all had a drink, refilling it from the rooftop tank while we waited, in mounting heat and trepidation, with no shade, eyes transfixed on the horizon, for the next tsunami to arrive.

It never came of course, but the looters who'd created the panic in the first place did as they had planned, working their way through the section of streets they'd targeted. They'd waited until the people who'd survived the tsunami had returned to their homes to salvage what they could find of value in the wreckage; after relatives and friends, precious possessions were the next things they looked for of course. The looters then set out to cause panic, literally running through the streets shouting out warnings of another tsunami coming, preying on survivors' biggest fear of all. Once everyone had run for their lives in desperation again, what they left behind was easy pickings for the looters, who were armed and very dangerous.

The twenty-five year civil war produced hundreds of demobilised conscripts every year, many of whom had no other training than in arms and using them to kill. Some turned to crime for a living and as I peered over some coping stones at the edge of the roof, I watched a team of six men systematically work their way up the street and through each building likely to provide something worth having. We kept very quiet and I had to lie on top of the dog and clamp its jaws tightly shut with my hands to stop it barking as they reached our building, and worked through the rooms below us. When we finally felt it was safe enough to climb down from what had begun as a refuge from nature, but had ended up as a hiding place from men, I noticed they'd ripped the expensive shower mixer from the wall of the bathroom. Through the open door of a ransacked bedroom I saw all the drawers of a tallboy were open, the technique of a professional thief with limited time, working from the bottom drawer up.

One of them had ridden the woman's bicycle away, and her shoulders sagged at yet another loss, body language she shared with many residents we passed on our way towards the centre of the town, who were returning after the false alarm, only to find they'd been robbed of the final few possessions they had left in the world. The bulldozer had been working hard scouring streets back to bare earth and foundations, just as if this had been an orderly and planned demolition, not a disaster of unparalleled proportion. Still not having spoken one word of a common language to each other, the woman placed her hands together as if in prayer, in what I'd always thought was a traditional sign of greeting, before we went our separate ways. But after I'd left them at the entrance of a humble two-roomed house with no windows or doors, I think she was just thanking me and had realised before I had, that what we'd been through together had formed quite a bond between us. It felt good to connect with her.

The road climbed towards the bus station overlooking the remains of the southern suburbs of the town on the end of a steep tarmac road, bordered on one side by the stone walls of a sizeable Catholic church. It had thrown open its doors and grounds to the dispossessed and the hurt.

Sheets had been rigged up over makeshift beds, to give shade to the injured, in the open air courtyard in front of the church, whilst the seriously ill, the dying and the dead lay inside the cool vaulted interior, all dappled in kaleidoscopic light streaming from the stained glass window, ablaze with scenes from the final days of Christ. In front of this uncomforting backdrop, two uniformed nurses, out on their feet with fatigue, were overwhelmed by the numbers they were trying to care for. Wounded survivors looking for medical help were continuing to arrive. I didn't join the queue.

Around two dozen red or yellow buses, parked at their stands, weren't going anywhere, and had been commandeered by people who'd lost their homes. There was a short arcade of shops designed to serve the traveller; looters had emptied them of anything edible, drinkable or of value, but a men's hairdressers had remained untouched and was even open for business. Amazingly, the hairdresser was pummelling a customer's neck and shoulders as he sat in the chair, a standard optional extra after a trim in these parts, with two customers waiting to be next. I sat on a low wooden bench outside marked 'Clergy Only', thanking God I was an undecided atheist, massaging an aching hip and swapping stories with a very serious French ornithologist called Lauren.

She'd been twitching ten miles or so inland when the river she was camping next to burst its banks, sweeping away her tent and equipment. She was obviously traumatised at what she'd found on her journey back downriver. In a hide thirty feet from the ground, she'd witnessed an extraordinary inland migration of the island's animals, and an outbreak of territorial fighting between the birds she'd been studying, and hundreds of newcomers. The island's coastal wildlife had sensed the tsunami's impending arrival hours beforehand, saving themselves en masse, while we had all remained on the coast in advanced human ignorance. The ever present, vibrant noise of wildlife had disappeared completely since the tsunami. I'd assumed the waves had drowned the land based animals and insects and destroyed the birds' habitat, not considering for a moment there'd been a massed retreat inland. Mongoose had gone missing before my final journey on the bike, the hard boiled egg I'd left outside his burrow as a parting gift untouched, and he was nowhere to be seen at first light when I'd run the Honda through Mr. Ranasinghe's open gates just three days before, in what seemed now, another lifetime.

Along with everyone else I'd met with another country to escape to, the French girl was trying to get north to Colombo and a flight home, assuming the airport was still operational. After I'd told her about the remains of the coast road south of the town, a taxi driver in earshot, working under the bonnet of a car confirmed that the road north was only undamaged for a short distance, to the point where a wrecked bridge had once spanned the same river she'd navigated.

Apart from being another camp for the dispossessed, with a rare opportunity for a haircut, the bus station seemed to have become a focal point and meeting place for several hundred people, even though nobody was going anywhere. Three rangy, barefoot men in their thirties with mean, bleary, bead black eyes were sitting opposite us, all dressed in filthy beige shirts and shorts, immediately recognisable as road workers. Lauren was aware it was a mistake, but like the rest of us, only had the clothes she was standing up in when the water arrived, and was wearing a cut down 't' shirt and shorts, which were cool and sensible garments for a treetop hide, but in public, left little to the imagination. The three men had been staring overtly at her long, golden tanned, slender legs, swigging from a bottle of Arrack they were sharing. I have to say I'd been sneaking the occasional glance too, but it was obvious they were discussing what they'd like to do with her, and it was making her increasingly uncomfortable. By the look of them, it wasn't their first bottle of the day. They'd just opened another from the obviously looted wooden crate between their legs, and their discussion had escalated to an argument, when a standard Nokia ring tone rang out from Lauren's tiny rucksack.

Everyone within earshot desperately needed to make a telephone call, so stopped what they were doing and looked at us, including the barber, who held a pair of scissors suspended in mid-air over his customer's head, the customer himself, and those waiting for a cut. Around five hundred pairs of eyes watched Lauren dig a slim black phone out of the bottom of the bag and begin gabbling excitedly into it. I had enough French to understand it was her mother, but after twenty seconds or so of France Telecom's satellite riding to the rescue, Lauren snatched the phone away from her ear and swore at the screen that was telling her the battery had died, along with all our hopes of borrowing it. Two of the drunks opposite had stood up and taken a pace towards us, while the third was taking some serious swigs out of the latest bottle. he'd stopped staring at Lauren's petite bra-less breasts and was now focussing his gaze, as well as he could, I guess, on a fat leather wallet displaying the edges of a healthy wad of rupees and Euros, she was stuffing back into her bag.

The conversation the two standing men were having had dropped to a whisper, and the third was taking even bigger swigs from his bottle, which looked to me like a man putting the finishing touches to some Dutch courage. Fights in this part of the world are unusual, invariably begin with a heated argument and some threatening body language, and sometimes escalate to fist shaking, more insults and possibly stone throwing from a safe distance. The very rare next stage is total, complete violence with no regard for self-preservation - absolute red mist - and I had no doubt the prize on offer in Lauren's bag was sufficient, under current circumstances, for stages one and two to be quickly dispensed with. The livid scar on the face of what was rapidly becoming apparent was the leader of this delightful trio, the taller of the two standing, matched the snarling curve of a cruel pair of lips and was, I'm sure, the legacy of a knife, or razor fight. I started to get very worried indeed when scar face began moving to my left, while his drinking friend on my right stood up and began to screw the cap back on his now two thirds full bottle of Arrack, with purposeful care.

Being outnumbered was of secondary concern to the presence of a blade, and I had no hesitation in suggesting to Lauren that an orderly retreat may be a good idea at this stage, before things got out of hand. She'd been studiously ignoring them for obvious reasons, and was consequently, oblivious to their threat. She was still trying to get some life out of her phone as the three men started spreading out in front of us, but she finally cottoned on when the man with the bottle in his hand sat down with an unsteady thump next to her, opened his mouth in a Saccharine smile, revealing betel blackened gums and the rotten brown remains of what had once been teeth.

I knew in my heart I should have gone straight to the station and that coming here was really just a displacement activity, all because I feared the worst about Marian's train. I didn't owe this French girl anything at all, but I knew if she stayed put there'd be trouble.

"Lauren, let's go down to the train station." I said, "See if anything's going to move anywhere."

She looked up, nodded, threw her bag over her shoulder and started to follow me down the hill. A flash of red caught the corner of my eye and I realised my sight was just about back to normal as I glanced across at an immaculately cream and crimson robed pastor leaning on a little balcony wall at the front of the Church, gazing at the scene spread out below him.

It looked like he was about to begin a sermon and I was thinking that might have been a challenging one to write given recent events, but this train of thought was interrupted when Lauren started shouting.

"Degage connard!" she screamed at the man next to her on the bench, who'd snatched the bag off her shoulder, but failed to get the strap past her elbow. I could have just kept walking down that hill, the thought crossed my mind in the blink of an eye that I probably should have, plus the fact that I was outnumbered and there were more than likely going to be knives to deal with. She was nothing to me, just a stranger in trouble like everyone else. It had turned into a tug of war with the bag and I was on the point of shouting at Lauren to just let it go and run, when scar face grabbed her around the neck from behind with one arm and laughing, started feeling her breasts with the other, as his mate untangled the bag's straps from her forearm.

I'd like to say it was everything I'd been through, all the horrors I'd seen, civilisation just melting away and the impotent, frustrated anger of listening to the looters ransack the house earlier that made me sprint back up the hill. The rage produced the adrenalin rush which helped me forget the hip, but I also knew how to get Lauren's phone working, and that meant I could call Marian's. I needed cash too, and both were inside that bag. I launched a big right hook at the side of the scarred face, which would have floored him if I hadn't hit him still running. It made him let go of the girl, but didn't hurt him enough to stop him pulling the knife I was expecting from a sheath inside his shorts. If he hadn't been so dazed, the wicked little thin blade would have been a problem, but I connected more cleanly with my second punch before he had a chance to use it, feet planted this time, better balanced, and as the straight right found his mouth, I felt his front teeth go at the same time as his jaw broke, the bottom half of his face imploding. He dropped to the ground very awkwardly with the sound of something important snapping, his head at an impossible angle to his neck. Blood flooded from his mouth down the sloping gritty concrete and I just knew from the look of him he'd never move again.

Lauren was losing the tug of war with the bag, but I suddenly had my hands full again. Scar face's mate had produced his own knife and had come straight for me, holding the blade above his head, ready to strike down, instead of in front of him, as he should have, ready to stab upwards. I don't know how much he'd drunk - he was angry - but he would have been much more dangerous sober. He slashed at me clumsily with the knife, left to right across my chest as I'd expected. The blade glinted in the sunlight as I sidestepped, it traced a glittering arc through the hot and humid air, and I caught him on the chin with a nice little uppercut and the knife skittered away across the concrete. It snapped his head back ready for the big right that was going to let him join his mate on the deck, but that little plan fell apart as my damaged shoulder dislocated with the effort of throwing the first punch, making a noise like a drumstick being ripped off a Christmas turkey. The arm went rigid, completely numb, and I couldn't move it after it shot diagonally across the front of my body, at the very moment the third guy leapt on my back, put a strong, sinewy arm around my throat and started clawing at my eyes with his long and broken, labourers' nails.

An unseen punch landed in the top of my stomach, just below the heart; I'd been panting hard already with the effort in the heat and it winded me badly. With my eyes screwed shut, waiting for the knife, a couple of glancing punches caught me in the face as I was twisting my head from side to side, trying to avoid the gouging fingers, then there was a loud crack, I was showered in broken glass and Arrack from the bottle Lauren had smashed on to her assailant's head and suddenly he was off me. I snatched the jagged, broken top of the bottle from her hand, but the guy who'd been on my back was out cold on the ground, and his mate was running down the hill, weaving through the pedestrians. The padre from the balcony above us was watching his flight, and as he disappeared around the corner at the bottom of the hill, the man in the white collar's gaze turned to me. He shook his head in disapproval, turned away and disappeared inside the church, as no doubt yet another black mark was entered in my record at his HQ, for my failure to turn the other, bleeding cheek.

My consolation prize was a kiss on the remaining undamaged one from Lauren, when I showed her how to access the reserve battery power in her mobile phone, by entering the correct number sequence, then hitting the hash key. After she'd spoken to her mother in rapid French for five minutes or so, she picked up on my increasing agitation and gave me the phone. I was pretty confident I'd remembered Marian's local cell number, but got nothing but a disconnected tone. I tried three other random numbers and Mr. Ranasinghe's landline with the same result.

After a couple of large Arracks from one of the bottles we'd liberated from the stolen case, Lauren had helped me with my shoulder, now black, yellow and blue, which thankfully slipped back into place quite easily. She made me a sling from a torn piece of tarpaulin we'd found on our way to the railway station. It was the end of the line, undamaged and cooler under the shade of the platform canopies. After she'd cleaned up the cuts and scratches on my face and shoulders with more of the stinging coconut whiskey, Lauren held my hand, looked me in the eyes and told me she'd moored her little boat a couple of miles away, next to a twisted girder railway bridge blocking the river it had once spanned. Having hidden the outboard in some reeds, she'd climbed up the riverbank using a deformed rail and the wooden sleepers still attached to it, like a ladder. She asked me to stay with her, travel back up the river and find a route to Colombo further inland.

The goods train that had been waiting in one of the station sidings for the arrival of the fated Colombo service before it could head north up the single line was still there, as the southbound service had never arrived. And now it never would. The driver, who was camped out in the cab of his locomotive, told us the railway north was wrecked in most places for over forty miles, that news had come through that the Colombo train's carriages had been found, near Hikkaduwa, scattered across three different lagoons half a mile from the track, and that there were survivors from the thousand or so passengers on board, but not many.

Along with my fragile hope, the afternoon sunshine was snuffed out by a dark grey, low blanket of heavy rain clouds. As the weather broke, a shiver ran right through me in the gloom of the afternoon and it felt like a giant hand inside me was crushing my heart. My chin dropped to my chest, and I only realised I was crying again as I tasted the big, salty tears rolling across my cheeks. I watched them join the fat raindrops disappearing into the light brown dust under my feet, wondering why I couldn't even picture Marian's face in my mind. I sat down in the dirt and devastation, not even noticing Lauren's arm around my shoulder. I was shuddering with the grief and loss, and the certain knowledge that I'd killed the man with the scarred face at the bus station. Lauren had heard his neck break too as he'd hit the ground. I'd taken a final look at him as we ran away down the hill, and I've seen that image every day of my life since.

Nothing I'd ever experienced before had come even close to the desperation I felt, squatting there in the pelting tropical rain. But, I'm afraid to say, the worst was yet to come.

8

The faintest pilot light glimmer of an early dawn was limbering up to light the furnace of another day, as I tied my shoulder bag onto the Honda's petrol tank, with some old coir string. I slid an open map with a route to the mountains under the coarse hair of the makeshift strapping, used a ragged old tea towel to wipe heavy dew from the plastic seat, swung my leg across it, and saddled up, ready to roll.

I gingerly prodded the kick starter with a sore foot, the twin cylinders' exhausts coughed, and the scorpion nest holes in the air filters that I'd plugged with pieces of natural sea sponge wheezed in sympathy, like an old smoker's early morning lungs. The smell of cheap petrol swallowed the oily tang of the puffs of rust-laden smoke expectorated from the multiple perforations in the rotting exhaust pipes. The worst were bound up with wire and thin metal cut from old food tins. One part of a rusted downtube repair still sported, baked on by the heat, the label from a can of lime pickle. We had ignition seeking combustion, which reminded me.

Of an earlier trial run along the coast road, when one big piece of hot, rusty metal gave up hanging on to the left hand exhaust pipe and lodged itself in between my first and second be-sandalled toes instead. The intense smell of frying pork that resulted, defied even the rushing air stream and I stunned a rural bunch of bus stoppees, as I appeared out of the distance at some considerable speed, screaming in pain like a manic, motorised banshee. Their heads turned as one as I hurtled past them, watching me weave out of sight around the next corner, furiously shaking one leg to try and halt the cooking process.

The memory of the pain produced a maniacal swing of the kick starter and a stentorian rasping from below, a mechanical convulsion, a backfire and I'd started a revolution, followed by a few more, then multiple combinations of the necessary sequences of four strokes were finally arranged and maintained in a semblance of order. All's well that ends well, as you like it.

I kept both fleet flat on the ground, turned to flip down the rear right hand footrest and strong fingers gripped my shoulder, as Marian expertly swung one leg over the pillion, the rear shocks settling gently under her weight. And it came to pass she tapped me on the shoulder to announce she was ready, I nodded back, eased out the clutch and ran the thumping bike down the hill past the bus station, where fellow early travellers were waiting for the first fast buses north to Colombo. A small shop was already open for them, selling single cigarettes, handfuls of sweets, and odds and sods to sleepy customers. A white dog with brown patches and mange, sat on one haunch in the middle of the road under the clock tower, the other propelling a hind leg in a languorous scratch, disturbing the fleas' breakfast. It stopped and yawned at us as we cruised past, speed slowly building out of town, leaving only a pall of dust, a flurry of leaves and scurrying whirls of sand that had found its way from the nearby beaches onto the pitted tarmac behind us.

Behind the ramshackle buildings of the fish market, early morning human ablutions were being carried out on the green open space where the town's first cricket XI played their Sunday matches. Whilst watching where they tread. And finally we were on our way to the mountains with a sharp left turn a few miles on, leaving the coast, and a huge advertising hoarding, extolling the benefits of an abrasive blue soap bar, behind us. All three of us settled into our long haul inland. My bare arms were cold, and the early morning and late night insects, unable to avoid our onward rush, hurt on impact, but the wind chill cooled the stings. It was still too dark to use the Bausch and Laumbs, and the only thing I could find to protect my eyes was a bright yellow dive mask, which made me look like Jacques Cousteau on wheels.

The countryside was flat, and the road dead straight ahead between rice paddies glistening grey in the soft half-light. The spectral graphite forms of hunched figures moved in the gloom, their working lives spent ankle-deep in water, their start was as early as ours, to get as much done before the heat of the day - just like us - except our harvest was miles, not rice.

The horizon glowed orange behind distant coconut trees as we approached a few buildings and throbbed through a waking village, early risers about their business, a purposeful few on their way to a communal water stand. A barefoot little girl in a worn yellow dress spotted our white skins, grinned and waved, clutching an earthenware water container under one arm, her greeting carried off by the wind. I smiled back and shouted hello with a guttural second syllable, forced out by the first pothole I failed to miss. The steering shimmied and an arm wrapped itself around my waist from behind as Marian steadied herself, and it stayed there as I tightened my stomach muscles with pitiful ego.

The venerable old suspension wallowed for a while after bottoming out, and we slowed for an 's' bend, snaking between two big irrigation locks in front of a man made lake. Now, how a brown Jersey cow managed to tease the glutinous white flesh from a broken king coconut husk at the roadside was a passing thought, while overhead, a huge dark fruit bat swirled into an ancient oak tree, the environmentally friendly reason for a little chicane in the road. Or was it just easier to bend the road rather than fell the tree? The flying straggler joined several hundred others settling upside down for the day, cloaking themselves in diaphanous wings, shading blind eyes, heads hunched into bony shoulders, looking like a heavy crop of giant, pendulous prunes. No doubt their stay within the shady cool of the magnificent canopy was made more pleasant by the digestion of their favourite custard fruits, freely available, as we knew, locally.

To our right, a sudden equatorial dawn burst open another day and yellow light the colour of broken egg yolk flooded the countryside with dazzling life. The instant warmth played with my goose bumps and the shivers that had been running along my spine since we set off, were reduced to a walk. The rice paddies threw off their dull cloak and shimmered with iridescent, shooting green in stark relief amongst the darker hues of the jungle backdrop. Further ahead beckoned the first dark foothills of the mountains, while down below I felt the ominous, familiar volcanic rumblings of the amoebic dysentery I'd picked up in the Rajasthan desert, some months before. It was the very last thing I needed at the beginning of a long ride. My bowels were putting up a threatening protest at the early morning pounding they'd been receiving, and I knew my instant deployment of tenacious sphincter control was only putting off the inevitable. The jelebi, a particular weakness of mine, had looked so good in the baker's teashop. I'd known only too well that street food I hadn't watched being cooked was a risk, but the glutinous sticky orange swirl got the better of my sweet tooth. I gave the smiling baker my five rupees and here I was, older and wiser, a lot thinner, and still paying a heavy price.

I'd resisted the immediate, cool glass of water always served to desert travellers, and ordered the safer tea instead, boiled together with milk and sugar, sterilised microbes, northern Indian style. But it wasn't a good sign when the proprietor waved his arm over a big black disc, and several hundred flies rose as one, revealing the stark white surface of a large bowl of sweetened milk, just as I swallowed the final piece of my forbidden fruit.

As more foreboding rumblings churned below, another lake appeared on our left, covered-in flowering lily pads, tall spiky orange blooms not waiting for a second invitation from the sunshine to open in magnificent splendour. Herons, cranes, waders and egrets dotted amongst them, heads lowered and to one side, studying the depths, waiting for their own invitation to breakfast. At the edge of the lake, just below us, around a dozen people washed in the shallows, the women wearing their husbands' sarongs, the husbands, small pieces of cloth, their children naturally naked, splashing around in the surroundings of mother nature's womb.

We waited for a dozen or so herded stragglers of water buffalo, big brown bovine beasts bombarded by swarming cattle flies, a few of which took a perilous passing interest in us, as their hosts plodded slowly into a muddy water hole, served by the lake's overflow. Here they would spend many hours ruminating, almost completely submerged except for eyes, horns, topknot and nostrils, manufacturing milk to be boiled for curd, which can apparently be thrown around with impunity.

Farm buildings connected by meandering dirt tracks were either side of us now, dotted with walkers joining us on the road, all making for the big town ahead as we moved on in a bit of a hurry, unbeknownst to Marian, due to increasingly urgent stomach messages, signalling an unwelcome early arrival of last night's dinner. I was only just managing to keep everything under control as we slewed to a halt at a bus stop, in front of the dubious delights of Chandra's Hotel Restaurant and a big, yellow, slab sided, utilitarian state bus. It honked at our impudence as we scattered waiting passengers, potential patrons and passing pedestrians in all directions. The contracting hot metal of the air-cooled Honda was ticking me off in protest at my maltreatment, as we mounted uneven steps up from the street. Here, a cook worked in an alfresco alcove, sweating over a hot stove manufacturing a small mountain of bowl shaped rice flour pancakes called hoppers, which were generating brisk breakfast business.

"Good morning, take a seat please." smiled the louche proprietor. He had nervous hands, which looked like they were already counting our money. He kept them busy sweeping back his greasy long hair then deployed them to brush away the crumbs of previous occupants from a melamine tabletop, before using them like a circus ringmaster to theatrically draw our attention to a vintage glass display cabinet behind us. Its closed glass doors entombed a bile generating selection of old cakes, buns and savoury pastries - 'short eats' in the local vernacular. Several generations and varieties of fly were incarcerated in the glass and wooden tombs, many dead, desiccated and on their backs, while their live descendents were frenziedly trying to escape back to their breeding grounds in the open drain running past the restaurant's entrance, just a few feet away from us.

"Bananas and tea, black please - that's the tea and not the bananas by the way." Marian ordered.

The longer I was spending upright, the more difficult it had become keeping things under control. There's only so long you can keep buttocks tense and clenched before they begin to atrophy, and Marian gave me a quizzical look as I disappeared past a smattering of seated customers in the direction of a brown finger, which pointed to dark satanic kitchens at the rear.

I waddled past an elderly tea wallah, who grinned at my Max Wall impersonation through clouds of steam, billowing from an ancient urn of copper and brass, burnished with tannin from decades of brewing. By now, all I could do was grunt and wave as the most welcome sign I'd seen all day announced the choice of Eastern or Western style toilets, still, somehow, just managing to hold what felt like the entire contents of Vesuvius inside me. I undid my belt and jeans button in fairly desperate haste, as customers' stares were replaced by kitchen staff's, occupying a derelict part of a building that in most other countries would have been condemned long before, let alone certified for catering.

Grappling with my zipper, at last I reached my destination, a misshapen, ancient toilet door, advertising the Western style device inside that I now needed beyond desperation. The door was so stuck in its rotting frame that I gave up my struggle with the wobbly old brass handle, and just booted it open with a kick hefty enough to tear the whole thing straight off its rusty hinges. It crashed straight into the splendid china toilet pan within, which exploded with the sound of a chandelier falling onto a marble floor, leaving only a few broken shards pointing skywards. I swore and whimpered simultaneously as the nose and whiskers of a gigantic black rat sniffed and twitched at me from a gap between the under leaves of an oversized thistle plant. Its mean, beady eyes watched my strange, frantic gate, trousers and undergarment now around my ankles, as I shuffled from West to East. Squatting, perched on raised footplates, I managed to orchestrate some sort of damage limitation, suspended over the keyhole shape in the floor, under a corrugated tin roof that made the crude privy, hotter than a docker's armpit. Beads of sweat formed salty rivulets that trickled from my temples and stung my eyes, as the searing heat of the previous day's dried red chillies, that I'd shared with Samanda the beach boy, wreaked their awful revenge.

With the mixed emotions of enormous relief and the externalising activity of humming Johnny Cash's *Ring of Fire*, I mused about squatting in this proscribed Eastern style being purportedly the healthiest position for not only defecation, but parturition too. Japanese elderly for example, rarely suffer the decay of Western hips, but for those not used to it, only a couple of novel minutes in this position produces a pain in the knees similar to having red hot butcher's skewers inserted either side, just under the caps.

I cursed my luck, as this was the very last thing I needed on such a journey, particularly one featuring a passenger with whom I was hoping to make at least a good impression, if not more. Through the open door and odour of ordure, the huge rat gave me a glance of unabashed admiration over its shoulder, as it slunk back into the kitchen through a neat hole in the wall, for what was obviously a regular visit along a well-trodden path. It was probably making a mental note to return later in a quest for any leftovers, which looked like being substantial, as turning the brass handle of the floor level tap had produced nothing more than a few fine grains of powdery grit, which dropped into the small cleansing bowl so thoughtfully provided. I fiddled with the spigot and swiped at the pipe praying for a healthy gurgling onrush of water to no avail, and began casting around in mounting panic, even for a few seconds masochistically contemplating plucking a few thistle leaves. But as temperatures continued to increase in every area, a change of tune and humming tempo to Lou Reed's *White Heat, White Light*, for some reason provoked sudden inspiration. The sacrifice of the Arabic, Chinese, Slovakian, Cyrillic and Hindu sections of my International Driving Licence provided a jobbing solution. Or big jobbing if you prefer; at least the rat would now have some reading matter to peruse during its elevenses.

Popping the somewhat thinner Driving Licence back into the valuables pouch I kept suspended around my neck, I extracted a black marker pen and regaining some composure, for the benefit of future visitors, took a moment to inscribe, above the shattered remnants of the Western style toilet, *All Turds Weighing 14 lbs or More, Should be Lowered and Not Dropped.*

I made my way back to the table and Marian's happy smile, feeling very much more relaxed than I had been going the other way, and sipped at the opaque brown tea that had arrived in old enamel mugs, while Marian delicately tapped an infestation of miniscule fruit ants onto the floor, from a bunch of tiny sweet bananas. She'd ordered fresh egg hoppers too, which arrived with a dish of ground black pepper that contained so many weevils it looked like a minimalist version of the Indianapolis 500.

The bike and our luggage had collected a confusing, eddying crowd of onlookers from passers by, being fed by an ubiquitous crocodile stream of schoolchildren stretching off into the distance. Long blue ties for the girls with dresses, blinding white in the sunshine; red bow tie, white shirt, and grey shorts for the boys. I chose the shyest little boy to start the bike for us, and his chest puffed with pride, the envy of his peers, as I showed him how to twist just a little throttle, and after only his second kick we were away, waving as the three of us settled down the road once more, the children's laughter melting away into the steady hum of the Honda's exhausts. We branched off the main road out of town towards the north west, green grass verges and stone walls smothered in striking red bougainvillea, hiding the British built chalets and bungalows of well to do residents, far from the farmland to the south of town. Warm air streamed across our skin now, Marian's touch light on my hips, steadying herself as we swerved past two white goats with black spots, chewing on something they'd found in a big pile of rubbish at the side of the road, and taking me back to childhood.

So sad once, a very small boy, I held my Father's hand as I kicked through the dry brown leaves of English autumn streets to see my Great Aunt's goat, because, he said, she was dying. And I wanted to say goodbye to her before she went to Heaven to be with the angels like my Daddy said she would. We walked over the shiny red porch steps through the little terraced house into the neat kitchen that smelt of roast dinners. Auntie Mabel was boiling her whites in a huge saucepan on the grey enamelled range, stirring the bubbling mixture with a pair of big wooden tongs and she smiled her hello down at me, wiped chapped red hands on her apron and hugged me tightly. Went out through the kitchen door through a big back yard to the wooden shed, where my friend the goat lay panting on a bed of straw, thin and weak. She raised her head to nuzzle me, flopped down again, breathless. Liked to play butting games in the yard, blinking at me from eyes with their strange shaped middles. I sat on the straw and stroked her bony head as it rested on my lap, and murmured a prayer to God under my breath, to ask Him please let my furry friend stay on earth a little while longer, because we liked to play together, and the angels probably wouldn't like the same games we did.

I heard Auntie tell Daddy that Flossie hadn't eaten for a month and a half, not even any of the big fat, late summer blooms of the yellow flowers that poked through the gaps in the neighbour's rickety old fence, as my tears melted into the coarse white hairs on my friend's head. I picked up some leek tops from the floor, another of her favourite treats, and she sniffed them as I waved them under her nose, opened her mouth to try and nibble at the green leaves but gagged, which was when I saw the strange white thing inside her mouth. I went running back in the house to tell Daddy what I'd seen and he came out to the shed, looked in Flossie's mouth and smiled.

"Go and ask Auntie for a crochet hook." he said, and I came running back with the strangely shaped little tool, Auntie following behind, still clutching her wooden tongs, one drooping orange stocking wrinkled at her ankle. I stroked Flossie's head, watching my Daddy push the little hook between her big back teeth, twist, tug, and then pull a thin piece of white elastic out of her mouth. Then, with a hand over hand motion like he was hauling a bucket of water from a well, inch by inch, a perfectly intact pair of my Auntie's giant bloomers emerged from Flossie's throat, stuck there ever since she'd tugged them from the washing line six weeks before. Auntie gave me a whole half crown for saving Flossie, which I clutched tightly in my hand all the way home as my Daddy told me about his pin up Doris Day, who went swimming every day in her Beverley Hills pool. She had a handsome young man waiting at either end he said, to pop a strawberry into her mouth after each length, which she never ever mentioned in her song I liked about The Deadwood Stage.

I put goats behind us as the road narrowed, the vegetation thickened and the traffic thinned, along with the tarmac. It was good to be away from the busy main roads where there was only one rule – whoever drives the biggest, fastest or most threatening vehicle has right of way, from any direction, at any time. The fact that roads are shared with pedestrians, cows, buffaloes either solo, en masse, or pulling carts; buses, goats, lorries, dogs in various states of activity ranging from sleeping to psychopathically rabid, street hawkers, cashew roasters, the occasional elephant, cyclists, rotivators pulling trailers converted into massed transit vehicles, monitor lizards, snakes, fruit sellers and every other sort of wild animal imaginable, requires a serious level of concentration. We rounded one blind bend to find a wizened, shrivelled old man with a long beard, matted and dirty, sheltering from the sun under an old oilskin draped across his head and shoulders. He was sitting cross-legged in the middle of our side of the road, back to the traffic, nonchalantly eating from a plate of curry nestling on the ragged sarong stretched across his lap. Marian wanted a picture so we stopped and were ignored, the old fellow oblivious to us, and everything else surrounding him. It was a miracle he hadn't been hit, and another that he was wearing an immaculately clean, white Dolce & Gabana shirt, the D&G logo emblazoned in large red letters down one side.

The surface of the road changed from poor to non-existent and back again in the blink of an eye, both of which were full of the dust and road debris that worked its way behind the RayBans. They'd replaced the dive mask at sunrise, softening the electric brightness into earthy pastel shades. Marian sounded happy humming a gentle tune behind me as we bowled along, around forty miles an hour, while the sun headed for the top of the hills with us. The Honda started to work harder as the road began to climb gently along the edge of a miniature valley between two small hills. Neat terraced rows of grey-green pineapple plants followed the contours of the valley floor, whitewashed farm buildings with red tiled roofs shone away in the distance. The three of us leaned into a long sweeping bend as one, emerging above the tree canopy to be confronted, suddenly, by the full majesty of the purple grey mountains that filled half the world before us, shimmering with white reflected light at their peaks, lit up and majestic in all their glorious, sunlit splendour.

A coir factory in the middle of nowhere was surrounded by huge balls of bright orange hair, being tossed across the road like ginger tumbleweed in the light breeze. Workers waved from their open air weaving workstations, strong new rope appearing like magic from the wooden machines clamped between their legs. The road steepened, the exhaust note deepened, the air freshened, cooling still and filled with the putrid smell of coconut shell, rotting in the factory's huge, swampy coir pits below us. Then suddenly, the sweet, familiar smell of cones and sap filled the shadows and dappled sunlight under the arched cathedral roof of a magnificent pine forest, as we entered the hill country proper.

We snaked around winding, climbing bends, my legs splayed away from the hard working heat of the Honda's engine, the toes of the foot pegs scraping the road, suspension bottoming out on a tightening hairpin bend.

Straightening up, we burst into scorching mid morning sunshine again, and a drop of a thousand feet or more appeared on our left, a swathe of emerald tea bushes carpeting the valley floor far below, dotted with the bright colours of pickers' saris. The mountains ranged ever higher, disappearing into distant haze, and we stopped to drink sweet, cold water from one of the silver streams that gurgled down the hillsides. Wild flowers and ferns sprouted from rich brown soil, between the dark grey rocks we sat on, under the shade of a magnificent Bo tree *, and we wondered if Prince Siddhartha Gautama had a view like this in Bihar, when he sat under the Bhoda tree at Bodh Gaya, and pondered on all the suffering in the world.

It took him a while to suss out the answer, realising that all existence involves suffering, and that suffering is caused by desire. So simple, and yet so hard to escape worldly gratification. I decided to put off a personal attempt at enlightenment yet again, in favour of snatching a sneaky glance at Marian's legs, and found it impossible to prevent them generating desire.

"What are you thinking?" Marian murmured beside me.

"I was just thinking", I lied, "with all those bushes down there, there must be somewhere to get a cup of tea." Actually, I was thinking Buddha couldn't have had anyone as lovely as her around, putting him off getting enlightened.

The dark black skin and chiselled facial features told me this was a Tamil lady, even if she didn't have a gold ring through her nose, who served us tea on a long white veranda, with high ceiling fans, reserved for visitors to a picturesque tea estate. Human traffic bustled outside the open windows, lithe women tea pickers at the end of their morning shift, carried huge sacks of the light green leaves they'd harvested, eternally picking two leaves, one bud. Two leaves one bud.

We sat next to each other in straw-coloured high-backed wicker chairs, the sweet smell of fermenting tea drifting towards us on the gentle breeze that had welcomed us to the mountains. Now it fanned the surface of the fragrant brown liquid, steaming in white bone china cups before us. Marian rested an open journal on her lap, chewing the end of a pencil, gazing at the strenuous activity before us.

The slow thumping thud of a giant diesel engine driving the factory

---

* Sri Lanka's Bhoda trees are descendants of the original, under which Buddha gained enlightenment. They are descended from a sapling taken to Sri Lanka by the Buddhist nun Sangha Mitra, daughter of the Emperor Ashoka. She was invited to the island to teach by King Devanampiya Tissa. The tree was planted in Anuradhapura around 27BC. It is still flourishing.

73

machinery beat like the heart of the operation, but it was the women pickers who were the backbone. As she wrote, I drank in every part of her, sipping the infusion, the tiniest buds from the bush, the most delicate flavour available, these Broken Orange Pekoe Fannings. Bargain auction price of $150 a pound, as long as you buy a few tons.

Having found out the level of wages on the tea estate, we dramatically over tipped the friendly waitress. At least everyone was provided for under a system not dissimilar to a kibbutz. Up in these mountains the hard work was all done by Tamil workers. The tea was only planted in Sri Lanka after a catastrophic coffee harvest one year. Dutch and British colonial planters had always struggled to get the indigenous Singhalese to work in the new plantations. With a sea full of fish and soil so fertile that telegraph poles sprout leaves, it's hardly surprising. When you can walk through the jungle and food literally drops off the trees onto your head, why move to the hills and work for a living? So Tamil workers were recruited to work on the estates, exacerbating ethnic tensions that have lasted for over two thousand years.

The Honda ran strongly, enjoying the drop in air temperature as we continued our climb towards the rocky peaks looming larger ahead, the mountain tops disappearing under fluffy cumulus, the engine beating rhythmically and I was so happy, I could have ridden forever with Marian close behind me, pointing at wonder after wonder. A monitor lizard disturbed from its sunny position in the middle of the road blinked, scowled and flicked a disapproving tongue at us, before scuttling into the undergrowth. An occasional bus or lorry packed with tea chests honked a warning before each blind corner, lorry cabs full of hitchhikers and often, more on the roof, everyone waving except for the hangers-on standing on back bumpers, clinging on to the lumbering, swaying vehicles.

We reached a small village with a little hardware store and to Marian's amazement, I purchased a shiny new toilet pan. I was sitting on it, drinking yet more tea, while arranging delivery to the scene of my recent destruction, with a note of apology and enough Rupees for a plumber to restore things to their former glory.

I dipped the hot oil stick, topped it up just a little and refuelled the Honda using an ancient brass oilcan, filled from a hand pump, on top of a fifty gallon drum. As our hare passed the friendly humming tortoise of an old Morris Minor we'd overtaken miles back, a big white smile from the driver, and a double thumbs up from us, I mused on the idiocy of inbuilt obsolescence. Just a little more wear and the sophisticated piece of engineering excellence beneath us, would be forgotten and thrown away.

Our society's acting as if we were the last generation there's going to be, and has wrought such vast and unprecedented changes on the planet, that we are personally ushering in a new period of geological history. Through population growth, urbanisation, travel, mining and use of fossil fuels, we have altered the planet in ways which will be felt for millions of years. The forthcoming Anthropocene (new man) epoch will replace the Holocene, and lead to the sixth largest mass extinction in earth's history. Thousands of plant and animal species are being wiped out in the first period of geological time shaped by the action of a single species. Natural, and human forces have become entwined, and the fate of one, will now determine the other.

The obscenity of planned obsolescence is more than a confidence trick of modern industry, it has become a fanatical obsession. Colluding politicians announce economic figures of expanding economies as if they were a success, rather than a direct measure of our systematic demolition and destruction of everything we need to survive here. And still, to this day, well into the third millennium, superficial politicians peddle the specious dogma of 'growth' - the very thing that irrevocably causes financial disaster - as the solution to recession!

The two most common elements in the universe are hydrogen and stupidity, but not necessarily in that order. There is a direct connection between this economic insanity, and the ongoing poisoning of every life system on the planet. IOU's are being signed that future generations will never be able to pay. Without a radical change in our hearts and vision, the earth will end up like Venus with its atmosphere of 96% carbon dioxide, charred and dead.

Henry Ford, the only American mentioned in *Mein Kampf*, owner of Edison's last breath * and the father of mass production, took a wholly different view. In his 1922 book *My Life and Work* he wrote:

"It is considered good practice, and not bad ethics, occasionally to change designs, so that old models will become obsolete. Our principle of business is precisely to the contrary. We want the man who buys one of our products, never to have to buy another."

This is an ethos all of us, not just industry, need to re-embrace.

Britain's industrial decline is due in no small part to this industrial

---

* Thomas Edison's last breath was collected and bottled by his son and given to Henry Ford as a gift. Describing the sun, Edison once said, "What a source of energy! I hope we don't wait until coal and oil run out before we tap into it."

trend. Its global reputation for high quality, long lasting products became, paradoxically, economically unsustainable. Fondly regarded in its UK birthplace as an anachronism, Sir Alex Issigonis's Morris Minor remains a highly sought after motor vehicle in Sri Lanka, where parts are still manufactured. Simple, infinitely repairable, cheap to service and run, big enough to transport a family, strong enough to deal with rough and ready roads and built to last indefinitely. Perfect. In direct contrast to the West's throwaway society, most of the East fully understands that a mechanical marvel such as a car, or a motorcycle, is an immense treasure, a privilege for anyone lucky enough to be transported by it, a precious product of Mother Earth's finite resources. So should all of us.

The road turned into a switchback ride, still climbing, but little dipped descents where the suspension had to work hard for its living, and then more steeply, down into the next valley, and we ran the Honda over a wooden bridge, crossing a tumbling river far below us, turned left and pulled up outside a long, low white building. Half a dozen boys stopped playing cricket with an old tennis ball in a big dusty courtyard, to stop and stare at the sun and saddle weary arrivals. Gentle yellow lights softened the late afternoon shadows in this Resthouse reception, where they answered my question - only one room available – which avoided another my heartbeats were racing to ask.

We padded silently on thin sisal matting, along an open passage running the length of the building, behind a skinny room boy in a white sarong. He swung open a big blue door into a room the low sun was flooding with golden light, through a pretty balcony framed with trailing jasmine. The gentle rush of water beckoned us outside as I placed a horribly greasy and probably virulent ten Rupee note in the room boy's hand, who didn't seem to care about the colour of my money.

"Sir, thank you. You can use the natural pool for swimming, cool off.

Take the path through the garden." he said, handing me an ancient brass key.

The noise of the river grew louder as the levers groaned inside the lock of the cast iron gate, and the hinges whinged as I swung it open and followed Marian through, and down a garden path. Which is better than being led up it. The grass beneath our bare feet was coarse and shorn and we dodged the occasional black pellets underfoot, before we came across their purveyor, a black and white goat sporting a bulging udder, being butted and frenziedly depleted by two nursing kids next to a big mountain stream. It was a small river really, tumbling down the hillside into a wide clear pool, surrounded by huge rocks, tossed there with an unimaginable force, thousands of years ago, smoothed by the water of millennia, all radiating the heat of the day. A shiver ran through my dive as my glowing, sunburnt arms pierced the cold silver water, and the current that ran through the natural pool sloughed the grime and sweat from me, like a snake shedding its skin.

"What's it like?" called Marian from her perch, where she'd found the last rays of sunshine, dappling one of the mottled grey rocks.

"Come on, it's as hot as a road digger's truss!"

Only the merest ripple of water and a little splash marked her graceful dive, and I watched her breaststroke power her way towards me underwater before she broke through the surface, shrieking with the cold, arms flailing, playful fists landing on my chest and shoulders.

"You terrible man, it's freezing"

I grabbed one wrist and a forearm to try and stop the assault, and a bit of a struggle ensued. I felt her suddenly cool, wet skin and the strength of the sculptured muscles in her arms, and I studied the shape of her slim lips. Her hair glowed in the sunset.

We gave up the physical struggle together, and finally ended the mental one of resisting the wonderful invader we'd been fighting for days. Her hands traced the shape of my hips and ran up to my shoulder blades, and I wrapped my arms around her freckled shoulders and pulled her towards me, eyes closing. Sweet warm breath, and a rushing wave of wonder full emotion washed through me as our cold, wet lips, finally met in earnest.

> I look at you,
> You look at me,
> I wonder, who do you see?
> I wonder do you see what I see, when I look at me?
> Do you see a mountain?
> Do you see a bore?
> Do you see a crazy kid and nothing more?
> Do you see a lover?
> Do you see a friend?
> Is this the beginning?
> Or is this the beginning of the end? Labi Siffre

9

The salt water had turned the rails and the big fat rivets on the remains of the girder bridge rusty. About two thirds of the structure was missing, the part I was standing on, propped up only by the twisted railway track that disappeared into the turgid brown river water about forty feet below. The red body of a large truck poked out of the water upstream where the river bent out of sight, the remains of a blue boat lying next to it, broken and forlorn. 'Bluestar' was crudely painted across the stern, which stuck out of the water at an unlikely angle.

A large yellow sign advertising packet soup on the side of one of the few buildings still standing on the opposite bank showed two huge, well dressed, smiling children eating from white bowls the same colour as their perfect teeth. Below it, two small children in soiled clothes stopped searching for something to eat in the deep piles of debris littering the bank, to watch a vicious fight between a small monitor lizard doing the same, and a black and white cat defending what it obviously regarded as its own territory.

There was an acrid smell of ash, mixed with the foetid stench of rotting vegetation and freshwater fish on the banks of the river, all killed by the salt water, that must have stormed inland here at least fifty feet high to have wrecked the bridge.

The heavy rain had been cleansing, reducing the humidity, the air freshening under the clearing skies overnight, but by morning, low, grey cloud had scudded over the coastline, then stopped overhead as the wind had died. We'd drunk the rainwater cascading from the station's guttering and filled the Arrack bottles Lauren and I had emptied together, before sleeping under postless mailbags on the platform's ancient teak benches. We'd set off at first light, both of us on different missions, after paying the goods train driver a small fortune to boil up some rice on the exhaust manifold of the massive diesel engine. With North / South travel so difficult, Lauren had decided to take her boat all the way up river to a gem mining town, and try to work her way back to Colombo, and a flight home, by road. She wanted me to come along too, but I was going to follow the remains of the railway line to Marian's train, wherever that led me, and she understood.

The air was still, and had closed in on us again. It was hot and oppressive and I was sweating freely as we climbed down the twisted rails to the dark ochre water using our feet and one hand, rumps on the wet sleepers, like children bumping on their bottoms downstairs. We held each other's hand in case one of us slipped towards the water, stopping for a breather when I recognised a pit viper in the river, bright green with inky black markings spilled along its back, highly venomous and very dangerous. It crossed from bank to bank with practised, liquid ease below us, passing a retreating monitor lizard swimming in the opposite direction, head above the current, trying to remove a clump of black fur stuck in the back of its jaws, with a flickering tongue. The cat was nowhere to be seen. I'd tightened my grip on Lauren's hand instinctively, and it felt so small and helpless, my fingers wrapping around it like a boxing glove.

I closed my eyes for a moment, wishing it was Marian's hand again. Held it gently while I kissed her eyes awake from a troubled dream in Kandy. Then later, knees bent beside each other in bed, propping up big wooden breakfast trays on our laps, scattered bright blue flower petals surrounding scrambled eggs, breaded seer fish, fragrant, fluffy, warm white toast, corrugated curls of yellow butter in ice, chef even found chives for the eggs from somewhere for us. Glass of Champagne, bubbles tickling, beautiful slices of fruit. I ate pieces of mango from the small of her naked back, sticky juice in tiny blond hairs around a long pink scar running down her spine. Teaching me lilting Dutch in her soft voice, propped up on one elbow, amongst crisp white sheets, teasing me in English, pale skin shining in the soft sunlight slanting through the wooden blinds, freckled and soft, and I kissed every brown mole on her body. Took a long time.

Lauren's little motorboat was still tied under our makeshift stairs, and she rowed with a small plastic paddle to a dense reed bed of Biblical size, through parts of peoples' lives the sea had washed upstream that were still being picked up from the banks, and carried back by the swollen current. A clothesline passed us, a row of garments still pegged to it, white school dresses undulating in the current as if still rippling in a long lost breeze. A green refrigerator door swirled by, three unbroken eggs still inside the holes of a neat shelf, trapped under a see- through Perspex lid. A pink doll's head with blonde hair and red ribbons tied in bows floated past, it's blue eyes staring unblinking at the clouds, mouth wide open, lips parted in an endless cry for her missing bottle. The Suzuki outboard and a flat-bottomed metal petrol tank nestled as safely as Moses among the reeds where she'd hidden them, and it started second pull.

I stood at the top of the opposite bank holding half Lauren's ready cash in my hand, waving goodbye to a very feisty lady indeed, who swung a wide floppy sun hat back as she disappeared behind bright green foliage bordering the river's bend. I felt bad about us splitting up, she was still going to be a vulnerable target and we'd shared everything, protected each other, she'd saved me from a stabbing, grabbed the loose knife, so all I got were punches instead of punctures and in the end, had saved the day at the bus station. She'd silenced my protests with a finger to her lips when she gave me the money, telling me I would need it more than her in the coming days, as she headed for civilisation, leaving me alone again amongst the devastation. Enough of the track remained in place for me to follow the line north, rails still attached to their concrete sleepers, which must have acted like ballast when the ocean hit. After three hours of walking, mostly under a canopy of coconut trees, I was yet to find one straight rail. Whole sections, sometimes a quarter of a mile long had been lifted and violently twisted by the immense force of the water, but with the pliant trees alongside preventing them being dragged inland, these huge pieces of track had dropped back to earth with the water's passing, and now lay in tortured, crumpled lines.

I trudged along the meandering tracks, speckled orange with rust, drinking from fallen King coconuts to conserve water, meeting a few people along the way. I slowly caught and passed a young couple holding hands, who looked at me as if I'd just landed from outer space, backing away when I offered them a drink. I came across an elderly gentleman later, in the middle of wilder, more open country, with a jute sack of pineapples, two of which I bought from him, preparing them with the knife that could have killed me. Lauren had insisted I keep it as a talisman, had scratched her mobile number on the handle and made me promise to get in touch when I could.

As I ate the sweet, juicy yellow fruit, a stunningly handsome hornbill glided down from an unseen perch to peck at the spiny discarded peel with its enormous beak, only a few feet away from me. And I remembered what Lauren had told me at the station about her Grandmother, who'd shared her love of birds with her when she was a little girl. She'd told Lauren that after her death, she wanted to return to the world as an owl. And nearly a year after her Grandmother had passed away, on the day that would have been her 97th birthday, a white owl had landed on Lauren's kitchen windowsill early in the morning. It had stared inside at her through the open window as she sat transfixed at her kitchen table, watching the bird, which had put its head on one side and blinked, calling softly. It arced its sculptured wings one after another, preening its flight feathers for nearly a quarter of an hour, before flying low across the garden, banking once in a semi circle as if reluctant to go, then soaring high and away, disappearing into forestry on the horizon. Granny takes a trip.

Out to sea on my horizon, the international shipping lanes between China and Europe that skirt the bottom of Sri Lanka remained as busy as usual. One long, grey vessel seemed to be steaming closer to the coast than the others. What looked like a sizeable green dredger was much nearer, beached close to a small village I reached around mid-afternoon. The sides of the steel hull and the stern were too high to climb to see if there was anything useful on board, so I carried on walking. Progress was slow as I had to pick my way through the untouched debris of flattened and broken buildings, and the familiar sickly smell of human decay that hung in the air. I passed a half closed doorway framing a young woman, sobbing, sitting on a pile of bricks in an old outbuilding that looked like it had been used for animals, and had somehow survived. She was breast feeding a baby on her lap, wiping her tears from the child's forehead with a cream coloured piece of cotton material she was also using to fan the face of a comatose boy, around five or six years old, lying next to her on some rush matting. Even from thirty feet away I could see the little boy was ill. His elder brother was outside, a very serious faced, obviously traumatised youngster, who was never going to see his father again. I gave him the pineapple I hadn't eaten, a twenty-rupee note and three quarters of the rice I had left over and kept going, fearful of what his brother's illness might be.

Further on, just a scattering of houses remained standing, but weren't habitable safely, with a dozen or so people doing what they could to survive. Several crude shelters had been put up using salvaged material, including broken asbestos sheets for walls from the collapsed roof of a large municipal building, tucked behind some coconut trees.

The going underfoot was tough, the decimated buildings covering the railway tracks completely. I was tired and hurting and wanted to rest. I would have stopped if it wasn't for the sick boy and the broken asbestos everywhere, and the fact that a teenager confirmed he'd heard Marian's train had been found in one of the string of inland lagoons set back from the beach, that run up parts of the west coast. It was about five miles further north. I followed his directions and veered off inland towards the first of them, half a mile or so behind the little town, skirting it in the direction I needed to go. The water was full of parts of buildings the tsunami had swept there, items of every description littering the muddy shore and shallow waters. A middle aged man with a mask and snorkel around his neck, and a maroon sarong knotted high up his thighs, was throwing broken bricks at a pack of thirteen pariah dogs interested in scavenging something to eat from what he was struggling to pull out of the water. I don't know whether the dogs had left along with the exodus of animals before the tsunami had arrived and had returned, or if they hadn't left, and had somehow managed to survive. Either way, without the normal plenty of human waste and leftovers around that they'd been used to scavenging from the small communal dumps dotted around towns and villages, (usually burnt once a week or so after wandering cows, crows, dog and rats had consumed anything worth having), the dogs had become cannibal, increasingly feral and dangerous.

I'd walked through the middle of a big pack two nights before, most of them sleeping, thankfully, on the warm tarmac of an intact piece of road I'd been following. I hadn't seen them in the dark until I was right on top of them. Three or four guarding the perimeter of the pack started to growl as I kept going, picking my way right through the middle of them. The hairs on the back of my neck were rigid, and I knew if I'd changed direction, or shown any fear whatsoever, I would definitely have been in trouble, particularly without a weapon.

Instinctively, I picked up a hefty iron post that had broken off some railings protecting a storm water culvert leading to the lagoon, and the dogs backed off twenty yards or so as I approached, helped by the man scoring a painful looking direct hit to the snout of what looked like the pack's leader. It was a lean brown and white mutt with strong shoulders and haunches, a fighter, half of one ear missing and numerous battle scars etched into its mangy short hair. I stamped my foot and shouted at them, waving the solid lump of iron about which made the pack retreat a little bit further, but they didn't leave, half of them just sat on their haunches while the rest skulked around, panting in the close humidity of the fading afternoon.

Leheeru was a baker who had lost his wife. he'd been cleaning his ovens on the morning of Poya day, while she'd been shopping at their little market and he was desperate to find her remains in the water. He explained that the dogs had been getting progressively bolder before I'd arrived, attracted by the sickly sweet smell of the five bodies he'd already pulled out of the lagoon and laid out on its gently sloping edge. I could see by the deep gouges on the arm of one female corpse, that the pack had already got the taste for human flesh. So, I broke my journey one more time, guarding the dead, helping this genial, gentle man continue his awful underwater undertaking, wading into the water each time he found another body.

The third the baker surfaced with, was that of a young boy; fish or crabs had eaten a great deal of his softer body parts, including his eyes and lips. There was nothing of him, and light enough to get out of the water on my own, so I waved Leheeru away, grabbed both the little boy's wrists and dragged him through the sand. I expect it was because his wrists were smaller than the others, but my fingers had sloughed off some of the soft tissue and sunk through to the slender little bones, a scaphoid snapping as the soft wet sand we'd been churning up with our feet made my uphill task harder. Once I'd got the poor little chap laid out next to the other seven, I washed my hands in the water and went into a clump of low scrub bushes a little further on around the edge of the lagoon, where I was out of sight of Leheeru and as sick as I could be on the pineapple and rice I'd eaten earlier. The violence of my retches made me involuntarily empty my ongoing loose bowels, so I had to clean myself up as best I could and was rinsing my shorts out, when I heard the first cries of the infant.

Maybe there'd been a conspiracy of silence about it, but I couldn't find out who'd left the little girl next to the corpses. Eventually, I have come to understand why. Someone looking after the girl must have been watching me. I believe the thinking was that a wealthy white foreigner would have the resources to help the little orphan, find her some food and care for her maybe, even adopt her, while the few desperate people in what was left of the town fought for their own survival. I expect they thought leaving her there would leave me with no choice other than to take on the responsibility.

Whoever had, was gone by the time I'd managed to pull wet shorts up damp legs and sprint back, but two dogs' hunger had overcome their fear and they'd got to the baby before me. Each had one of her limbs in their jaws and were shaking the screaming little child like a rat, trying to break the other's grip. I leapt on top of one of the dogs and it let go of the baby, locking its jaws into my arm instead. I tried to grab the second, but it span out of reach and ran, dragging the baby away by one leg, leaving a trail of blood in the sandy yellow soil, before it was leapt on by the rest of the pack. I gouged into an eye of the first dog's head with my thumb, which made it let go of my arm with a scream, but it turned to come at me again with three others from the pack that now had the scent of blood. More were chasing down the dog with the baby - I'd screamed at Leheeru for help and he'd heard, but was still swimming towards the shore about fifty yards out.

I killed two of the dogs quickly with one blow each from the iron post, stunned the third, I heard its skull crack like a stone shattering a windscreen and I broke the back of the one eyed one. It kept coming at me in its blind fury, suddenly released from pent-up years of fear of humans, even though its back legs had stopped working, dragging itself with its front, but it was no longer a threat. I sprinted across to the gaggle of other dogs that were fighting over the baby like hounds that had caught a fox, while others fought each other for position in furious dogfights at the sides. I used the post like a baseball bat, killed and maimed six more of the frenzied dogs but I was too late to save the child. I broke both jaws of the second of the first two dogs that still had the baby in its grip and it ran off screaming in pain, both jaws dangling from its face.

Only the body and one leg remained of the little girl, and as I picked up the tiny little torso, her intestines spilled out of a gaping wound in her stomach. With the post I'd dropped, Leheeru killed another of the dogs that tried to grab a mouthful of the guts, and another that had been feeding on one of the corpses. He tried to catch the pack leader which had the little girls' head in its jaws, but couldn't. After he gave up the chase, doubling over, panting with exertion, the dog loped to a safe distance in the brush and with a wary eye on us, began hungrily devouring its prize, the sound of its teeth grinding on the bone of the skull, clearly audible.

I have never forgiven myself for walking those few yards, just for privacy from a stranger, just to avoid my own embarrassment, pandering to my pitiful little ego. I have never forgiven myself for wasting precious seconds pulling on the wet shorts, and I never will.

On my knees in the reddened soft sandy soil with what was left of the little girl in my arms draped, and bleeding all over me, I heard the most awful primaeval noise I have ever heard come from a human. I turned and saw tears streaming down Leheeru's face; his mouth was open, but he was still panting from his frantic swim, killing the dogs, and the chase. And through the adrenalin, and the terrible turmoil of the images of what had occurred in less than a couple of minutes, I was shocked to realise that the sound had been coming from me.

10

I ducked under the flight path of a huge sand wasp as she droned past, clutching another load of gritty soil for her small ice cream cone nest, tucked high up in a corner of the Resthouse bathroom. I flicked the two drowsy daytime mosquitoes I'd caught, hanging out in the damp folds of the shower curtain, into a pristine new spider's web. The sand wasp's neighbour stole warily from her vantage point at the centre of her overnight creation to investigate the bounty, suspicious of the lack of struggle from the new arrivals. All this insect industry was interesting an envious, beady black-eyed gecko that cursed its luck and scuttled away across the whitewashed plaster wall in disgust. I stooped to the inevitably chest high mirror to ask myself why it is one always seems to find something that's been lost, in the very last place you expect to come across it?

Water from the external plumbing, warmed by the sun, ran from the old brass shower head for a few fleeting seconds as I braced myself for the icy blast that would follow, piped directly from the mountain stream and capable of engorging nipples to the size of rifle bullets in seconds.

The suds from the soft water were a treat though, as was the huge, fluffy white bath towel. I dried myself under the ceiling fan of the empty bedroom and tried on the new trainers I'd tucked into the tank bag. I checked each one carefully for scorpions and snakes, both of which like to overnight in dark, warm, concealed places, and thoroughly object to intruding human feet. Surreal, Lilliputian moment waking in gloom on the morning we started this trip, to see one of my old shoes, stripped to its carcass, being slowly transported across the teak floorboards of my bedroom by several hundred ants, in the direction of their nest. *de gustibus non est disputandum*. Must have been the drugs.

I was wiggling my toes in the unfamiliar, reptile-free footwear, watching the morning sun brushing mist from the Eastern face of the mountains behind Marian. It played amongst the copper highlights of her hair as she tilted her head towards the warmth. She sat at a long refectory table laid for breakfast on the pastel yellow painted veranda, dark wooden floorboards polished by decades of waxing and countless feet. Laughter lines danced at the sides of her mouth as she smiled at me, chin cupped on the upturned palm of one hand, She wore a white t-shirt with a cartoon moon in a dark, star spangled sky. Her elbow rested on the crisp white linen tablecloth, where she sat between two concrete pillars under furled storm blinds bleached by the sun, completing the frame of a picture that took my breath away.

Speckled boiled brown eggs, hot buttered toast and sweet strawberry jam were the taste of home and a breakfast I will never forget, the flat of Marian's hand soft and cool on top of mine in the middle of the table. The bright blue eyes of a wheelchair bound elderly Austrian further down the table twinkled at us. He offered the lure of cigarettes, politely declined by Marian in perfect German, while I swore under my breath in English and made do with secondary smoking as we chatted over coffee and several decades of our three countries. He reminisced of living through the late 1930's in Hitler's Germany, the Reichstag fire, *crystalnacht* and the purges.

"You know how they started rounding up the Jews, then began arresting the gypsies and the travellers, and we all kept quiet when they turned on the communists and the trade unionists as well."

"If I'd been in this then." he said, slapping his hands on the arms of his chair, "I'd have been wheeled away next and that would have been that, but I learnt the English word, 'hackneyed', it is hackneyed, yes?, to say there was no-one left to speak up when they finally came for us. But it's true, and we must continue to speak of this, in case it is ever forgotten. Einstein knew, he learnt the lesson and spoke out famously of course, * but too late for so many of us. We couldn't believe it when they began raiding the clubs, God in Heaven, Himmler sometimes brought his boyfriends to ours, we just never expected it."

He was quiet for a while, staring into nothing but memories and we

---

* 'the world is a dangerous place, not because of the evil things men do, but because of those who stand-by, look on, and do nothing.'

sat with him until Marian prompted him back to the present, so we could visit his past and he held us with his story, wrenched from the centre of a shattered heart.

"I was nineteen, and very much in love. He was in the year below at our University, studying music, the piano. He was so beautiful, blond, brown eyes, tall and slim and so graceful, so sensitive and gifted, so gifted with the music, he could take you to Heaven."

"It was our anniversary, two years we'd been together but we'd argued that night in the club, too much to drink. Daniel accused me of looking at another boy but it was meaningless, I mean I was just looking, not to touch, but the argument got worse so I left our table, I strode over to the boy and I kissed him, just to spite Daniel then I took him outside, around the corner to a little bar, more so I could cool down before I went back than anything else."

"When I did, half an hour later, the club had been raided and I watched from the shadows of a doorway everyone inside being thrown into the lorries. Daniel was one of the last, he looked so fragile, so scared. He was the only person I have ever truly loved. I tried, but no-one ever knew exactly where people were being taken; East to where the camps were - we were beginning to hear of what was going on there and then the war started of course. That was the trigger for it all to worsen; as soon as Britain declared war Goebbells said, 'Now we can do anything we want.' And the camps became so bad."

"I didn't fight, I wouldn't fight, I was an Austrian, Germany's war had nothing to do with me, but I ended up as a guard, at Krakow of all places, and three years after the raid on the club, I met Daniel again. I didn't recognise him, couldn't have, he was so sick by then but he recognised me of course. I was guarding a work party laying railway tracks outside the camp. It was so cold, the prisoners were glad to work and I was stunned when one walked towards me and spoke - prisoners were not allowed to do that - then he touched my arm gently. His hands were rough from the work, but still so slender and beautiful, I recognised them first, then he looked into my eyes and in a moment we were back in Berlin, together again, and I was so desperate to hold him, and kiss him after all that time, but the other guards were already watching what was going on."

"I have always loved you," he said. "I've missed you so terribly."

"And then he was gone, running. Away from me, towards some woods, a hundred metres or so away. I heard a guard behind me cocking his rifle and Daniel stopped and turned to me, smiling, hoping it was mine, and I called out to him across the frozen field, told him I'd never loved anyone else, and that I never ever would, and my words reached him just before the bullet from my rifle burst both our hearts."

****

Now fully out of retirement, the Honda seemed pleased to see us, albeit protesting a bit at the thin mountain air it was being asked to work with, but I wiped the tropical novelty of mountain dew from the seat and it fired up backwards twice, then eventually in the right direction, and the low white building that Marian and I would never really leave, disappeared to nothing in the old bike's sepia stained mirrors.

They say there's a first time for everything and even when we got quite close to the lorry ahead of us, it took a while to work out what the strange shape was, swaying about in the open back. But in the end there's no getting away from the wrinkled skin of an elephants arse, its owner standing high and proud next to her mahout, leaning quite precisely into the mountain bends. She seemed perfectly at ease in her elephantine taxi, pink and grey spotted trunk sprawled across the yellow tin roof of the driver's cab as we eventually accelerated past when she'd opened her bladder, turning the lorry's slipstream rather moist and yellow.

The strip of tarmac narrowed and clung to the precipitous side of the mountain we were climbing. To our right, the road was bordered by bright red Agapanthus blooms behind deep kerbstones and beyond, an endless vertiginous mass of open space over the treetops of the coastal plain where we'd begun our journey. Split by the glassy sliver of a snaking river thousands of feet below us, the jungle canopy sprawled away to the sienna strip in the far distance, where it met the sapphire water that reached seamlessly up to join us in the blue skies, high above the southern Indian Ocean.

Ten minutes later we'd made the train we'd wanted to catch with time enough to enjoy the restrained morning bustle of the tiny provincial mountain railway station. Marian stooped to peer through an ancient wrought iron barred window and in her soft, lilting accent explained our requirements to the ticket clerk, whose eye whites and teeth gleamed in the gloom under the Roman numerals of a beautiful big clock on the wall of the stationmaster's quarters. I pushed the Honda onto the platform in front of the parcels office for inspection and clearance for transport and parked amongst baskets of chickens, sacks of rice, coconuts and a big pile of pineapples, and a crowd gathered immediately around us, Marian attracting most of the attention as usual. An ancient telegraph machine, another wonderful clock and assorted old railway paraphernalia cared for, highly valued and polished, glinted in the shadows behind a smiling white haired parcels clerk, who explained the formalities from his seat behind a huge battle scarred, ink stained oak desk.

"You must first remove all petrol and provide some rope for lashing the guard." he explained. The rules seemed a little harsh on subordinates, but after the usual lengthy and tortured administration, we swapped a handful of greasy rupees and the torn cardboard back of an empty Gold Leaf cigarette packet I found on the tracks, for two stopping tickets to Kandy, the island's mountain capital.

Marian clutched the multi-coloured sheaves of paper bureaucracy we got along with the thick cardboard tickets and a complimentary piece of string, which we used to attach the back of the fag packet - transformed into an official dispatch note with a heavy black stamp - to the only part of the rusting handlebars not covered in sinewy, Singhalese hands. Their owners jostled for a chance to fantasise about riding the big blue twin – an unusually large and rare bike on the island.

I asked the clerk who accompanied me outside to oversee the boarding preparations, for a stopping schedule. His eyes rolled to the heavens before he delivered what sounded like a considered guess, while a further distribution of bank notes enhanced the local economy, and some brand new scratchy coir rope appeared within a couple of minutes. Under the close scrutiny and covetous murmurings of a dozen white clad mountain villagers regarding the surgical quality of Victorinox steel, I used my battered Swiss army knife to undo the jubilee clip at the bottom of the fuel pipe where it joined the carburettors. With apparently nothing better to do, we began to exchange pleasantries, short and tall stories and rudimentary jokes, while the bright red petrol slowly trickled into a variety of hastily gathered containers.

As I placed each one on the concrete platform at my side, it was surreptitiously spirited away as its replacement, handed to me with timing designed to distract the removal of its forebear, began to fill. Serene and relaxed, Marian stood on an old teak platform seat, polished to a sheen by endless posteriors. From her vantage point, and through her professional photographer's eyes, she surveyed the scene and recorded the conspiracy for posterity in black and white, through the lens of a small, neat old wet film Leica. Preparations finished, and the bike still parked in the middle of the small crowd adjacent to where the guard's van was predicted to come to rest, there was time to wait for our mountain chuffer. So I went in search of yet more tea, strolling past the neat white painted buildings divided by an exit gate where the original ticket clerk, whose teeth I recognised, hurried out of his office to meet me. Doubling as a platform attendant, he scrutinised me and my rectangles of purple cardboard covered in the tortured hieroglyphics of Singhalese script, as if seeing all of us for the first time.

He removed a chunk from the body of the tickets with a vicious metal implement I would have liked to borrow to clip my toenails, as the scissors on the Swiss army knife were the only ones I possessed, and exclusively reserved for my Mengelesque mosquito experiments. I asked for a second opinion regarding where we were going to stop and received an interesting variation on the original theme. I'd learned it was always best to ask the same question in three different ways here, before taking a view, and to remember that more often than not, the majority answer was the least reliable. But everyone we asked seemed to agree we had one hour to wait for the train at little Haputale station, where a brightly whitewashed platform cafe served thirst quenching ginger tea of both taste and colour. It was brewed and served with one arm, a smile of welcome, and a nod of thanks from the efficient proprietress, who clasped a young sleeping son to her breast throughout the process. On the top of a glass display counter in the shady cool lay a cut branch of green bananas which looked unripe, but a peel and peep inside one revealed perfection; sweet reward for my grumbling tummy. Not strictly a tree, but a herb, what an extraordinary plant the banana is, its six month life cycle one of nature's wonders.

I handed over a tiny sum, the coins disappearing inside a colourful sari top, stuffed the middle finger of a bunch of bananas in a back pocket of my jeans and carried two white cups of steaming tea back along the platform to find Marian still on her bench, engaged in a conversation in Dutch with a slight, wiry chap of advancing years.

"Ah, this is your husband?" he asked, switching to English as I handed Marian her tea. We looked at each other to see who was going to field the question, and Marian volunteered.

"No, we're not married."

"Then you are betrothed?" he asked me with an inquiring smile.

"Just travelling companions; but who ever knows what life brings us?" I replied, resisting a glance at Marian.

"Are you travelling on the Kandy train today?" I asked him, deflecting further speculation.

"No, I am waiting here for my sister, for fourteen years. She is coming on the next train, from Croydon."

"I'm sorry, where?"

"Croydon, in England, it is near London in a county called Surrey. You are from London, your wife - I mean this lady here has told me so. Perhaps you must know my sister, she has been living in Nelson Road, number seventeen, since 1990."

They got bored waiting for me to find an inspired response to his confirmation that it's a very small world, switched back to Dutch and lost me in seconds, so I left Marian to follow up his revelation, and withdrew to the gingery fragrance of the brown brew. I was absorbed by the eclectic mix of passengers trickling onto the platform past a forlorn, disabled lottery salesman, slumped inside his homemade cart. I bought a ticket and shared my bananas, lifted a little boy onto the Honda's seat and became his hero when I let him scratch off the ticket's little silver squares to give us luck and his face lit up when we were Rs.50/- winners.

Beyond the roof overhanging the track, the midday sun was really beginning to flex its muscles, hardening the softer morning light with dazzling strength, flattening the landscape's perspective from cubist depth, to flat, stark, colour wash. And talking of Cubism, I'd recently learnt from the broadsheet *Colombo Times*, what must have been substantial chunks of the UK's Lottery Fund had been invested in some Picassos 'for the nation'. Tucked away in another, rather older institution, The British Library, is a copy of Giovanni Papini's *Libro Nero*, written in 1951, where the author, a confidante of the artist, records Pablo Diego Jose Francisco de Paula Juan Nepomucemo Maria de los Remedios Cipriano de al Santisima Trinidad Martyr Patricio Clito Ruiz y Picasso's confessions.

"The people no longer look for consolation and exhilaration in art. The cunning, the rich, the idle and the distillers of quintessences want the new, the strange, the original, the extravagant, the scandalous. And I, from Cubism onwards, have satisfied these gentlemen and these critics with all the changing oddities that have come into my head. The less they understood, the more they admired me. When I am alone with myself, I dare not call myself an artist in the grand and ancient sense of the word. Giotto and Titian, Rembrandt and Goya were true painters; I am only an *amuseur public*, who has understood his times and has profited as best he could by the imbecility, the vanity and the covetousness of his contemporaries. This is a bitter confession to make - more painful to me than you may think - but at least it has the merit of being sincere."

My eyes narrowed in defence of the stark light glinting from the shiny steel rails below me, which gently whispered of an approaching locomotive. Twelve matt red oxide coloured railway carriages shimmered through the heat haze into my watercolour, removing it like new scenery entering from stage right. They were hauled into place by a throbbing diesel locomotive, which brought the carriages to a shunting stop, brushing the perished black rubber hose dangling like a broken armband from a sad, rusting and redundant water tower, joining the many of us, mourning steam. The open grey lavatory door at the end of a second-class carriage came to rest directly in front of our slatted wooden platform bench, three metal embarkation steps led up from the platform.

Human life appeared on board, dissipating my still life illusions, a young man scouted for the toilet, glanced inside but withdrew mysteriously quickly, back the way he came. Moments later he reappeared though, clasping from behind the not insubstantial hips of a fat blind man whom he steered towards the toilet. The blind man waddled, arms akimbo, feeling the passage walls like a cat's whiskers in a tunnel. They entered the compartment together in what must have been a very tight squeeze and I wondered if the helper's duties extended to aiming the flow from the blind man's penis, or perhaps it was merely consultative and hands free, more like *The Golden Shot*. They'd slammed the door and the smell of baked, stale urine, wafted across the platform, which rather put me off continuing chomping the moist sweet creamy herb, the rest of which I donated to a patient brace of crows, ever present scavengers of the East, who cawed in appreciation, stabbing truculently at the banana's remains, with their black sickle beaks.

Here at the end of the line, some over zealous shunting, preparing the train to retrace its tracks, slammed the guards' van into the last carriage, jerking the whole train, just as the blind man reappeared on the top step of the open doorway. His helper made a vain grab from behind, only managing a tenuous grip on the back of his charge's shirt collar, which detached with a loud rip, as the vast bulk of the blind man plunged the not insubstantial distance to the platform, where a stack of wooden cages containing several hundred baby chicks, exploded instantly on impact, as if made of balsa wood. The ensuing chaos of the noisy, chirping, massed escape, provided the perfect diversion for my conspirators and I to hide half a dozen varied containers of petrol, passed through the window from the wrong side of the tracks, behind the stacks of magazines, mailbags and general incoming cargo being ticked off by a clipboard-wielding goods van guard. He checked the back of the fag packet on the handlebars, then added one motorcycle to his recently reduced inventory, as I trussed the machine to the side of the carriage with yards of coir rope.

The guard's opinion of the train's stopping schedule conflicted with the assured prophecy of the ticket clerk, which differed to the prediction of the parcel clerk. Fluffy baby chickens rushed in and out of the Parcels Office, the Railway Protection Force Office and the Ladies' Waiting Room where Marian had disappeared and several dozen gave the guard and I a chirpy, ankle height welcome as we crossed the threshold back into the shadowy cool of the Stationmaster's Office. Here, chaired by the uniformed, sage like Stationmaster himself, we entered the committee stage of our train's stopping schedule and reached a unanimous verdict based on what appeared to be a combination of calculation, experience, divination, recollection, intuition, prayer and hope.

Back outside, a wiry, efficient looking fellow, immaculately dressed in pressed white business shirt and trousers in shining silvery 'staprest' material, swung nimbly from the platform onto the oily vibrant bulk of the diesel locomotive. Good to see the engine driver so smartly prepared and I wondered if he knew where we were going to be stopping, as I'd put quite a bit of time and effort into planning this journey. I decided to give the first carriage marked 'Clergy Only' a miss, as acquisitive orange clad men were to be avoided on this trip, and the Buffet car was next, where soft drinks, having warmed up nicely on the platform, were being stacked inside by barefoot staff preparing for the alleged six hour run through the mountains to the island's interior. Flies, cockroach carcasses, soot, grease and general grime of substantial age and depth covered just about everything.

The second and third class carriages offered the choice of broken fans, comfortable, padded seats covered in plastic for sweaty backs and bum clefts, or hard but slatted and cooler third class benches, which numbed the arse completely after a few miles. I found what I needed in a second class carriage further along, which actually had a working overhead fan pointing at two opposite facing window seats, beneath a stern stencilled sign announcing they were reserved exclusively for 'Elderly and Pregnant Mothers Only.' They were on the platform side, which was just what I needed, with the added benefit of them being in shadow for the majority of the journey. Posh.

I borrowed a stick of chalk from a khaki clad porter, trousers rolled up above his knees, trundling a sack trolley heaving with luggage. He watched

me quizzically as I chalked a big white cross on the side of the train directly under our window. Another train throbbed in to the station from up
country and a couple of minutes later, with the single line clear ahead,
Marian was leaning out of the same window, taking pictures of the platform sliding past us and an embracing couple, one from Haputale, the
other bearing gifts from Croydon, surrounded by suitcases and a sea of
baby chicks.

A warm breeze toyed with Marian's hair as she leaned through the window humming to herself, studying the scenery and I stole a sneaky look at
her curves, all the way from her slim, strong shoulders right down to the
tips of her toes and suddenly, my eyelids were heavy from lack of sleep
and the mountain air. The train had by now rocketed to a fast running
pace, but slowed back to a crawl as the smell of hot coconut oil wafted
through the carriage from the Buffet car behind us. I followed the smell
like the cartoon kids in the Bisto gravy advertisement, to find a cook toss-
ing a few onions and dried red chillies into a smoking frying pan, in the
intense heat of a rudimentary kitchen.

He ladled a watery omelette mixture over the fizzing vegetables from a
grimy green plastic jug. The lacy thin egg mixture cooked too quickly for
the grinning cook's assistant, who was lazily slicing white bread rolls, into
which an expanding pile of cooked omelettes were waiting to be placed.
The finished articles were stacked on a steel tray in mountainous arrays.
This gave the countless flies inhabiting them, plenty of grip and room for
manoeuvre for their salivating, regurgitive consumption.

With such a lead over the roll slicer, the cook was glad of the diversion
I provided and an opportunity to practice his English.

"Where you from?" he said.

"I am from Burning Bottom."

"American?"

"Venutian actually."

"I am cook omelette for beesfast."

"Jolly good they look too."

"What is your name pliss?"

"Egon Ronay."

The cook repeatedly rolled the name around his tongue, started another omelette and after a bit of practice he was pronouncing the name with
some aplomb. Whilst digesting this newfound information, he reflectively
removed a large bogey from his left nostril with the index finger of his left
hand. Using the same digit with delicate dexterity and no attempt at

removing the offensive nasal detritus still located on its tip, he picked up the edge of the wafer thin omelette, and dropped it into the waiting jaws of a sliced bun held open by the still grinning cook's assistant. It seemed rather like a nurse holding open the jaws of a recalcitrant dog, allowing the vetinary surgeon safe access for the insertion of a pill deep into the patient's throat. At least the bogey will be hidden from the unlucky recipient I thought, who turned out to be me, as the assistant pushed the 'special' omelette bogey bun into my hand.

"For you beesfast. No rupee OK?"

"OK, thank you."

I decided to take my leave before they expected me to consume the horrible thing in front of them. Like the chicken I was expected to carve as the honoured guest at a village feast the other day. Tramped through the jungle for miles at the invitation of a friendly young chap, to find all thirty odd residents of a small village waiting for me at a long table, in a palm thatched ceremonial meeting house.

At the head of the table, a burnt and blackened chicken was placed before me that had obviously died of starvation long before being cooked to a cinder in an underground clay oven. I sat next to the head of the village and a pile of wooden plates was placed at my elbow. Then the headman motioned in sign language that I was to carve the flightless famine victim, with the huge machete he placed at my disposal.

One gentle blow from the massive implement, more suited to felling a coconut tree than the precision required to divide the pitiful bird's corpse thirty ways, was enough to shatter it into hundreds of pieces, shards of blackened bone flying to all corners of the room. This was more to the benefit of the village dogs than the gathered throng, who had to make do instead with their standard dinner of vegetable curry, coconut sambol and boiled rice. The two bottles of Old Arrack I'd carted along saved my honour and the day, the strong alcohol promoting quite a party for villagers used to home made palm wine. Picking our way through the dark on the way back, stopping for a breather with my young guide, it also provided enough Dutch courage for his question.

"You like to see Cobra, King Cobra now?"

"It's a bit dark don't you think, they're rather dangerous aren't they."

"This one not dangerous, but big for you." he replied, stroking the end of an enormous tumescence, poking up against the thin cotton of his sarong.

I eventually found my own way home.

"You tell everyone Egon Ronay was here OK?" I called over my shoulder to the breakfast chef, as I swayed away up the corridor.

"Yes, yes, Egon Ronay, goodbye, bye, bye,"

The train was accelerating hard and as I negotiated the swaying floors in the connecting doorway where the two carriages met, I could hear the cook repeating the name over and over like a religious mantra, in time with the clicking of the steel wheels below us. I bowled the offending bun out of the open door at the end of our carriage with a little bit of off-spin, getting quite a bit of grip and turn off the omelette seam before the whole thing came to rest, intact, on a patch of grass at the side of the track, awaiting the first scavenger, ovine, bovine, canine, feline, porcine, ornithoid, goat or human, unlucky enough to come across it.

Standing on the top step of the doorway, the train began to rock, sway and roll, full diesel ahead, and I gripped the sturdy boarding handles on either side, to ensure I only watched the blurring landscape and didn't become part of it. Chiaroscuro colours bled into each other, and I remembered Joseph Turner once held his head out of an English train window, facing the steam engine and driving rain, and later that day, painted what he saw. It turned out to be one of his masterpieces, the blur adding greatly to the scenic beauty. And in his opinion, the loveliest skies to paint were those over Margate. Lucky Kent.

I ducked out of the way of a ragged branch being beaten back to the forest carpeting the hillsides on either side of the train. The landscape dropped away to valleys far below, thronged by the ranks of blue green mountains in the distance, as if lining up for our inspection. We passed some open water, carpeted with pink and lilac blooms. A dragonfly of exquisite beauty and metallic green hues held perfect station in the turbulent billowing slipstream just in front of me, before it twisted its head like an owl and scudded away, zig-zagging back to its predation above the lake.

We flashed by a fresh water stand pipe and the small hamlet it served, and I saw a dozen lives in half a second, in a variety of personal activities from laundry to showers, to quenching of thirsts. Further up the track, a pretty barefoot teenage girl walked along, balancing two dripping water containers. Under the crook of her left arm was the neck of a traditional pot bellied earthenware water jar, its base resting on the top of her hip, weight evenly distributed, poetry in motion. In her right hand she held an ugly old plastic oil container, arm drooping, handle probably cutting into her hand. Her dress was beautiful native cotton batik, her shirt a cheap and gaudy imported rag, featuring Donald Duck. The transition of the rural

97

Singhalese from ancient custom to modern tat, is more than a crying shame.

The tragedy of Asia for me is not so much that such shirts are valued higher than silk, that cooling coconut thimbuli, is eschewed in favour of Coca-Cola, but the false values that have been imported with them. Droves of directionless Westerners seek enlightenment in the East, milked by the 'export gurus' in their contrived Ashrams, while local populations crave satellite TV and learn to speak English from atavistic game shows.

Marian was sleeping, and I sat down gently next to her, studying her face in every detail and remembered yesterday's evening the same way. I let the warm glow deep down inside me, envelop us both. The train slowed, the distant hum from the diesel's throat deepening as the climb steepened and curled around tight mountain bends. At times I could see the whole of the side of the train through the window without moving from my seat, here on our narrow track, threading amongst the peaks which vaulted into glittering aquamarine skies, in the thin mountain air.

Our fellow passengers had settled into the journey and quietened down with the gentle, swaying movement of the train, which had now taken charge of all our lives, imposing its own pace upon us, and rocking me to sleep too, my eyelids getting heavy and losing their battle with gravity. Up front in the distance, the train hooted at a cow straddling the track and I drifted off, holding Marian's hand, her head turned towards me, soft breath on my cheek and I couldn't remember the last time I'd felt so happy.

I dreamt of a journey in the front seat of a bus early one chilly dawning, mist cladding trees lining the road. All the seats were full, but the passengers behind me were silent, and I had a feeling it was because of me. Their eyes burnt into the back of my neck while my feet were cold in my leather sandals, so I warmed them on the metal engine cover in front of my foot well, these seats always the last taken in the heat of the day, because of the heat from the engine. The driver had fashioned a gaudy shrine, garlanded with flowers in the compartment that once housed a roll of destination signs at the front of the bus.

Buddha sat sedately cross-legged next to small pots containing offerings of rice and sweet smelling frangipani blossoms. The small lime-green-painted cavity featured hidden down lighting and was incongruously flanked by a picture of the pop singer Madonna and massive red, yellow and green lamps, more at home on the roof of a Kenworth Freightliner. These were linked to the indicators and brake lights, quite handily in fact, as the driver alternated between flooring the brake pedal and accelerator along the narrow twisting roads we travelled. Every time he stamped on the former, screaming brakes were accompanied by the sickly smell of scorched asbestos, the exhaust brake throbbing its protest, and additional red lamps further illuminated the shrine, and even Buddha's eye sockets. Every time this happened the driver turned in his seat, expressionless, to stare at me and I was afraid, holding onto the metal seat frame with sticky palms.

The road ahead worsened, became dusty and turned out to be coastal as the sea appeared on the left, before we entered a series of blind switchback corners hewn into rock. A full light display accompanied our fiercest braking session yet. Buddha's eyes were extinguished as he toppled on to his back, while the driver furiously pumped his middle pedal to stop the wheels locking. I held on for cheap life as the big yellow bus slewed sideways and out of the driver's control towards a bullock cart, overturned in the middle of the road. The poor beast had laid down its burden and was on its side, dead, tongue dangling grimly from its last gasp. I braced myself for the impact and a jolt and a squeal of the train brakes woke me as we came to rest under the shady roof of Ohiya station.

The high mountain air was cool and filled with the musical chants of food vendors queuing on the platform to board the carriage, working their way through the train, with zealously competing chants, "Lunch packet, lunch packet, lunch packet," or "Orange, orange, orange, orange," the tea ladies lilted, "Chai, chai, chai, chai, chai" and the definite winner, was a man with a deep woven basket full of crispy spiced lentil doughnuts, neatly wrapped in cones fashioned from pages torn from old schoolbooks. His quick fire delivery featured an extended singsong, uplifted final syllable, "Wadi, wadi, wadi, wadi, wadeeeee!"

Amongst the throng competing manically for our transient business, my co-conspirator had spotted my cross chalked under the open window, and without saying a word, passed in the little folding wooden picnic table we'd borrowed from Mr. Ranasinghe. It fitted perfectly between our seats, followed by an improvised clay ice bucket, incredibly, filled with ice, plus two chilly pint bottles of Lion Lager to go with devilled king tiger prawn starters. They were fresh from the skillet, blackened strips still smoking from inside perfect banana leaf pouches, held together with tiny bamboo spears, which we used for cutlery. Marian was as stunned as everyone else on our carriage, hugging Samanda through the window and kissing me on both cheeks, and her laughter lifted everyone's mood in the carriage, which had by now turned into a restaurant car, picnics and snacks, lunch packets of rice and curry filling the air with spicy fragrance. Marian slid one of the small bright orange flower blooms Samanda had scattered around the edge of our table into her hair, as I poured beer into two pot bellied clay tea cups. We toasted serendipity, and ate.

Samanda reappeared a few minutes later with two neatly wrapped leaf packets of sear fish steaks, a green banana and coconut curry, with warm, fluffy steamed rice and a separate stack of puffy hot puris on a bamboo skewer, practically hurling the latter through the window at me, as our departing train gathered pace. We shouted our thanks down the platform, waved goodbye, rounded a corner and Samanda and Ohiya Station were gone.

We finished the last of the beer after we'd eaten, throwing the clay cups, pieces of bamboo, banana leaves and some leftovers out of the window to await scavengers and the rain, which would dissolve it all back into the earth from where it came. Alas, the pointless, thin, plastic bags that began to appear on the island only a few years ago, are carelessly tossed into the environment in the same way natural wrappings have been for thousands of years. With no infrastructure to deal with their disposal apart from the toxicity of occasional burning, the build up of plastics scar the natural beauty of the island, the product of a technological society inflicted on another without the culture or knowledge to deal with it, destroying in a few short years an environmental balance that took tens of thousands to perfect.

Christianity, Buddhism and Hinduism have much in common. All are founded on the belief of happiness in another world, while preaching a life of humility, devoid of sin in this one. The major difference is that Christianity teaches that life on earth is transcendental, leading to a disembodied existence in a spiritual state. Judgement Day even foretells destruction of the material universe. As technology fuels massive, accelerating change in Western culture and society, the teachings of the Christian church are becoming less influential, but the state of mind where the natural world is regarded as a disposable resource remains. Plastic bags are only a small indicator of a dangerous infection from a global epidemic of frightening consequence. Throwaway world, throwaway society. If the teachings of the Buddhist and Hindu church follow the patterns of religion's falling influence in the West, the belief in rebirth and consequent wish to preserve resources in consideration of the unborn, will probably also diminish.

Mounting piles of discarded plastic could be just a temporary aberration. The saving grace for the new environments they pollute may still be that, particularly where reincarnation is central to religious belief, its followers look upon the world as a property conferred to them for all time and one they must preserve - based on a selfish premise if nothing else - for their future incarnations. Hinduism has inbuilt logic and commercial self-preservation. The Hindu habit of hoarding money, following a moral commandment that no more than one quarter of income should be expended, provides Hindu society with its own social security system, and the comforting knowledge to its adherents that every incarnation will benefit from a sizeable inheritance.

In just about every Hindu household, even westernised ones, there is a shrine devoted to Lakshmi, the God of prosperity. In many Hindu shops and businesses is an image of Ganesh, the elephant headed God of commercial and financial success. Conferring such religious discipline and moral commandments in money-making globally, may well be the only means of survival open to the human race in this planet's doubtful future. If it's not too late already. As the West, and increasing numbers of other regions of the world are infected by the suicidal economics of relentless industrial growth, and the absurd accumulation of possessions, Mr. Ranasinghe was abiding by his religion. All human unhappiness, Buddha taught, is rooted in possessions, and Mr. Ranasinghe had told me before we left, that he'd just given his house and property, his rice paddies and everything else he owned to his son. I'd asked him how he was going to live and laughing, he'd said,

"Don't you see? Now, at last, I am free!"

The roar from the diesel engine ahead of us fell another octave as it used every horse at its disposal to drag the slowly rolling stock up a steep cutting towards the high planes. Even though I was expecting him, having cut a corner out of the train's route in a frantic taxi ride, when Samanda hit the side of the slow moving train with a thump, clinging on to our window frame like a limpet, it did make me jump, but nowhere near as high as his athletic leap from the grassy banking above us. The look on Marian's face was worth his effort though, and I'm sure Samanda blushed when he got another kiss from her, having delivered more cold beers from a canvas rucksack, freshly-picked wild mountain strawberries with buffalo curd, a Thermos of coffee and four delicious Champagne chocolate truffles in two little cardboard boxes, announcing they were with the compliments of the Swiss Hotel. Well, thank you.

Samanda jumped off the carriage's running boards with Mr. Ranasinghe's folding table under one arm, disappearing into wreathes of thick black smoke from the exhaust stack, which billowed away down and across the deep green wooded valley far below us. Here, the trees gave way to the dense emerald of high grown tea plantations and the bright lime green of rice paddies, clinging to the banks of the silted brown river coursing along the valley floor.

Far in the distance Adam's Peak stood majestically high, the Buddhist pilgrimage site with a Christian name, the gilded monastery at its top a glinting, tiny golden speck. So many legends surround the mountain and over thousands of years, millions of feet have climbed to see the tiny depression at its peak, said to be Buddha's footprint, which rests under a tiny golden pavilion. Muslims claim it's Adam's footprint, where he first set foot on earth, having been cast out of Heaven, standing on one leg on the mountain's peak in penitence, until his sins were forgiven. Under colonial rule before the Dutch arrived, followed by the British, the Portuguese even tried to instil the belief it was St. Thomas's footprint and just for good measure, Hindus claim it's Shiva's. During April and May, countless rainbow swarms of butterflies take their final journey to the summit, which is also known as Samanala Kanda, for this very reason.

We began our own, long, seven kilometre climb to the peak around midnight, in time to reach the summit just before the sun rose majestically behind us, casting a triangular shadow that lengthened across the jungle canopy far below. One of the interwoven legends of Adam's Peak says that where the tip of the mountain's shadow comes to rest at sunrise, lies the site of the Garden of Eden. Standing there on top of the waist of the world, at the beginning of another glorious day, holding Marian's hand, I felt we were already there. And I realised in that moment that I'd found what I had lost in the last place I expected, because I'd stopped searching for it, a long time ago.

11

I never smoked again. I drink now. In fact, I've been drinking for the
five years and thirty-four days it's taken me to find the courage to
write these words. I'd never seen a monk smoking before. It looked so
odd, I guess because of the timelessness of his simple maroon robe,
the yellow shoulder bag and the incongruity of the cigarette in his mouth.
He was leaning on a furled umbrella the same colour as his robe, stuck in
the soft, light brown earth beneath our feet. The blue tobacco smoke hung
in the thick, still air, and smelt as sweet as ever; I was going to ponce one,
even though I knew it would taste of ash and burn my lungs, still sore
from their saltwater rinse three days before, but I felt sick again and didn't
fancy the nicotine rush after my enforced abstinence either. I borrowed his
plastic Ronson though, and walked slowly down the slope of freshly dug
soil towards the plump middle aged woman at the bottom, who needed a
light.

She wore a pretty cream dress covered in beige flowers and was sitting,
bent legs splayed out akimbo at the bottom of the grave. The dress was
covered in the damp soil from the waist down, the material stretched tight
between her knees, on which she was resting her two daughters' heads,
twins, about seven years old I thought.

One looked quite peaceful, as if she was sleeping, wearing a dress similar to her mother's, only her sunken eyes and blue lips giving away her
drowning. Her sister's arms were bent and outstretched though, rigid in
rigor mortis, her left hand looked relaxed and careless, but her right was

103

still gripping something she'd held just before she died. What it was, shall remain a mystery. She had blue lips like her sister, but her expression was serious, slightly troubled, and if her eyes had been open, it would have looked just as if she was asking her mother a question.

She was gently cradling their cheeks and caressing the side of their faces, their necks, and jaws and under their chin, as if she was trying to gently wake them from a deep sleep. I knew though, that she was tracing every part of their faces, so she would never forget what they looked like, in their lives together and here, en route to their next. I hoped she had a photograph of them, but I doubted it. Poverty isn't only hunger, poor education, sickness with no doctor. It's also not being able to look at your dead child's picture. And she would dread her own future soon enough, because poverty also means your children are your pension.

A woman who loses her husband is a widow, a man his wife, a widower. A child without a parent is an orphan. But what is a parent who loses a child? What of parents who lose all their children? There is no word I can find for this in the English language, none to accurately describe her grief. If there are any, I wouldn't even dream of insulting her by trying. She looked up momentarily at me and shook her head in assent as I pointed the lighter at the three incense sticks sticking out of the ground between the girls, and smoke of a different sweetness joined that of the tobacco at the graveside.

The Queen of the Sea had been stationary at some signals when it was punched off its tracks three hundred yards from the nearby beach by sixty feet of water, the dark matt-red carriages she was hauling, snapped apart, then spun over and over inland by the surging water.

I'd stood next to one that didn't seem badly damaged at all, just a few big dents in the side where it had rolled before coming to rest on the side of a boggy ditch. The Queen herself, a big two tone blue and white diesel locomotive, hadn't been moved quite so far and was practically unscathed, just some superficial damage to a couple of climbing ladders on her nose.

The holiday train had been packed with around one thousand five hundred people that Sunday, many of them families. After the first wave, survivors from the surrounding area actually clambered up onto the carriages in an attempt to get above the second that followed close behind. Others, including the few that had managed to get out of one carriage, climbed onto the roof of the sole surviving house it had come to rest against. Strangely for an island race, few Sri Lankans swim, which must have added to their absolute terror, along with the passengers who were still alive, but trapped inside the carriages, watching the second tsunami closing on them. I'd never known fear like it in my life, rooted to that spot where I was convinced I was going to die, when the scare the looters had invented swept through the town. I remained humiliated by my funk-driven inertia during that experience.

By the time I'd limped my way to the scene, the search for survivors from the train and the surrounding area was being called off, and work was underway to bury the rapidly decaying corpses of the eight hundred and two bodies that had been retrieved by then, in a mass grave close to the scene. The majority were women and children, laid out in haphazard rows in the clothes, and postures in which they'd died. I joined locals, tourists, travellers and train survivors looking at them all, in what for me was a fruitless search for the white face I so desperately wanted to find, but was dreading to see.

The tsunami had stopped short of their Pagoda and the monks brought process, structure, prayer and dignity to the massed burial. Someone had the foresight to take pictures of the unknown and the unclaimed. The faces of those who could not be identified were photographed before burial, the hundreds of images eventually posted on the remains of long, upright walls nearby, to join photographs of the missing, with contact details of the friends or relatives who left them there. They were simple messages. 'sophie Patterson, aged 3, missing. Please contact Bob +447896 228916 or Neptune Hotel'. Ironically, there was no photograph of my photographer for me to add. I did my best writing a description of her, and added Lauren's phone number and an email address.

The grave had been dug in the shape of a huge wheelbarrow, maybe eight feet at its deepest. It was desperate, but the only solution, and the senior monk in charge brought great authority to the simple ceremony he conducted, his fellow monks chanting as they poured water over the bodies to be buried, before we shared silent prayer in memory of those of all faiths who had died.

Five diggers waited at the base of the grave as the constant procession of bodies were carried down the slope to their final resting place by relatives, friends or volunteers, in scenes of tragic poignancy. A father in a pale blue polo shirt was weeping, but so dignified, cradling his young son in his arms, without the strength to carry him down the slope, where he knew he would have to let go of him forever; one of the gravediggers, in a railway worker's shirt and shorts, understanding, hurrying up the slope to meet him, relieving him of his terrible burden with caring gentleness.

A chubby little boy, maybe three years old, perhaps even younger, in a torn brown shirt and underpants, spittle flecking the sides of badly split and swollen lips was beyond crying, his forehead creased, standing at the side of his mother's twisted corpse in anguish, still trying to wake her. Someone had placed a blanket over the naked lower half of her body, to protect her modesty in death, and shroud the unborn child she carried in her swollen womb. I had picked some hibiscus flowers to throw in the grave; I was so hungry, I must confess, I ate quite a few of them (they taste of raspberries and rhubarb) and realised how quickly I'd reverted to a hunter-gatherer.

I walked over to the little boy, knelt next to him and he let go of his mum's arm to help me take the flowers apart, and we gently scattered the pink and red petals over her, and his unborn brother or sister, together, and I held his hand as they were carried down the slope. A little cooling breeze sighed across us all, disturbing the petals, and they swirled around his mum's body, fluttering down to make a little trail so many others were to follow. And just at the right time, her final journey seemed beautiful. The little boy stopped pulling on my hand to follow her and the creases on his brow disappeared. A novitiate monk, probably eight or nine years old appeared from nowhere, and led the little boy away, disappearing through the crowd; the monk in charge, his eyes full of compassion, met mine and for a few seconds we spoke in silence.

Only a few bodies had shrouds of any kind, the relatives of those that did, had used anything they could find - saris, blankets, sheets, sarongs, even rugs, making the bottom of the grave suddenly kaleidoscopic when breaks in the heavy low cloud allowed the bright sunlight to join us. A row of children had been laid next to each other, looking for all the world as if they were just asleep. One pretty young girl's head was shaken by the dark yellow soil being shovelled across the row of tiny faces, that no-one would ever see again. Her hair had been lovingly brushed, and shone like silk. Next to her in the row was a skinny little boy in a checked shirt and shorts, legs splayed, still covered in the ashen slime from the bottom of the bog, dried in lumps, whitening his skin. Lips that would never smile any more, would never be kissed, their own children never to be, became memories as they slowly, agonisingly slowly, disappeared under the rich ochre soil of their homeland, while the grief of the bereaved at the graveside, drowned the solemn silence of our witness.

12

I was basking like a lazy shark on my back, just nostrils and knees floating above the water, under the gaze of Buddha himself. His massive
white cast concrete effigy surveyed the bustling mountain capital of
Kandy, the Temple of the Tooth where he'd stashed one of his molars,
and my aquamarine swimming pool from his vantage point on the top of
a hill, to the south of the city.

I kicked with my feet, disturbing the placid smoothness of the water, the
ripples flashing dappled sunlight on the whitewashed walls behind an
elderly, white haired, white skinned gentleman. He was sitting alone on a
polished cast concrete bench at a small table, set under the delicate shade
of a mountain ash tree, amongst the beautifully manicured poolside gardens. He was the only other guest present, and was wearing the plain drab
olive of military uniform, unadorned with distinguishing marks of rank,
unit or country,

An early morning waiter, incongruously dressed in eveningwear, strutted
the length and width of the pool to deliver a very large vodka and tonic to
this enigmatic figure. I swam past, watching him out of the corner of one
eye as with the precision of well-practised habit, he poured half the tonic
on top of the crackling ice cubes at the bottom of the tall glass. The resulting fizz sent a thick slice of green skinned lime fizzing upwards on the crest
of an effervescent wave of carbonation. He extracted the fruit between
thumb and forefinger, squeezed gently and rubbed the acetic juice around
the part of the rim of the glass, where he was about to place his lips.

"I like to see a man preparing an aperitif properly." I said, as I passed by him in the middle of another relaxed backstroke length of the deserted pool. He looked down at me with a smile, twisted, then dropped the lime back into the frosted glass, poured the remainder of the tonic and raised it in a friendly gesture, before downing a sizeable part of its contents.

"I'd enjoy it more with a pretty woman sitting right here," he called back, patting the vacant seat next to him. "Cheers! That's what you say in England isn't it." he said, without it being a question. "I've always liked toasts for breakfast. Care to join me?"

I levered myself out of the pool from the deepest end, weakened arms reflecting the severity of my morning's efforts, and accepted a crisp blue towel from the efficient attendant, who paused long enough from his poolside cleaning duties to inquire about the temperature and condition of the water. I assured him everything was fine and took the seat I was offered.

"What'll you have?" the American asked me. "Tea, I suppose?"

"No, I'll have a Cognac and a coffee if I may, thanks." I said, draping the damp towel around my neck and shoulders, defending them against the low morning sunshine, mounting a sneaky attack, slanting under the branches of the ash tree.

The waiter disappeared with the new order and I found out this big man served on the staff of Lord Mountbatten in the second world war, and had been based in Kandy.

"This hotel was reserved exclusively for WAAFs you know," he told me, looking up at a balcony above us. "Women only, we couldn't even get past the lobby, especially at night, let alone into a room. So, sixty-two years after I left here, I decided to come back and stay in the only room I ever wanted to get inside."

Another vodka arrived along side a Cognac in a big cut crystal balloon glass, next to a bone china coffee cup and a battered, but glorious sterling silver pot, sugar bowl and milk jug, set out on pristine linen covering a silver tray, garnished with a maroon and cream orchid.

"She was a pretty young English WAAF, we worked in the same office for six months or so, but on different floors and fraternising wasn't really approved. There wasn't a lot of time off either, but what days we did get, we spent together, walking in the mountains around here, snatching trips to the hill stations and so on." he recalled, staring into the pool, with only an occasional glance at me.

"Then she got posted to Africa out of the blue, when the Japanese were sweeping everything before them over there," he said, waving an out-stretched arm northeast, in the general direction of Burma.

"We wrote, but the mail wasn't very reliable and it was, oh, three years later before we saw each other again, after it was all over. Well, there'd been a great deal of water under both our bridges and I guess we were different people by the time I looked her up in England, on my way back to the 'states."

"Where did she live?" I asked.

"With her parents, in a little village not far from Nottingham. You know, Robin Hood and all that stuff." he said, smiling at me for the first time, while preparing his second vodka with the same attention to detail as the first.

"It was a freezing January day when I arrived at the house. I must have looked a bit of a mess - I'd travelled half way around the world to see her and it was obvious from the reception I got from her mother when she let me in, that I wasn't really welcome. There'd been a lot of trouble with local girls and American fliers from a nearby airfield and it hadn't done much for transatlantic relations. Caroline was still as pretty as I remembered when she came down the stairs to greet me, but..... more distant somehow. They'd prepared a wonderful English tea for me though, a pile of muffins and fruitcake, excellent hospitality considering the rationing at the time. There was a roaring log fire in the big sitting room where she took me to meet her father. I shook his hand and sat down when he offered me a seat on the sofa in front of the fire."

"The trouble was, I didn't realise they had a cockatiel as a family pet and they let the damn thing roam around out of its cage. It must have been right by my feet on the carpet, because when I crossed my legs, somehow I kicked it straight into the damned fire. Went up like a torch, squawking and flapping its wings to try and get out, the poor little thing." He grinned at the memory, the passing of the years had obviously diluted his remorse.

"So what happened?"

"I high tailed it out of there before they killed me. We wrote to each other a couple of times, but then it petered out. Love's like that sometimes you know; you get over it though, time's a great healer - and I've had a helluva time as a bachelor. You married?"

"No, I'm not. Can I buy you another drink?"

"That's nice of you but no, later maybe."

He struggled up from the seat with the help of an ebony cane I hadn't noticed, propped behind the trunk of the ash tree. With a painful looking limp and a list to port in compensation, he tacked across the open lawn of the pool's garden and disappeared inside the hotel. I stared into the fruity cognac and swirled it around the glittering glass, wondering if my destiny was the same as his. Old age with only memories for company, boozing at breakfast. I made a mental note to always check the carpet for wildlife on the loose, when in the company of prospective father in laws.

I twisted the controls of the giant faucet and the torrent of hot water ceased to tumble from a chromium showerhead the size of a dinner plate. Pulled back the heavy curtain and stepped out of the deep, cast-iron, Victorian bathtub - one of civilisation's greatest virtues, hot water; you don't miss it until it's not there like so much, and finding an unlimited supply after months of deprivation is total luxury; shaving is elevated to sensuality.

An electric hair drier in these latitudes is a spurious absurdity for a male, but this hotel was a class act, so I used it, if for nothing else, the novelty. I was standing overlooking a vibrant Kandy street scene below the hotel window, legs bandied akimbo, while an eddying rush of electrically heated air from the ancient brown Bakelite machine removed the final vestiges of moisture from my scrotum. I've yet to find a more effective method of drying one's balls.

I span round at the cackles from the doorway behind me to see Marian laughing her head off again, next to a maid trying not to, clutching clean pressed sheets to her shaking bosom. In a rush to grab my towel, I lost my footing on the shiny wet floor tiles and my grip on the hair drier and crashed to the floor, buttocks parting as I trapped the whirring electrical device beneath me, which momentarily roasted my balls, while sucking up water from the floor through its air intake, straight into its heating elements. There was a muffled thud, a bright blue flash of earthed electricity, and a pall of acrid smoke from my groin region.

The two ceiling fans in the main room of our suite immediately began to slow over my spectators' heads, indicating my testicles were responsible for blowing the hotel's fuses. Marian's look of concern at the explosion which had just occurred beneath my naked body was momentary, the merriment both reinstated and increased as she flopped back onto the bed, trying to stop her sides from splitting. The maid managed to stammer,

"Excuse me, come later." on her way to the corridor outside which echoed with her stifled titters, which increased in intensity the further she believed herself out of earshot.

Full of fear of the worst, I got to my feet, unplugged the smouldering hairdryer, pushed the bathroom door closed with an outstretched toe and sat on the edge of the bath, making a tentative examination of two of my most precious possessions. Unbelievably, apart from a mild reddening of the skin in a couple of areas and a ball bag looking like the aftermath of an Australian bush fire, all seemed remarkably well. There is a God. I wrapped a big white bath towel around my waist and emerged sheepishly, red balled and faced.

"You OK?" she said with a suppressed smile on her face, revealing the two dimples that lived slap bang in the middle of the laughter lines at the side of her mouth.

"Yes, I'm fine, I'm sorry about that but it's, well it's just the easiest way to dry things you know."

"I'm sure you're right, but I think its best I make my own examination." she said, pulling the towel from my waist.

Later, I joined a small crowd surrounding a disreputable looking fellow trying to sell a herbal remedy for snakebite in small brown glass bottles. His demonstration of the preparation's dramatic healing powers began by allowing another fangless viper to bite his arm, after which he feigned a rapid breakdown of his central nervous system, performing convincing convulsions on the sandy ground at our feet. During admirable death throes he beckoned weakly at me of all people, to save his fading life by administering a dose of his medicine. The bottle I held to his lips had barely exuded any of the miraculous milky fluid within, before his mortality was sufficiently salvaged to enable his final sales pitch to coincide with the frenzied customers he had planted in the crowd earlier.

A short way past the medicine show, in a sort of no man's land between street performance and a line of beggars further ahead, was a young boy dressed in a royal blue pyjama top with white piping, several sizes too big for him. His bare heels had worn through the folds of the trousers, which were too long for his skinny legs. Over his shoulder hung a bag of worldly possessions and a small drum, which he beat with stiff fingers in time to the same plaintive song he'd sung to us, and the other passengers on yesterday's train here. He recognised my white face too and momentarily stopped the performance to smile and say,

"Hey, there, good pineapple, thanking you much." before starting the verse again with renewed vigour. I dropped a two rupee coin on the piece of cloth he'd laid out before him and smiled at the memory of the practical Marian buying some fruit and giving it to the hungry-looking kid, in case he had a pimp in the next carriage, ready to relieve him of the collection he was making after his performance.

Lots of entertainment in this busy town on my way to its cricket ground, and I missed Marian's company already; she was with Samanda, making travel arrangements for her photo assignment up country. he'd got ahead of us while we climbed Adam's Peak and to Marian's delight, agreed to accompany her as an interpreter. I reached a rotten row of aged beggars crouching in soiled rags, hands outstretched to passers-by, mouthing silent ministrations from toothless gums in the timeless posture of their profession. A dark skinned Tamil woman stood at the end of the row holding a lighter skinned, naked baby in her arms, probably borrowed or worse, one she was being paid to look after. Unashamedly, she twisted the boy's arm behind its back to make him cry as she thrust him towards me in one hand, the other outstretched, palm upwards. Her frustration at not being able to speak my language came out in a sort of nodding grimace, which soon become a scowl at my failure to believe her lie.

The sound of a big crowd grew larger with my progress up a wide track leading to the cricket stadium, where I joined a long queue until finally a skinny arm stretched through a hole in the corrugated iron wall below an engagingly prosaic, entirely erroneous hand painted sign saying, 'ticket Window'. The calloused hand removed the twenty rupee note I offered it, and like a crooked fairground ride owner returned two single rupee coins and a hand printed slip of paper bearing the legend 'stand Only 8/-Rs. This was accompanied by the most revolting ten rupee note in Buddhadom, still damp and greasy from its former owner's sweaty palm, stained an oily brown, barely recognisable as money. The crude piece of paper allowed me past a moonlighting bank guard still in his employer's uniform, sporting an old Lee Enfield strapped to his back. While tearing my piece of paper apart, he breathed the vaporised contents of the half empty, half bottle of Arrack stuffed into his back pocket before waving me around a corner to face the backs of the rearmost row of people in a small stadium crammed to the brim with a standing sea of sweating humanity.

Far below me was a parched open area of mud, which probably used to support the green life form known as grass. The plant life inhabiting the arena was more akin to shaven African savannah than the traditional emerald swathes of an English cricket ground. Nevertheless, upon this surface a President's XI was trying to remove the number two and three batsmen of a visiting team from their dusty crease, while more fans jostled and poured into the ground behind me, pressing forward into an area that had obviously reached capacity some hours before. I was quickly engulfed in the seething morass around me, unable to prevent myself being slowly moved away from the entrance gate by the force of the huge numbers pouring in behind me. I was powerless to escape to the rarefied roofed enclaves of the Rs/-30 seating, in the white painted stands shimmering in the distance on the opposite side of the ground, like the mirage of an unobtainable oasis, in a desert of discomfort.

The fact that my height allowed me to stand head and shoulders above most of the rest of the crowd around me, quickly turned out to be a mixed blessing. An unimpeded view of the cricketing action was immeasurably offset by the target practice my head received, from the bored and disaffected drunks behind me. To gathering applause, a half-masticated leg of chicken knocked the straw hat from my head into the arms of some spectators several rows in front. Despite my shouted pleas, a game of Frisbee began, which continued clockwise around the ground until my hat disappeared from sight, having completed around three quarters of a lap. With my arms pinned to my sides in the worsening crush, I couldn't even remove the lumps of curry and rice from my hair which, now the unseen assailants behind me had found their range, were starting to hit the mark with increasing regularity.

It wasn't long before the ever-present flies found the attractive array of debris accumulating on my head preferable, no doubt, to whatever they'd been devouring previously. They were only pausing in their feast to hover a few inches above my now roasting bald patch, in order to avoid additional incoming salvoes of foodstuff which, with each direct hit, enhanced the flies' already eclectic menu.

Screams of delight, whistles, applause and drumbeats around the ground greeted the fall of another wicket, while down the front, several hundred big firecrackers, tied together in a huge bundle were thrown towards the boundary rope, landing unseen behind the legs of an armed policeman.

The half a dozen burning fuses were enough to set the rest off, which exploded with something akin to the shootout scene from a cheap Western. The policeman, probably thinking he was under attack from separatist terrorists on one of their forays from the north of the island, dropped to the ground and primed his weapon in one movement, only to receive a fusillade of orange peel and catcalls from the crowd he was supposed to be controlling. The smell of cordite that hung in the air was about to be joined by a batch of the real thing by the look of it, as the policeman, now

113

back on his feet and suffering a severe sense of humour failure, began waving his machine gun around as if choosing which particular section to mow down, in hot tempered cold blood.

The crowd directly in front of him formed a crescent shape, backing away in fear of being shot, while another huge roar went up around the ground as a new batsmen's stumps were shattered, first ball. The consequent surge, ebb and flow of the crowd behind me, gave me a chance to free my arms and remove the larger lumps of food from the top of my head, although the hot sun had already encrusted a lot of the curry in my hair. My personal escort of flies rose in a cloud and high dudgeon at being disturbed from their dining, and as I flapped my hands around above me in a futile attempt at preventing their resettlement, I noticed a white outline on my wrist, where my watch should have been. Along with the several thousand people sharing this hideous incarceration, I continued to be slowly pushed around the ground by new ticket holders, or to be more precise, further victims of the ticket seller and guard's little racket, pouring through the entrance. The game had obviously sold out hours before, but as the homemade tickets continued to sell well, every new arrival was in turn, pushed forward by those arriving behind them, jostling for position. We moved en masse with a restricted shuffling movement of tiny steps, as if all part of a giant manacled chain gang being herded back through the gates of our prison.

A complete vegetable samosa whizzed into my left ear and exploded, scattering its stodgy filling over a wide area, indicating my attackers were having to resort to heavier ordnance for their artillery as I moved further out of range, and I couldn't help wondering what was going to be next on the victuals agenda. Twenty yards or so to my right was a wide gap in the sea of black haired heads around me. I had earlier assumed this to be the location of a dividing fence and was quite worried about people being crushed up against it. Myself amongst them. Another big surge in the crowd, this time from behind me, thrust me forward and to the right, to within twenty feet of the gap and a couple of rows of heads next to it mysteriously disappeared from sight. Another couple of shuffles and all was hideously revealed as the majority of the energetic flies dining in the remnants of my hair, deserted me for dessert in the unrivalled pleasure of the open sewer that ran downhill from the rudimentary toilets at the back of the stand, to a verdant green area of luxuriant grass growing just inside the boundary. The liquids just seemed to soak away in this highly fertile area, where the more solid parts of the slurry solidified in the heat, rather as a lava flow slows as it cools on its journey down the slopes of a volcano. The smell was completely appalling.

The crowd between me and the edge of this river of excrement was now only two deep and the wafer thin veneer of civilisation was quickly revealed, as one poor chap lost his footing and fell headlong into the mire, landing on all fours. Several opportunists amongst his neighbours of seconds before seized their chance, using the poor fellow as a human stepping-stone to reach the other side of the ten-foot wide trench, pushing him deeper into the gruesome, turgid slime oozing along the bottom. Now, completely covered, this unfortunate, like The Creature From The Black Lagoon, stood up and began throwing abuse and sticky handfuls of ordure at the miscreants concerned.

One innocent victim on the opposite bank was hit on the cheek by a flying turd and turning to shake his fist in admonishment, was pushed from behind by unseen hands to join his attacker in the mire, where they engaged in an awful variation on mud wrestling. All local attention was diverted from the cricket to the ensuing judo style battle, the protagonists trying to make each other lose their footing, each successful manoeuvre being greeted with delight, laughter and rapturous applause from onlookers lucky enough to have a ringside seat.

Meanwhile, the policeman down the front had been joined by three colleagues, who were making arrests, charging into the crowd in a flying wedge formation, dragging spectators out, seemingly at random. One particularly deep foray into enemy territory had the knock-on effect of increasing pressure in the section of crowd next to me, forcing a decision. The gap over this trench would be possible to jump with a run up, but without any room there was only one course of action. I removed one of my sandals just in time as I was knocked flying forwards, sinking one foot into the middle of the liquid midden, to just below the knee. Several others were neither tall, nor lucky enough and were skittled headlong into toilet torrent, while I managed to plant my other foot halfway up the opposite bank and lunge forward to grab one of the outstretched arms high above me.

I gripped one chap's hand who hauled me half way up the steep side of the trench into a position where I was totally and literally in his hands. A smiling accomplice appeared at his side who calmly unscrewed the clasp attached to the silver bracelet on my wrist, pocketed it, then dropped to his knees and crawled away between hundreds of pairs of legs. His partner in this opportunist crime let go of my hand, grinned and waved goodbye as I dropped backwards into the furious melee that had now erupted amongst the newcomers behind me. My fall was broken by two fellow unfortunates who, to the unbridled delight of the onlookers on both banks, disappeared completely below the gruesome surface, under my not insubstantial weight.

I found running water at last from a brass tap, polished by thousands of hands before mine, seeking water from the standpipe it served. It was located behind the main stand, where I was escorted around the boundary by several thousand flies and two policemen, who couldn't help laughing at me as they kept station several yards upwind. One spends so much time in the East dwelling upon one's bowel performance, but never did I dream of having an opportunity to study so many other peoples' at such close quarters. The lady I disturbed doing a spot of washing on the smooth grey stones surrounding the standpipe, lent me her blue bar of laundry soap, with which I worked up a gritty navy lather, probably the final denouement to a once proud hairline.

She was joined by several onlookers with a rare opportunity to study a semi naked white man at close quarters, sporting such strange features as pink nipples, light brown chest hair and freckles. Particularly interesting as each feature was slowly revealed from beneath a solid layered caking of ordure below waist level and food above, moistened and eventually removed by the abrasive blue detergent concoction. It wore straight through a favourite Tin-Tin & Snowy cotton 't' shirt I was scrubbing once, in a matter of seconds.

The flies gradually dispersed, as did the brown coloured effluent topped with blue froth, running gently away into the undergrowth behind the standpipe. Another big roar from the crowd inside the tin-walled ground woke a mangy pariah dog from its midday sleep, in the thin noon shadow of the stadium wall. One baleful eye peered at me as it sniffed the air, scratched away some of my former head inhabitants who'd made a fly line to the open sore on the side of its neck, shifted position slightly, then continued its dognap.

I thought perhaps I'd come across a madder one to keep me company on the way back to the hotel because the cricket quite frankly, had lost its appeal. As I assumed had the bowler, from the jeers, hot on the heels of the cheers, ringing out from inside the ground. I stood up and rinsed out my shirt and myself down with the kind washer woman's bright red plastic bowl, and I bowed low as I returned it to her along with the rancid ten rupee note now even more in need of her efforts and I was rewarded further, as with palms pressed together I received her whispered blessing.

I strode off with dripping shirt and shorts, back down the hill past the medicine man who was now lying motionless, propped half upright in the arms of a tame stooge who was holding the small brown bottle to his partner's lips, in front of a brand new, hushed and expectant crowd.

"Hey, mister!" called a familiar voice from behind me, and the smiling boy in the blue pyjama top appeared at my side and in the hand he held out towards me, were my wristwatch and silver bracelet.

"For you, yes?" he said, shaking his head from one side to the other in the confusing movement that means yes in the East and no in the West.

"For me, yes, thank you, where did you get these?" I asked, strapping both back on my wrist.

"My friend, he is a thief, I owe him for them now."

"It's just a cheap watch you know and the bracelet's not worth much either, it's only Indian silver."

"Yes, I know, if they were good things you not get them back." he laughed.

"Well, that's refreshingly honest dishonesty I suppose, how's your singing going?"

"Not bad, I still learn good Singhalese songs, I am just here from India."

"You speak good English, where did you learn it?" I asked, as we started the walk back towards the centre of town.

"From the man I have been working for the year; but he is gone now, back to America. He buyed me in Bombay."

A rickshaw driver pedalled a gaudily painted tricycle slowly past us, whipcord hamstrings standing out from the backs of lean, muscled legs and knobbled knees. He raised his eyebrows and nodded towards the top of the hill leading through the centre of town. I declined his unspoken inquiry and waved him on, as I wanted to try and dry out a bit, walking in the sunshine.

"What, you mean he bought you for sex or something?" I asked, wondering if there was after all going to be a price, or an offer, attached to the return of my possessions.

"No, he likes ladies, many ladies my boss, I roll his smoking joints and change language for him. I forgetting the word." he said clicking his thumb and forefinger together in exasperation.

"Interpret?" I offered.

"Yes, interpreter, I am interpreter. But main job is joints. He smoked a lot and I get him the best prices for hashish too, show him where to go, away from the hippy peoples. My boss, he paid for me $300 dollars, American. All I have to do is always have one joint and a match ready when he wants a smoke. I give it to him and roll the next one ready. Always one ready. That is my main job."

"Not much of a career really is it? What's your name?" I said, stopping to face him, holding out my hand.

"Varmaramaswarmi." he said, clasping my hand with small, cold, strong, bony fingers.

"What do people call you for short?"

"Ram."

"Well, it's nice to meet you Ram. Are you hungry?" A big grin split his thin black face and he shook his head again in the affirmative.

"OK, let's have some lunch then."

We strode through the smoky traffic up the hill of Kandy's thriving commercial sector, while Ram revealed more of his childhood. A story of survival in Mumbai's docks, the struggle for life and constant hunger, surrounded by the vast tonnage of food that pours through a sea port, always in view, hanging from dockside cranes, but out of reach, whether high in the sky or on display in the shops and markets. He begged for food and work, cigarettes - anything to trade - from incoming sailors with money to spend in port. He ran their errands, took them to the pimps who controlled the dockside hookers and picked up and practised the sailors' languages along the way.

We walked along high kerbed pavements full of over spilling merchandise. Every third shop seemed to be a greengrocer of plenty. Every day of Ram's early life seemed to be one of hunger. Today, it was only every other. We stopped to look at the neat displays of fat vegetables from the rich soil of the high country that surrounds Kandy, and to talk of the droughts and deserts, disease and despair of northern India where farming communities are more like fortifications from which men launch daily attacks, in the ceaseless war they have to wage against nature. Unending battles fought against dust storms and cyclones and disease and locusts and drought.

Mountains of dried fish, silvery brown, hummed with insect life and a smell of their own, as we passed a shopkeeper with honest eyes who beckoned me inside with practised inculcation. We bought two slices of water melon weighed on big balance scales with shiny brass weights, and sat facing the street with our backs propped up on the tall sacks of dried peas, lentils and rice of different grades, stacked in front of dozens of big tin trays of dazzling spices. Their fragrance mingled with the heady smell of tea from the shop next door, packed to the ceiling with plywood chests, boasting the names of the growers' estates as we saw how far we could spit our pips into the street. Ram won by a mile as one of his landed in a wooden box on the back of an old man's bicycle, freewheeling away from us down the hill.

Once we'd reached its top, we turned right and as the shops got bigger, more expensive and air conditioned, within a short tourists' walk of the main hotels, my strides became more purposeful and Ram's more timid, until he stopped around a final corner, confronted by the twin white pillars and polished marble floor of the hotel's entrance. The large uniformed doorman smiled and nodded a greeting at me, while planting his hand firmly on Ram's chest, as he tried to follow me into the lobby.

"Not you. Get out of here."

"He's with me." I explained to the doorman.

"I am sorry sir, no scallywag natives like this are allowed in the hotel, particularly ones that smell, like him. If you would like to speak to the manager about it, he can wait here, we have the other guests to think of."

"He's not a native, he's from India and he's my guest for lunch." I said, fingering a carefully furled, rather damp fifty rupee note.

"Of course sir, if only you'd mentioned this fact earlier, please accept my apologies." he said, relieving me of the note with a practised flick of the wrist. Like a lizard's tongue catching a fly, he pocketed it with one hand, opening the glass door with a theatrical flourish and half bow, with his other.

We crossed the lobby to the lift under a high, vaulted ceiling and pressed the 'call' button, which lit up with a red glow to Ram's delight. He prodded it several times, while he lifted his legs up and down like a sentry on parade, fascinated by the feel of the thick, soft carpet under his bare feet.

"That lady, is pointing at us." he observed, pointing back, and following his finger I saw this morning's room maid in animated conversation with a pair of smirking desk clerks, all looking in my direction.

The ancient lift creaked the last few inches into position, and I swung back the old latticed metal doors. Ram had been mesmerised by the mirrored walls of the tiny cubicle reflecting our images to infinity and back, and so scared by the lurching of the shaky ascent, he gripped my hand with the endearing fear of a tiny child and held tight all the way through the double mahogany doors of room 304. Marian sat at a small desk working through the maze of bureaucracy required for her permit to the north of the island. She looked up with a smile and surprise at my early return, and small companion.

"Hello. Who's this?"

"This is Ram, I am returning a favour, by buying him lunch."

He was despatched to the shower with strict instructions, a warning about the slippery floor, a fresh white towel, a spare shirt and a pair of Marian's shorts, who enjoyed my morning's report. I kissed the side of her neck then held her tight as she confirmed her assignment to the war zone in the north was on. Which meant we had to part, and I wondered how my heart could sink so far, yet thump so hard in my mouth, leaving no room for my tongue to say what I wanted to, and I just blurted out,

"Maybe we could meet down South again Marian, when you're back." and my mouth stopped beating for dreadful moments, until she squeezed her arms tighter around my waist, hid a tiny tear in the corner of her eye by pressing her head on my shoulder, and whispered,

"Yes, I'd like that very much."

We knew I'd never get a permit even if it was appropriate for me to go, which it wasn't. And how dangerous it was around the LTTE stronghold in Jaffna where she was headed with a journalist, to take pictures for a magazine story on middle class Tamil Tiger soldier girls, fighting their war of liberation. A surprise was the enterprising Samanda had been hired by the same magazine too, officially employed as interpreter and general factotum.

Conversations and luncheon mastication ceased as all eyes turned towards our odd threesome entering the palatial dining room. The floor manager showed us to a table discreetly located behind one of the wide pillars that supported the lofty roof, under which the hollowed out acoustics of conversations restarted. A waiter appeared on my left with a handful of menus and an invitation from my American acquaintance from the pool, to join him for lunch.

"Hi there, sit down, please, how's the cricket going, introduce me to your friends." he gabbled, obviously pleased to have company. Smiles and handshakes all round and after our drinks arrived, we joined the short queue for the buffet, Ram studying his reflection in the shiny white porcelain of the huge, crested, bone china plate in his hands, which was probably worth enough to keep his family in rice for months.

A noisy flock of Japanese tourists were being shepherded from their air-conditioned tour bus past us, to a long table in the restaurant.

"Never trust the Japanese." our host whispered in my ear, glancing in their direction. "Don't ever trust them, that's my advice."

I nodded at him sagely and concentrated on selecting a perfectly ripened slice of papaya and some Parma ham for starters. Marian was some way ahead of us in the line of prospective diners and was removing food from the mountain Ram had stacked on his plate.

"So what is this young man's story?" the American asked, looking at Ram back at our table, while cracking the big red claw of a lobster. I scooped the sweet pastel orange flesh from the yellowy green skin of my papaya, as Ram recounted the same story he'd told me on the way to the hotel. As she listened to the sad tale, I studied Marian's face, and wondered how I was going to live without it. And how it would have felt if she'd said no.

An elderly Japanese couple with bad skin, holding hands, stopped at our table to smile at Marian and bow in greeting.

"Hello Mr. and Mrs. Keama," she said, introducing us all, Ram waving a fork, chewing happily, next to our host who could barely conceal his discomfort.

"We are very pleased to meet you." said Mrs. Keama, her husband nodding in agreement as they walked away.

"Do you know what a Hibakusha is?" asked Marian.

"Something those Japs are eating?" our host replied.

"A Hibakusha is someone who survived the atomic bombs dropped on Hiroshima and Nagasake. Mrs. Keama was eighteen and survived Hiroshima, because she happened to miss her usual tram to the city centre that morning. She lost most of her skin and all of her hair and stumbled around the burning rubble amongst the remains of the dead, wishing she was one of them."

"Mr. Keama was twenty three, he was an engineer who was working in Hiroshima at the time of the attack and survived, although he was badly burned as well. He and the few survivors in his group travelled back home to Nagasaki, and arrived the day before the bomb was dropped there. The bandages covering the burns he got at Hiroshima were scorched off in the blast at Nagasake. Both lost their families, their homes, their health, everything. They have never had children, because they were worried about the genetic effects of the radiation that hit them. When they were well enough to work again after the bombings, they struggled desperately to find a job, because employers discriminated against them."

"No-one thought they'd live very long, or if they did, they'd take too much time off sick. They're covered in scars from head to toe, literally; some of them have never healed and just like lepers, they've had to fight all their lives for respect and every penny they've got. The past is gone forever. Your past and the sacrifices all of you made then, gave us the freedom we enjoy today and I appreciate that, very, very much."

"But it's long past the time to forgive. The bitterness you've got inside you is doing you harm. I'm not asking you to forget what happened, I'm not asking you to do that, but just try to forgive these people; they're not your enemy any more. Mr. and Mrs. Keama never were to begin with."

****

A cool evening breeze wafted across the polished mahogany floor of the hotel's communal first floor balcony, and through the wickerwork of my planter's chair. I swung out the leg rests from under the arms, nestled down deeper and put my feet up, watching a dark chorus of magpies spiral in tight formation. They swooped, black darts across a soft pink sky, shading to orange towards the hills behind the big lake, which slashed the reflected beauty of the changing sunset into neat ripples. Along with the rest of the corvin family - rooks, crows and jackdaws - much-maligned magpies pair for life and live in hierarchical societies. With brain / bodyweight indexes matching chimpanzees, they have extraordinary observational abilities, often work in teams and will defer instant gratification for larger rewards. They mourn their dead, and dance in ritual to celebrate the life that has passed. I'd watched one dropping stones into a deep pothole earlier, patiently raising the level of the rainwater that had drowned the worm floating on the surface, until the bird could reach it. It wasn't learned behaviour.

The softly lit Temple of the Tooth shimmered on the lake's surface too, glowing in the fading twilight, as the oil lamp man made his nightly rounds, lighting braziers on the stucco walls. The birds ascended for the last time in perfect symmetry before a final dive towards the big banyan trees whispering in the wind in front of us, where they settled at last to begin the roosting songs that would entertain us for an hour or so.

On the far side of the square between the lake and the balcony, silhouetted against the last of the light fading away across the water, was a working mother, and her baby elephant, trudging slowly up the road. Their Mahout was talking away to the youngster, one hand on its spiky back, as it gripped its mother's tail with its trunk, while she carried a big pile of foliage for their evening meal in hers. As they plodded towards their quarters in the Temple grounds, I slit open the side of a fat white envelope with a letter inside, handwritten on hotel stationery.

Room 276.
December 11th., 2005

It's been a long time since I met a girl as special as yours, nearly sixty years in fact. You look very good together, make damned sure you keep hold of her, tight as you can and don't ever let her go.

She has wisdom, beyond her years and I thought I might be bold enough to give you some of the little I've learnt in my lifetime.....

Life isn't fair, but it's still good.
When in doubt, just take the next small step.
Life is too short to waste time hating anyone.
Your job won't take care of you when you're sick. Your friends and family will. Stay in touch.
Pay off your credit cards every month.
You don't have to win every argument. Sometimes its better to agree not to agree.
Cry with someone; it's more healing than crying alone.
It's OK to get angry with God. God can take it.
Save for retirement with your first paycheck.
Make peace with your past so it doesn't screw up your present.
Look after your knees. You'll miss them when they're gone.
It's OK to let your children see you cry.
Don't compare your life to others. You have no idea what their journey is all about.
If a relationship has to be a secret, you shouldn't be in it.
Everything can change in the blink of an eye, but don't worry, God never blinks.
Take a deep breath, it calms the mind.
Get rid of anything that isn't useful, beautiful, or joyful.
Whatever doesn't kill you really does make you stronger.
It's never too late to have a happy childhood, but the second one is up to you and no one else.
When it comes to going after what you love in life, don't take no for an answer.
Burn the candles, use the nice sheets, wear the fancy clothes. Don't save it all for a special occasion, today is special.

Over prepare, then go with the flow.
Be eccentric now, don't wait for old age to wear purple.
The most important sex organ is the brain.
No one is in charge of your happiness, but you.
Frame every so-called disaster with these words: "In five years, will this matter?"
Always choose life.
Forgive everyone, everything.
What other people think of you is none of your business.
Time heals almost everything. Give time, time.
However good or bad a situation is, it will change.
Don't take yourself so seriously. No one else does.
Believe in miracles.
God loves you because of who God is, not because of anything you did or didn't do.
Don't audit life. Show up and make the most of it now.
Tragedy in life doesn't lie in not reaching your goal, it lies in not having a goal to reach
Growing old beats the alternative - dying young.
Your children get only one childhood.
All that truly matters in the end is that you loved.
Get outside every day. Miracles are waiting everywhere.
Envy is a waste of time - you already have all you need.
The best is yet to come.
No matter how you feel, get up, dress up, and show up.
Yield.
Life isn't tied with a bow, but it's still a gift.

It's been a pleasure to spend time with you both and I hope you will not mind doing me a little favour as by the time you are reading this, I will have moved on.

The young man I met at lunch has hope and honesty in his eyes, something sorely lacking in the world these days. When I spoke to him, he told me that, most of all, he'd like to see his family again. That goes for me too, but as a lonely old bachelor, I'm just hoping to see them all again in the next world.

Please find enclosed an open air ticket and some cash for the young man to play at being the prodigal son in Bombay. As you're heading for Colombo, perhaps you'd be kind enough to humor an old man and administer this small gift to the boy on my behalf.

Merry Christmas, my best wishes to you all for the future and happy travels.

Best wishes,

Bernard Ballantyne.

Ram sat on the arm of Marian's chair next to mine, studying the words written on the bright colours of the Air India ticket, followed by those on one of the twenty dull green one hundred dollar bills, spread out on the low table before them.

"What do the words mean?" he asked, looking up at her.

"You're going home." she said, "To your family." gently brushing Ram's hair back from his forehead.

Two days later, Marian and Samanda, Ram and I, all four of us holding hands, made a strange foursome on the station platform. Conversation was minimal and difficult with the early morning noise of trains coming and going, the crowds of travellers flowing past. A young woman fainted, was sick on the platform, a distraction. I wished we hadn't hired one of the human limpets that work the platforms there. The young boys fling themselves at the sides of fast moving trains arriving at the platforms, scrabbling for grip, risking their lives for a few rupees reward, clambering in the windows, the trains still moving, to claim seats for their customers. It would have given us something to keep us busy, something to organise. Everything I'd rehearsed to say to Marian seemed stiff and difficult, and Ram and Samanda standing between us in the midst of all the chaos really didn't help. So we just said goodbye, hugged briefly, and I watched her gracefully walk away from me with Samanda behind, down the platform towards the boy guarding their seats. She stood on the bottom step of the dark red carriage, waved once, smiling, and was gone.

I'd managed to find some Christmas wrapping paper and was glad I'd sneaked the old *Falling in Love Again* '78 safely into her big aluminium camera case, after she'd packed and treble checked all the equipment. I asked myself if I couldn't say it, could I have wished for a better messenger than Marlene? But standing there holding Ram's hand, I felt more than the sadness of parting from someone you care for - something didn't feel right and I realised for the first time it was a sense of foreboding that was troubling me, more than anything else.

Unless you're the one planning to leave, or terminally sick maybe, it's rare you ever realise it's the final time you're going to see someone, rarer still to recognise, this is the last time you'll ever make love with them. People die, move on. Relationships can end suddenly, things just change.

She didn't look out of the window at us. I had wanted her to see me. One last time. Because I knew already in my heart, I'd fallen for her. Wanted so badly to say, I couldn't bear to wait until the 26th. Missed her smile already, that made those little creases at the sides of her mouth.

And I was still with her, in the warm breeze that had dusted us with jasmine petals and scent, through the soft, dusk lights under the golden roof of the Temple in Kandy. Warm, gentle, brushing lips of a shy kiss, petals falling, hands on each other's hips. Wanted to stay there forever with her, in that perfect moment. And I got my wish because in my mind, I never have left. You see, people do fall in love, and it starts when they reveal their vulnerability, people do belong to each other and that's the only chance anybody's got for real happiness.

The butterflies she'd let loose in my stomach, flew after the back of the guard's van, deserting us in the shady cool of the station, dissipating into the stippled, smoky heat haze that danced above the sunlit steel rails beyond the platform canopy. A small knot in an empty stomach had replaced them by the time I fired the old Honda back into life. Bursting with excitement, Ram hopped onto the vacant seat behind me. We threaded our way through the frantic traffic and found the winding road that descends down from the mountains towards Colombo, its fortified airport, Ram's flight home and his family's escape from poverty.

As we left the seething metal mayhem of Kandy's streets behind us, I was already missing Marian, wondering how I could possibly wait until Boxing Day to see her again. I was humming Lennon's *Beautiful Boy*, and feeding in a bit more throttle as the roads cleared on our long descent to the western coastal plain. I sang the lyrics silently in my head, the only way I could hear them above the noise of the bike's exhausts, and the rushing wind.

But life is, of course,
What happens to you,
While you're busy making other plans.

13

The air oozing north from the equator was so heavy with moisture, the corpulent sky had sunk all the way down to earth under its bloated load. We walked through fine mist, veils of dense white cloud shrouding the top of the canopy, and blanketing the thick tropical vegetation. Every plant and tree wept gently, as moist, warm air condensed on cool, early morning leaves; the jungle forest too, was mourning the loss of so many.

The normal, vibrant sounds of bird and animal life were muted, the bright colours of flowers subdued as I followed the teenage boy along the narrow footpath. The soles of his improvised flip-flops were made from old car tyres, and with every step, his right foot left the neat, apposite print of *'Michelin Pilot'* in the soft, damp earth. My eyes were open, but I was blind to the journey, just doggedly following the same two words in front of me, hypnotically repeated over and over again as we climbed gently, threading our way through the tearful jungle.

I'd turned my back on the grave at dusk and walked away from the mass burial, but I hadn't really left. The images were still stark, far more potent than the ones I was seeing. I felt so guilty and I still do. Guilty that I had survived, when so many hadn't. As I witnessed the wasted potential of so many perfect young lives that had disappeared in front of me, guilt exposed the fecklessness of an itinerant life that had amounted to nothing. It was a difficult confrontation in so many ways.

When we finally reached the hospital I was in pain, out on my feet, and too exhausted to be surprised at its size. It was the fourth and final medical centre we'd come to, where victims and survivors from the train had been taken. It was a large Ayuverdic hospital in fact, set in beautiful countryside, surrounded by mountain ash and coconut palm. In their shade we picked our way through several hundred injured people, their friends, helpers and family, camped out along with the homeless, the deranged, the hungry, the lost and the lonely. As with so many municipal buildings on the island, each of the hospital's three storeys had high ceilings, no windows and pillared dwarf walls, all open to the elements. They also shared the same neglect and crumbling decay as the island's overarching military budget took precedent, year after year, over all others. Inside, the wiring was ancient, exposed in many places, damp and dangerous. The overhead fans caked with glutinous dust hadn't stirred for years. Without their help, the torpor of the breezeless day could do nothing to stir the foetid air above the mass of humanity overflowing from jam-packed wards into crammed corridors. The wounded, the dead, the injured, the dying, the shocked, the traumatised, their relatives and the bereaved huddled together in pain and collective despair. My fading hope of finding Marian alive finally disappeared when the three white women we'd been told were here, turned out to be Portuguese mission workers, who'd been on their way to a Catholic church centre in Galle. Along with every other survivor I'd asked, they couldn't help me. I'd worked my way systematically through the crowded grounds, the morgue and every other room containing its overspill, and then every ward, walkway and corridor on each floor of the overwhelmed and chaotic, but somehow, still operational hospital. The surgical ward I'd ended up in on the top floor had six or seven times the numbers of patients it was designed for, but the section I was in was reserved for the seriously injured awaiting surgery, and post operation recuperation patients, and was a little less crowded.

I even found a small patch of floor space at the end of the ward and sat down, trying to ignore the cries and moans from the injured, and the painful protests from my hip, thinking that lives lived out here amongst nature's seething, endless struggle of violence and death were not more stoical than ours in the West. But that perhaps they were more accepting, closer to the fragility and transience of life than the sanitised and cosseted view many have of death in the West where the rhythmic emotion of life and death are more often than not only really experienced in hospitals, at weddings, funerals and Christenings. The majority's Buddhist beliefs on the island, and teaching of multiple reincarnation in the struggle towards the ultimate goal of Nirvana, was also helpful in the acceptance of impermanence and the certainty of death, followed by the prospect of rebirth. Events had been so huge though, so shocking, so traumatising, that I just wasn't sure if it was making the loss, pain, bereavement or grief in these hospital wards and corridors any easier than if it had happened on say, England's Atlantic coast

I dozed for a while, sitting on the concrete floor at the end of the final ward I'd checked, with my back propped up against one of the battered, chipped and trolley-gouged grey painted walls. I woke to a numb left leg and buttocks, shifted a bit to get some blood flowing and pins and needles into the limb, while I held my head in my hands and my tears back, reminding myself again, that if all of us inside the hospital labelled our troubles and threw them in a big heap to exchange, I'd soon be snatching mine back. I was hungry as usual, but not as much as the sick and starving rat that limped wearily past me, dragging a blood stained, discharge encrusted dressing along the floor with its mouth. Its grey, balding skin, stretched tight over tooth pick ribs, was only just hanging on to a few remnants of patchy fur, its tail crusty, entirely hairless. It really would have been a kindness to put the animal out of its misery, but nobody, including me, either had the heart, or frankly, could even be bothered, and it was left alone to wander off and dine in piece on its distasteful find.

I felt the rat wasn't the only one being watched, and as I looked up, my eyes met those of a boy in mid teens who was studying me with big, soft brown eyes as he lay on one of the narrow metal beds. Its coir mattress leaked coarse ginger coconut hair out of one torn corner onto the floor. He was bare chested, wearing a dark green batik printed sarong and had one big fresh rectangular pink dressing that ran from the left side of his waist to just above his left nipple, and a smaller square one covering his right hand side, above his liver. His curly black hair was thick on the top, trimmed close at the sides in a cut reminiscent of an early Little Richard. He was weak, probably still dopey from an anaesthetic, and was propping his head up with his left hand to see me better. I thought he was beckoning me over with his right, and I got up off the floor with the athletic grace of a ninety year old to speak with him, thinking he probably needed a nurse and to see if I could spot one, but all he was doing in fact was trying to draw my attention to the badly injured patient in the bed next to him.

The right hand side of this boy's face was traumatically damaged and misshapen, the closed, infected eye nearly white, weeping pus, huge and

129

swollen beyond the level of his forehead. His nose had been crushed and pushed left, the nostrils caked and blocked with black dried blood, above a severely swollen upper lip that had a boomerang shaped hole in it, exposing deeply gouged gums and the stumps of broken teeth. His mouth and lower lip seemed to have been pushed down his face with the impact of whatever had hit him, or whatever he'd been flung into inside the train, and it was also caked with dried blood, swollen and misshapen. Sticking out of the side of his mouth, held in place with white surgical tape covering a lot of the left hand side of his face, was a long plastic tube, attached to a green elbow piece leading to a larger tube, that disappeared behind the bed. I assumed it was delivering oxygen, but it may just have been keeping the youngster's airway open, or draining his lungs of fluid maybe, I couldn't tell.

I looked back inquiringly at his neighbour, who was nodding and continuing to point at the horrifically injured boy. I had no idea he was conscious until the small part of his left eye that wasn't covered by the piece of tape that ran laterally across it, from the bulbous and bruised bridge of his nose to the side of his cheekbone, fluttered open and peered at me. He made a movement with his badly damaged mouth and through the plastic tube, and the hole under his nose, he whispered my name.

The shock was so great it felt like my heart somersaulted in my chest and I had to grab the end of the metal bed to stop myself from falling. I tried to compose myself, think of the right thing to say, but I couldn't formulate any words in my mind, or my mouth, and in the end, instinct overcame emotion, I perched slowly and carefully on the edge of the thin, coarse mattress and I just held Samanda's hand as he drifted in and out of consciousness.

14

Leaden grey skies had trapped an oppressive, humid afternoon heat in Colombo's harbour, and a turgid oily sea had assumed the clouds' torpid colour, melting the horizon in grisaillic light. My shirt was glued to the back of the plastic seat, less than a minute after choosing where to sit on the lower level of the flat-bottomed double decker boat I was taking back down south.

Most of the passengers were leaning on the rails above, enjoying the views from the upper deck, a big pile of their assorted luggage surrounding the old Honda. It was lashed to two of the splintered wooden columns that supported the peeling roof of the old boat, which looked more suited to a disco cruise down London's river Thames than an ocean voyage. Oily puddles slurped with the small swell across sections of the lower deck, and nautical debris of buckets, bits of rope and plastic bailing scoops fashioned out of old cooking oil containers, slopped around in the rainbow film of the surface. A pile of coconuts sat next to an old oil drum offering passengers drinking water of dubious quality, by a greasy, steep stairway dotted with rusty tools and broken components, leading to an ill-fitting hatch above the engine room of this decrepit old tub.

The salt encrusted window next to my seat was stuck halfway down its runners at an odd angle and rattled in time to the engine's drumming under my feet. The toot of a klaxon from the bridge above was followed by the thump of a thick rope hitting the narrow walkway just outside the window, as rising revolutions orchestrated our departure.

A puerile deck hand pushed us away from the concrete quay with taut tendons, using a sodden length of bamboo. The propeller screwed into the frothing water, stirring a salted stench of rancid rotting filth from the polluted harbour. The bloated corpse of a large dead rat tumbled momentarily in the bow wave as we increased speed, heading out towards the Indian Ocean. The open-ended overhead stowage lockers above me shook the fibrous remains of a few moth eaten, mouldy life jackets onto the floor, as our slimy concrete berth slipped away behind us.

As the coastline receded, an Indian family, their sightseeing over upstairs, took shelter from the stiff sea breeze in some seats on the opposite side of the central gangway. Bringing up the rear of the colourful procession, the father spotted my watch, grabbed and turned my wrist to see the time, a socially acceptable habit, particularly on public transport. He inclined his head to one side in thanks, accidentally bumping a rusted overhead fan with his head, before joining his family in the noisy chatter of a journey's beginning. The fan whirred into life with the sudden impact, turning slowly towards me on its cyclical gear, and just as the welcome cooling breeze streamed across my upturned face, the blades, caked in black oily fluff, ground to a halt as quickly as they'd started.

A large black spider emerged from the motor housing in high dudgeon and hastened around the perimeter of the blade's battered wire cage, surveying the remnants of its web, securing the remains of its hard won maritime larder, wrapped in their silky shrouds, suspended in little hammocks, from the ceiling of an arachnid morgue.

A dugout outrigger fishing boat rushed past us towards the wide harbour entrance, its skeletal shape skimming the water like a predatory pond insect. A huge V8 car engine and gearbox was swivel mounted, grafted onto its stern, an extended prop shaft ending in a brass propeller instead of a differential, the whole assembly used to steer by a wiry fisherman of phenomenal strength. He must have been stone deaf standing next to the open stub exhaust which jutted from the manifold, next to a rubber hose dangling from the water pump straight into the ocean, greedily sucking supplies from the biggest radiator in the world.

We weaved our way between water traffic of all shapes and sizes. Leviathan oil tankers being tugged to skeletal steel loading platforms by tiny tenders, freighters at anchor awaiting their berths and dhows and junks waiting for cargo, or maybe enough wind to carry them to their destination. It seemed fresh here behind the harbour walls, but strong enough beyond them to whip white caps from the heads of waves of major proportion, spraying them into the air, while their former owners mounted ram raids against the rocky sea defences.

"My name is Kumble." announced a voice, distracting me from the disturbing vista. I turned from the window to see the middle-aged gentleman on my right, tugging at the tip of his wiry grey beard, looking at me from underneath a floppy white sun hat bearing the legend, 'tiger Beer - Never Run Out!'. His beaming beatific demeanour indicated he was unaware, or unconcerned about the bloody great waves crashing around ahead.

"Hello, pleased to meet you." I said, raising an arm in greeting, throwing a quick fixed grin in his direction, before re-riveting my gaze on the heaving water in our path.

"You were at the match in Kandy. I saw you there - most unfortunate incident." he said. "We won the game, in the end."

I turned to face the man again, who was now adjusting the peak of his hat to a jauntier angle. In the other hand he held two heavy glass tumblers.

"Would you care to join me in some gin?" he asked, producing a large bottle of Bombay Sapphire from an old Gladstone bag gripped between his feet.

The V8 outrigger had now reached the open sea a few hundred yards ahead and pitching wildly, turned back towards us which, damn it, I thought, is what we would surely have to do too. Nothing but the biggest ship or an even bigger fool would venture out into wild seas of that proportion. With a bit of luck, assuming we got straight back to the berth we'd just left, I could catch the late afternoon southbound train. If not, I decided to overnight in the city and ride back down the coast to Mr. Ranasinghe's guesthouse the next day.

"Yes, thank you, I will Mr. Kumble." I replied, "It looks like we'll have to turn back don't you think?" I asked, nodding in the direction of the angry ocean.

"No, I don't think so, the crew say it was much worse on the way here." Mr. Kumble replied, "Wait until we are a few miles offshore, then we'll have some fun I can tell you. You had better take a drink now, while you still have the stomach for it."

I took the glass of neat gin from his shaking hand and recognised the detached eyes and spirited breath of a man who was at least one sheet to the wind, which was probably a good place from which to work towards two. The litre bottle was about two thirds full.

"Cheers!" we toasted, and the fiery spirit left a hot trace all the way down to my stomach. Conversation had ceased between the other dozen or so downstairs passengers, who were quickly being joined by many more from the open upper deck. We all looked, transfixed at the maelstrom ahead as, my God, the closer we got to the open ocean, the more vicious it looked.

So this was what the waiter meant in the restaurant at lunchtime. I'd followed the sign in a Colombo back street to a dark, steep, creaking stairway, descending into the brilliant neon glare of a basement vibrating with life, which ceased the moment I crossed the threshold. Over a hundred male Muslim faces looked at the kuffar in stony silence with expressions ranging from fear to loathing, and I knew immediately how the Alien must have felt when it popped out of John Hurt's stomach for a run around the dinner table.

I'd sat at the only empty, plywood table, my progress followed by everyone's eyes, swivelling in turning heads, seemingly all attached to one big neck. A waiter appeared and managed a smile.

"Yes, please?" he asked, head wobbling from side to side.

"What's good?" I asked back.

"Everything good here, where you from?" he replied. My shoulders sagged slightly.

"Tipperary." sprang to mind.

"Where is this place?" he asked.

"It's a long way away. Worth the trip though, you'd like it."

A huge blackboard ran the length of one long wall in English and Singhalese, above the heads of half a dozen busy cooks in an open kitchen. Interest from my fellow diners waned a bit when the waiter delivered a hot Masala Dosai on a gleaming stainless steel plate, everlasting, unbreakable.

I asked him for directions to the jetty for the ferry south; he'd looked me earnestly in the eye and held my arm, shaking his head and saying,

"No ferry yesterday, big storm came from Batticaloa direction. You no go today, still big wave, very big wave. Stay here. Have good vegetable curry for dinner. Go tomorrow."

The crispy rice pancake, freshly cooked and filled with delicately spiced potato was superb, and I'd taken the latent heat out of the sambol side dish with a frothy sweet lassi, but I was already wishing I hadn't dismissed the waiter's warning. Because as we entered the open ocean proper, a sheet of spray enveloped the boat which pitched suddenly, and violently, as we were tossed upwards like an empty bottle onto the crest of a huge wave from where, with mounting terror, I saw a landscape of endless, blue-grey liquid mountains. The term 'watery grave' took on a newfound, personal and significant meaning.

I gripped the glass of gin between my knees and grabbed the wooden frame of my seat with both hands as momentarily, the boat was suspended in mid-air, the giant wave having suddenly rushed away from underneath us, and we free fell through clear air for awful moments, plummeting into the grey twilight of a darkened, molten morass between two walls of furious water before smashing, like a broken fairground ride, into the bottom of the trough of insanity we had dared to enter. Below my feet, I heard the muffled splintering sound of something very large and wooden, breaking. All I could see now surrounding the boat, were towering walls of angry, sloping water. No sky, nothing but water. Mr. Kumble's baby started crying, its brothers and sisters started screaming along with many of the passengers, and I had to dig deep not to join in. I was only on the old tub because my buttocks were so battered from the lunar mountain roads, and the fact that the Honda's rear suspension had given up even pretending to make an effort a long time ago. I hadn't fancied the slow southbound train in this humidity either, and thought the afternoon boat would offer a nice, breezy, relaxing sea cruise.

Appalling shudders ran right through it as the helmsman, who had obviously survived the impact, attempted to steer a course up the sheer side of the next wave we were facing. I'd managed to wedge myself against the row of slatted wooden day trip seats in front of me, bracing myself with all four limbs, and looked again at the derisory provision of life jackets, stifling a manic staccato laugh at the pitiful remains of faded canvas covers, rotting in the wooden racks above our heads. And I couldn't remember seeing a lifeboat either.

Three of the ramshackle side windows had detached themselves from their runners and disappeared, and a fierce wind ripped through the deck, carrying sheets of vomit from the remaining inhabitants of the upper deck, one of whom was either a vampire or had lunched on water melon, as their cascading effluent was bright red. The gale lifted everything loose into the air, including a pack of playing cards from somewhere, that swirled around Mr. Kumble, who astoundingly, remained standing, legs akimbo, knees bent, gripping one of the upright beams for support, ignoring his terrified young family completely.

"You are a Christian?" he asked me, above the raging wind, which continued to blast spray and sick through the open windows. Apparently oblivious to the furore surrounding us, he drained his glass, motioning a hurry-up signal at me, making little circles in the air with an index finger,

135

to do the same. Seemingly absentmindedly, he deftly snatched a queen of diamonds out of the air, as I swallowed the last of the clear liquid, nodded in reply and managed to get my glass back to him.

"Then according to your religion, you should pray for deliverance, should you not?" The boat was continuing its climb at an absurd angle up the wall of water towards a glimmer of sky, and I was pressed back into my seat, knuckles white, feeling the engine revs drop beneath me as we neared the top of the wave. We then fell, sickeningly again, my stomach trying to orchestrate an unscheduled reappearance of lunch, marinated in gin, before we cannoned into rock hard water and again, just beneath my feet, was the extremely worrying sound of large pieces of very important timber splintering.

"The crew, they are Buddhists you see." continued Mr. Kumble, who, with a balancing act of superhuman proportion, dispensed two more large drinks, without spilling a drop. "They will not be afraid. They believe their death is preordained; if this is their day to die, then they will accept this. Why turn back? There is no point for them. You are from the British islands I know, southern England I think".

Our watery roller coaster ride reverted to the ascendant as another sheer mountain of water faced us, up which we were borne, still floating, by some miraculous intervention, and I grabbed for the glass in Mr. Kumble's outstretched hand, spilling half of it, downing the rest in one gulp.

"Yes, London. Where this gin is from. May I have more please, I'm afraid I've spilt most of this one?" Despite my throat being on fire, even though it wasn't Dutch gin, I was definitely accruing some courage.

"I was there in 1971, visiting some family." he replied, timing his next pour to coincide with the helmsman knocking off the revs again as we emerged once more into daylight, on the crest of the latest Himalayan peak of water we'd been climbing. Land had disappeared from view. In fact there was no view except for the towering seas surrounding the precipice on top of which the frail little boat teetered. I braced myself again for the headlong plummet into the unfathomable trough below. The shattering impact as we finally hit the bottom, jolted my window, that had resisted all my efforts, squarely back onto its runners. Thankfully, I managed to struggle to my feet long enough to slam it shut and lock it into position, as dodging the noxious liquids being whipped in from the upper deck, without spilling any of the morale boosting gin, was becoming trickier by the minute. I lost my footing on the soaking oily deck and was thrown back into the seat, just as another glassful was thrust into my hand.

"I became very interested in love in England." Mr. Kumble shouted above the storm. "In fact, I even tried to fall in some, but failed. It is very big business I think. Look at your popular music. You see, in our Hindu society we do not have either. For you Western peoples, it is the most important thing; it seems to rule your lives. We have absorbed many parts of your culture into our society. We eat your potatoes and we use your computers and of course the tobacco you brought us too. All these have caught on very well, but love has not interested most of us at all, you see?"

"What about your wife Mr. Kumble?"

"That's quite alright thank you, she doesn't speak English."

"No, I mean, don't you love your wife?"

"Of course not, our marriage was arranged, long before we met. Everything is worked out nicely in advance you see. My parents took an advertisement in a newspaper and negotiated with my wife's parents. Then our astrological charts were produced and studied, we were introduced and married soon after. Sometimes, something like your love can come along in these situations. I am sure it never did for us, but I live in hope", he said, eyeing the few other female passengers, as if about to strike lucky at any moment.

Another terrifying impact shattered another window further up the deck, showering passengers with nuggets of glass. Sheets of salty spray immediately breached the broken defences. While Mr. Kumble continued to refresh our tumblers, he was managing to remain upright in the middle of the surging maelstrom, the crook of one arm wrapped around a wooden pillar. The rest of us sat hunched forward on our seats like passengers on a runaway train, gripping the back of the one in front, feet braced on the legs underneath, as if waiting for derailment or the finality of the buffers at the end of the line.

"We sometimes have 'love' marriages you know," continued Mr Kumble, who was now quite drunk. "But we always worry about such arrangements. They are like a stick of incense. They smoulder away and smell wonderful for a while, but then they burn out and you cannot light them ever again."

A large piece of thin planking splintered above us, detached itself from the roof and crashed onto the empty seat next to me, followed by a cloud of sooty black dust which had been accumulating behind it for many years, awaiting its moment to anoint me.

"But the fragrance of smoke can affect a whole room, or even a building Mr. Kumble." I said. "Sometimes, the perfume can last a very long time, because it gets into the fabric of the place, it becomes part of it."

"I see what you mean. Yes. It is hard for me to understand, do you understand? Are you having some love at the moment then?" he asked.

"Yes, I think I am." I said, to both of us.

The boat began to pitch more wildly into smaller, faster waves, being driven by an increasing wind and the propeller was being exposed in open air more and more frequently. Freed momentarily from its hard slog, the engine raced manically, the prop shaft bearings grinding as they overheated. Two thirds of the passengers on our deck had managed to drag themselves to the open stern handrails. Here they slumped, wrapped around them, as the wind whipped the contents of their stomachs back over themselves and their neighbours. They were all too ill to care, or even notice the additional contributions splattering over their heads from the more intrepid seasick, leaning over their own handrails on the upper deck.

"Look at those poor fellows." Mr. Kumble said, as a wave broke right over them. "In our legends, Hanuman didn't have all this trouble crossing little bits of water like this. He jumped the Palk Straits in one big leap you know."

"Was he the monkey chap who flew over here, spying for Rama or something?" I asked.

"That is quite right, you know the story?"

"Refresh my memory Mr. Kumble."

"Shall I also refresh your glass? We must finish the bottle, look." he said, holding it up in the dim light, pointing at the final inch of spirit, slopping around the bottom. Resistance was futile.

"Hanuman was sent to Lanka, you see, the old island capital, to spy on the demon king Ravana. he'd kidnapped King Rama's wife, Sita, if you remember - and imprisoned her, for a long time." explained Mr. Kumble, somewhat slurring his words now, and having trouble handing me my final ration, with the boat suddenly beginning to lurch from side to side.

We toasted General Hanuman, emptying the glasses.

"Sita was raised by King Janaka but she wasn't his real daughter you know - no, she sprang to life from the ground when he was ploughing the land. Did you know that? Well, Hanuman was caught spying, and the authorities set his tail alight. But he escaped at that very moment, jumping from house to house, and set light to the whole city, which was burned to the ground."

"Then, there was a great cosmic battle," Mr. Kumble let go of the wooden pillar and began furiously waving both arms above his head in a dra-

138

matic, drunken depiction of his story "...and Ravana, who had ten heads and twenty arms was....." was the last I heard of my drinking companion's story as, with his arms still flailing, the boat was suddenly tossed extremely violently to one side by a huge wave breaking on our right. Mr. Kumble was instantly knocked off his feet by the impact and tossed with some force into the big pile of coconuts in the walkway behind us, most of which had displayed amazingly tenacious angles of repose, by remaining together throughout the storm. The back of his head slammed into one coconut with enough force to crack it, squirting milk into his hair, while propelling his false teeth four or five feet across the gangway, which I plucked from the air with a diving reflex catch of staggering athleticism under the circumstances, worthy of the great English wicketkeeper Alan Knott, even if I say so myself. They were slimy, smelt of gin and paan and worst of all, were quite hot.

Mr. Kumble meanwhile, like an upturned beetle, made several futile attempts at regaining his feet. His struggles loosened dozens more coconuts, which flew around like pinballs in the violently pitching boat, as I offered him his dentures with one hand, and a lift up with the other. But in less than half a second, the next wave that hit us knocked me onto my knees, where hairy coconuts snowballing through the oily vomit soup underfoot, pinged off me like cannonballs. Mr. Kumble's previously garrulous lips mouthed a few silent words between newly sunken cheeks, his head wobbling with the effort of trying to get up. One glassy eye peered at me, but he quickly gave up the struggle, waving me away with a dismissive gesture, before slipping into the spread-eagled, unconscious coma of a major drunk, on his bed of coarse-haired, oversized nuts. There he stayed for the next ten hours, as the rest of us endured the torrid journey south, where the bow eventually found calmer seas just before dawn, finally slicing through still water, as we lost our way, and reached our destination.

Oddly enough, this wasn't the first set of flying dentures I'd encountered on this trip. The gut-rot I'd picked up in the Rajasthan desert, had sent me in Jodphur, where the amoebae had really started to take control, to Sardar market in search of raw opium, one of natures best cures for bowels needing incarceration. Drinking the sap of the poppy seed head melted into warm water, results in industrial strength constipation with, it has to be said, not unpleasant side effects. I'd travelled through the desert mostly by train, largely suspended in a semi-squat above gruesome 2nd class toilets playing host to several trillion germs and diseases, to which I contributed virulent amoebic dysentery.

I'd arrived at the open market by camel taxi, sliding off the rough wooden planking of the flatbed cart pulled by an ill-tempered ship of the desert. The driver had only just managed to win a tug of war with the truculent creature, which begrudgingly came to a halt at the edge of the market, next to a four foot high pyramid of garlic, neatly stacked on the ground, on top of a square of jute sacking. An enormous white cow was taking advantage of the garlic owner's absence from the pitch, by contentedly munching its way through the mountain of fat, fresh, pungent bulbs. I pondered the dietary effect on the flavour of tomorrow's milk as the camel joined in too, definitely improving its hideously appalling breath. It was only marginally more rancid than the foul stench emanating from the rotting remains of what passed for teeth inside the driver's mouth. He was blatantly pretending not to notice his grumpy beast of burden's free lunch, by concentrating on directing me towards the fabled opium vendor, whom I was led to believe plied his trade deeper inside the chaos of the sprawling market. Throughout the process, he augmented the delights of his oral perfumery, with evil smelling bidis, the smoke from which enwreathed us both like a cloak, with its acrid, pungent smell.

I was surprised to note that behind the cow were two rudimentary and disorderly queues, an alien social concept in this part of the world at the best of times. They featured two groups of a couple of dozen people jostling for an improved position, and their turn to try the various lenses, frames, shapes and sizes from a selection of second hand dentures and spectacles. The arrays of glasses on display were of mostly ancient design and the neat rows of grinning dentures, yellowed with age, use, and poor cleaning regimes. They were all arranged on the makeshift terraces of a dusty green baize sheet covering the short, squat, balding stallholder's rickety trestle table.

Such was the allure of his stock, he was having to impose restraint amongst his prospective clients, by lambasting them with verbal broadsides, whilst brandishing a large stick at those foolish enough to break ranks, jockeying for position amongst the impatient throng. He was otherwise busy at the far end of the stall, helping two patrons on consulting stools with empirical amateur optometry, using a cracked and filthy vanity mirror and a crude, hand painted Hindi equivalent of an optician's A-Z board.

As I watched the process with fascination, the previously toothless old man at the head of the queue for denture trialists, suddenly grimaced, doubling up, coughing and gagging simultaneously. The horrible, gummy, breathless sucking noises he made quickly worsened, indicating rapid suffocation due to the fact he'd managed to ingest the upper denture plate he'd been trying, obviously several sizes too small.

Even though the old man quickly developed the pallor of a white man's bruise before sinking onto all fours, with what sounded like an extended death rattle, the stall holder seemed to be in no hurry whatsoever as he ambled across to the prostrate figure. With what seemed to be practised, somewhat bored and detached insouciance, he lifted his stricken prospective client back up to the standing position, then executed a perfect, though perhaps unnecessarily violent Heimlich manoeuvre. Like a fighter pilots' ejector seat, the garish false pink gums were jettisoned skyward through a glutinous parabolic spray of saliva, rivulets of mucus glinting in the sunshine, before the gruesome assembly of yellowed, brown stained, pre-owned teeth, overcome by gravity, made a neat impression in the sandy desert soil beneath our feet.

Without a second glance at his panting victim, whom he simply dropped back onto the ground where he proceeded to throw up, the stallholder retrieved the offending object, checked for structural damage, chipped, cracked or loosened teeth - for which I have no doubt there would have been an immediate charge. Using spittle of his own, theatrically exhumed from the depths of his smoker's lungs as polish, he lackadaisically buffed up the offending article on a rather distastefully soiled shirt sleeve, before reuniting it, between the thirty or so other clenched teeth on display, with its lower partner in crime. Service with several smiles.

Customer care at the opium stall was delivered with more of a fixed grin, the proprietor obviously being rather too fond of sampling his own wares. He was clutching an aged silver pipe and was completely out of his nut in fact, slumped, crossed legged on a stone wall, next to a fine old pair of Victorian balance scales. On a small folding wooden table in front of the polished brass chains and dishes, was a lump of Kashmiri Twist hashish the size of a slightly deflated rugby ball and a dollop of fresh, sticky, jetblack Chinese opium not much smaller. He cut both in half for me and after jettisoning some redundant warm clothing to make room in the already minimalist shoulder bag I lived from, I had my first self-medicated infusion of the raw opium at a tea stand five minutes later. It was rather like drinking warm, diluted mud, but it did, temporarily at least, halt the inexorable takeover of my digestive system by the Rajasthani parasites.

In combination with the dark resin from the northernmost extremity of the country, the downside of this self-administered prescription was that the next couple of months or so were effectively lost to me. As was about four stone of body weight, nearly all my remaining possessions of any value whatsoever, and most memories of an eight-week peregrination down the west coast of India, during which at some point I acquired a particularly humiliating tattoo, which must have seemed funny at the time.

Remnants of the old north-south hippy trail survive to this day, and a living can still be made buying hashish from India's northern cities (generally Mumbai for Pakistani Black, Kashmiri, Chitrali and Manali variants, whilst the Delhi black market is often the best source for Afghanny * and the more esoteric Nepalese derivations).

Heading south on the well-trodden trails, this can then be sold in multiples of tolas (10 grammes) to northbound travellers, the burgeoning numbers of tourists on Goa's famous old hippy beaches, or traded for Kerala's (India's southernmost [and only Communist] state) famous marijuana.

If you actually manage to complete such a North-South dope dealing trip in one piece, conscious, and even more unlikely, solvent, the opportunity does then present itself to reverse the whole process by buying Kerala grass in wholesale quantities, turning around, and following the same trail and sales opportunities northbound. Surprisingly substantial numbers of Westerners still ply this subsistence trade, usually having cashed in their air ticket at some point, never to return home.

One of the few memories I do have of this diarrhoeal / opium / hashish fuelled odyssey, begins with half eggshells adorning a large spiky cactus plant, outside a traveller's cafe in northern Kerala. For the uninitiated, the eggshells signify the availability of psilocybin mushrooms on the menu. The bowel binding properties of egg consumption, along with the rather more cerebral benefits of a 'special' omelette, proved impossible to resist. When in Rome.

Waiting for the chef to weave his 'magic' on the omelette, I'd traded some of my remaining 'O' with another diner, for what turned out to be a batch of dynamite Kerala grass.

Following a substantial meal heavily laden with the fungi in question, and washed down with a speckled 'bhang' lassi for good measure, my dining companions watched in amazement as I loaded up a sizeable communal stone chillum, with what I had no idea was enough of the bright green, sticky herb, to poleaxe an elephant. Under the stunned, withering gaze of

---

* 'the vast majority of Afghanistan's high quality hashish production was diverted to Russian black markets during, and ever since their Army's occupation of that country.

a sizeable international audience, I persisted in defiantly smoking the entire contents through a regulation wet cotton neckerchief, even though the wiser, more experienced heads surrounding me, declined to share the damned thing. Pure bravado saw me finish the lot, overcoming lungs feeling like they were inhaling a thermal lance, and something akin to a warp drive, twin turbo-charged Disneyland firework display going off in my head.

Slamming the chillum back down on the table to a desultory smattering of sarcastic applause, I grabbed what I thought was a glass of water, and downed in one, what proved to be a very large, neat Indian rum - a drink I've never been particularly happy with. It quickly proved to be my final undoing. My fellow diners' estimation of me plummeted still further, following my immediate announcement that I was going outside to get some fresh air, particularly, it has to be said, as we'd been eating together at a long refectory table under the stars, all evening. It was only after I'd managed to get to my feet, that I remembered this, catching a glimpse of the night sky as I collapsed into unconsciousness on the flagstone floor. I remember the taste of the blood and the grit in my mouth, along with the feel of the few remaining objects of any value being removed from my pockets, then very little else, apart from residual flashbacks of spectacularly colourful dreams, for some days afterwards.

****

The same skinny deckhand who'd pushed us off the dockside at Colombo appeared again, yawning, whilst scratching tousled hair, then stretching - all indications that incredibly, he'd been sleeping deeply through his passengers' collective nightmare. He hitched up his sarong, rubbed sleep from his eyes, and splashed the anchor into placid, glassy grey water of crystal clarity. It sank out of sight into beds of tall and graceful sea grass being caressed by gentle currents, eddying to and fro, twenty feet or so below us. It was hard to believe this was the same journey. In the burgeoning light, I could make out a small shoal of blue wrasse just below the surface, darting away from the snaking anchor rope in communal paranoia, before returning for a closer look as it tightened and pulled the boat to rest, a condition my body was not yet ready to recognise.

Ahead lay the spectral shape of high land above the soft welcoming lights of the harbour; as morning's first light tinged clear skies behind the hills, the advancing sunrise dimmed the stars above us. The air was so still, the dawn chorus of birdsong and raucous parrots' screeches flew across the water from the treetops ahead of us, accompanied by the dreaded muffled thud of the Imam's microphone switch being turned on in the town's mosque. I knew that harbinger of loudspeaker doom so well, from my stay in a hilltop hotel overlooking the city. It announced the end of sleep, and presaged the gruesome, body fluid curdling torture of the daily, badly amplified wail to prayer, from the Muslim world's answer to the egregious 1980's punk act, Auntie Pus and The Sceptic Discharge.

Lying in that hotel bed, pillows invariably clamped to ears strategically plugged prior to retiring, I finally decided, after endless, sleepless debate, that death by bazooka would be the most satisfying end for this man. Not the merciful, unknowing explosion of a marksman's direct hit, nor the symbolic opening disposal of the minaret. That would have removed the very canned speaker system I hoped would record his final, highly blasphemous pleas for mercy, as I demolished the entire edifice surrounding him piece by piece, with unerring accuracy. But there we are, there are worse things in life. It could have been Wogan, and it's a testament to the civilised friendliness of the vast Singhalese majority in tolerating the all-pervasive inculcation to pray, for just five percent or so of the town's population. In England, it's silently transmitted by short wave radio, into the homes of the devout.

Having lost every navigation light, the crew seemed to have salvaged the caution they'd thrown to the tropical storm's aftermath, which we'd fought all through the night, by waiting here for the silvery half light to strengthen, and illuminate the narrow entrance between the coral reefs, that gave the harbour its protection. I looked around the boat in wonder and disbelief at our surviving the seven-hour journey that took over fourteen. My skin and clothes were stiff, cold and clammy, sticky with dried spray, sick (unidentified donor[s]), spilt gin and the sweat of raw, uninhibited fear. Every joint in my body was aching from the effort of pinning myself into a tiny space, braced on my seat between a hull and two stanchions for most of the night, like a starfish with rigor mortis.

Mr. Kumble's youngest daughter, sporting a big red disc in the middle of her forehead, watched me over the shoulder of her dozing mother. Under her emotionless gaze, I removed the bright yellow flippers I'd taken from my bag and donned, along with my mask, during the worst of the storm, when it had seemed certain it was a matter of when, not if I would end up in the clutches of the wild water tearing at our fragile vessel. I'd wondered how it was going to feel to have water filling my lungs again after all this time out of the womb. I'd never have made the coast in a million years of course, I knew that, but so certain was I that we'd be going down, I thought I'd have a better chance of fighting my way to any piece of debris with the flippers and the mask. I'd felt surprise at my impending death's location, more than any fear of my final destination, but overwhelming frustration and despair at the thought that Marian would never know why we reached the end, before we'd finished our beginning.

My feet began to tingle with exquisite pain as they renewed their acquaintance with a blood supply. I took the mask and snorkel from around my neck, pulling them over a pulsating head containing a tongue about twice its normal size, that seemed to have sprouted hair overnight. I struggled to my feet, feeling nauseous, head swimming and thumping, the pitching of the boat still a physical threat, and it took a few moments to realise I was again standing in a large puddle of human effluent of every type, which was coagulating in the lowest, middle part of the deck where I was struggling to remain standing. It rose in small eruptions between each toe, with the consistency of warm toothpaste.

Miss. Kumble smiled at me and giggled, holding her nose as I lifted up one foot dripping with slime, before she buried her head in her mother's shoulder with sudden shyness and I realised quite suddenly, I was delightfully, deliriously happy to be alive, with land in sight, here off the south western coast of Sri Lanka. I squeezed past Mr. Kumble who was snoring loudly, snuggled up to two big armfuls of coconuts, popped his dentures into the breast pocket of his shirt and dodged the motionless overhead electric fan, stopping to admire the symmetrical perfection of a brand new web, decorated by beads of dew glistening in the soft morning light. Its architect waited patiently dead centre, for a well deserved breakfast catch, after a night time's athletic labour in challenging conditions, and I wondered if spiders wished they could sit down for a bit, and put their many feet up. Maybe they do.

I emerged from the lower passenger level on the open deck aft, to a scene more than suitable for inclusion in Dante's Inferno. I picked my way with a bursting bladder over stricken and stirring bodies, to cast modesty and good taste over the side, with an arcing stream of urine, into my own reflection. Sorry fish. An elderly gentleman on my left gave me an old fashioned look, while scrubbing the front of his teeth with an index finger, in a futile, yet endearing attempt at dental care.

The first proper light of the day stretched over the hilltops and infused the sea with an indigo blue, further illuminating the teeming life that sur-

145

rounded us. A big shadow moved under my frothy dissipating reflection, the wide, dark mottled wingspan of a huge ray, ten feet wide or more. It was cruising so close to the surface, I could almost bend down and touch the purple markings on its soft and silky wings, as it glided effortlessly out of sight under the hull. A sleek, flashing silver barracuda accelerated away from the boat, chasing a small shoal of incandescent flying fish, which burst through the surface of the water, open wings whirring in their attempts to escape the fastest fish in the ocean. I followed the battle out of sight as they skipped and skimmed their way across the bay, crossing two deep, dark furrows in the molten lead surface of the placid sea.

I followed the lines, plotting a course a couple of hundred yards nearer, and was rewarded as the glistening blue-black backs of a pair of sperm whales, following the coast broke through the surface and breathed out, close enough for me to smell their fishy breath, topped by bursts of spray. The following, relaxed, sighing intake, was perfectly audible for the precious seconds of their presence, before two giant flukes appeared above the surface as they turned in perfect harmony, altering course away from us and were lost from sight, diving towards the deeper waters of the open ocean, far beneath the tortured surface that had tormented us all night. Here, inside their heads, the ton or so of milky oil, from which their name derives, would solidify into wax, protecting brains the size of soccer balls. This oil is used by NASA, the only substance known to them capable of lubricating and protecting their fragile, high technology equipment in the absolute cold of outer space.

My head turned like a flower towards the brilliant sunshine that suddenly spread like buttermilk, spilt across the saucer of the bay. Even our yawning anchorman had been mesmerised by our visitors from the deep, but the sudden, bright light broke the spell and wide awake now, the boy winched the anchor, and several pounds of sea grass back aboard, as the engine rumbled into life below. With a puff of black diesel smoke from the stern, we nosed ahead over the still water, following two shrimpers towards a long wooden jetty, dotted with an eclectic collection of vessels. At our berth were the myriad colours, luggage and goods of a hundred or so passengers waiting to board our boat for its return journey, lambs in quiet patience for their slaughter.

We moored between the chaotic unloading of the two shrimp boats, the auction of their live night time catch already under way, plastic crates of wriggling crustaceans lining the end of the jetty, which led to a single pot-holed street containing about thirty shops and restaurants. A giant sign advertising Gold Leaf cigarettes at the back of the narrow sandy beach had been daubed with the slogan 'Cancer is the best cure for Smoking' in bright red paint. Trickles of it ran from the bottom of the letters, down the chin of the gaudy movie star peddling the pernicious weed, making him look consumptive.

Piles of cargo, coiled mountains of rope, pickup trucks, lobster pots and a big crowd of interested parties, hawkers, hangers on and people with nowhere else to go filled the jetty, the numbers swelled by our arrival. Like the walking wounded from a forward battalion back from the front line, we disembarked, stooped and quiet, haunted by the vivid trauma of our shared experience. A smattering of white faces were smiling, expectant, dotted among the prospective outbound passengers, jostling for position to board first and secure favoured seats on the ferry's return journey.

"Big waves, don't go!" I advised them, before slumping unsteadily onto a stool at a food stall for a speculative breakfast. A street market that began with fish at the end of the jetty where the trawlers and shrimpers were moored, moved to vegetables about halfway down and stretched away into the distance, ending in the town itself and old Dutch fortifications. I watched the cook boil the black fermented tealeaves, condensed milk and sugar altogether in a battered aluminium saucepan, while contemplating my survival, wondering what exactly is the mortal coil? I don't want to sound like some sort of seafaring wimp, but to this day I know we were teetering on the very edge of capsizing countless times on that journey, in pitch-black darkness with no real chance of survival. I have never been much of a sailor, always preferring the air, with its birds-eye view of a country, but if I could survive a journey like that I thought, I could survive anything any ocean could throw at me. I wasn't to know what was coming - no one knew.

Chicken quarters and four plump silvery sardines smelt very good on the charcoal grill next to the sweet corn I'd ordered, along with a couple of vegetable samosas, deep fried in fragrant coconut oil for good measure. The kill or cure breakfast was accompanied by the hot, sticky sweet tea that arrived in a thick glass tumbler. I watched the Honda being manhandled off the boat and propped up against a huge bronze propeller, which was too big and heavy for the pickup sent to collect it. I got a cheery wave and a fully restored smile from a slightly delicate looking Mr. Kumble, carrying a souvenir coconut under one arm, as he shepherded his family towards a battered waiting taxi.

I waved back as my sweet yellow corn arrived char grilled, dusted in chilli powder, and my first big slurp of tea didn't actually make it down my throat, just soaked into my tongue and cheeks. The second gulp barely moistened a parched, cracked throat and some of the third actually made it all the way down. As my mouth lit up with the first mouthful of the moist, warm and hot chilli sweet corn, I ordered two more teas.

And I wondered if she was still asleep, curled up on her right side, breathing softly. Wide awake, I'd held her like that all through the night as she slept in Kandy, my knees tucked behind hers, silently whispering prayers of thanks to the gentle rhythm of the overhead fan, and my solemn promise, that I'd never, ever, ask for anything again. If only.

I'd dozed off at first light and dreamed again of the swan on the moon-lit water, which darkened as I watched the young bird caught in some barbed wire, trapped in the fast moving river's weir. There was a walkway across it, narrow and slippery, on which I knelt above the current and the struggling bird, reaching for the wire wrapped around the tip of one wing. But the water cascading over the weir kept getting higher, and the more I leaned over, the further the swan was below me, until vertiginous fear made me pull back. To find Mongoose sitting close by, beckoning, leading me to the safety of the bank. When I turned, the swan had disappeared, and I was full of dread.

****

The sun was drying the Honda's seat out nicely as I contemplated reuniting it with my battered and bruised buttocks, and singed bollocks. It had been a wonderful trip around the Southern Province and through the mountains, but I was tiring, mentally and physically of all the travel and wasn't looking forward to the final forty miles or so on the cratered coast road.

It wasn't so long ago a Briton would travel no more than two or three thousand miles in a lifetime, often never beyond thirty miles from the place they were born. During Queen Elizabeth II's reign, the average has risen from under a million at her post war coronation, to between three and four million miles in a lifetime. Even further for some.

I'd travelled on one of the first Boeing 747's, transatlantic, London to Miami. But sitting in the plane in the thin air of velvet skies, high over Greenland, heading for home on the top of the world, east into the dawn, I realised the privilege I was enjoying, could never be for the many. And my heart sank, knowing what the engines spewed in our wake must surely suffocate the very planet all its prospective passengers wanted to see.

As a kid, farming in Devon, in the West of England, I couldn't work out the point of killing all the life in the soil, reducing it to sterility, then using oil products to force plants to grow in the lifeless medium we'd created. And chemicals to kill the ones that weren't wanted. I could never get to grips with the logic. I still can't. All based on the fear of running out of food, as Britain so nearly did, separated from its Commonwealth larder by world war two. Never again. Rationing of the 1940's and '50's supplanted by consumer insanity, the perverse dogmatic lunacy of constant economic growth, the mantra of pathetic politicians lighting the blue touch paper, hypnotising themselves with their ephemeral delusions.

Good people of the East look at what we've done with horror. Nobody seems to connect the 'teak Garden Furniture Sale' notice pinned to their local lamppost with the end of rainforest in Borneo. And all the life that lives within it. We're in the process of cornering, and Hoovering up the last remaining fish in all our oceans. Is it any wonder the lengths the Taliban were prepared to go to, to try and stem the relentless flow of what they saw as the infection of their culture and society by destructive Western influences? I have great sympathy with some of their extremes; what other choice did they have, other than in desperation, to ban the television, films, discs and tapes, the harbingers of their cultural doom.

But due in no small part to their misguided pursuit of violence, the world now, has suddenly shifted. The freedoms I have enjoyed in my lifetime will soon be memories of the platinum plated age my generation has been lucky enough to live through. It's so hard to imagine freedom if you have been brought up to expect it. As a British citizen, I can travel a third of the way around the world to the USA without a visa, and from any British airport car park on my return, as a European, I can swing a leg over my motorcycle and ride, unimpeded, all the way to the Russian border. Or even to the Iranian border should I choose to do so, through many countries where freedom has only recently been realised, mainly through the desire of Eastern Europeans to enjoy the same right to uninhibited travel as their Western counterparts.

In *Hope against Hope* by Nadezhda Mandelstam, one of the best books written about life without such freedom, the Russian poet Osip's wife wrote about a conversation with her fellow dissidents in the Soviet Union in the 1930's, that for some reason had turned to train travel. She was describing to them how in Britain, people were free to buy a ticket for any destination they chose, and travel there without official permission. Her friends laughed at her with derision and scorn; how could the authorities possibly surrender so much power to citizens?

She was right, of course, but we have taken our natural rights so much for granted, that we never give such freedom any thought at all. In its pursuit, with their authorities too weakened to prevent them, eventually of course, the Berlin wall was torn down by the very people it was built to corral, contributing substantially to the end of the Cold War.

Even in my lifetime, my freedom to travel has grown enormously. A majority has access to a car, most of us have experienced foreign holidays and long distance travel became cheap and accessible with the 747, Boeing's first jumbo jet. Money now crosses borders in freedom too, in ever increasing quantity. In my Father's 1960's passport was a page where he was required to record all the money he took out of the country. It was a criminal offence to take more than £50.

Nowadays, in a daily miracle of global co-operation and co-ordination, we can all buy food and goods that have travelled by air to our local stores, from around the world. Prosperity that would have seemed impossible to previous generations has been a part of our normal, everyday life now, for decades.

I may have had my doubts about the viability of massed, jet propelled air transit, sitting on an early jumbo jet, but I never would have believed two airliners would eventually be used as flying bombs, to destroy New York's World Trade Center. It is a gross oversimplification to say these most extreme of extremists are in essence, fighting the largely Christian West in their religious belief, not only in an attempt to protect their culture and way of life, but for the very survival of the planet. However, it is a significant part of the conflict's complexity.

Because of the attack on New York, travelling through an airport is a very different experience today. We still have freedom to travel, and haven't yet reached the point of needing permits to do so, but we are certainly now, for the first time, under surveillance all the way. What the authorities can monitor, they invariably end up wanting to actively control, and we now travel by air, road or rail, observed. Our vehicles are tracked on our roads, by number plate recognition cameras, across the majority of Britain, barring all but the most remote districts. The impending schemes of bureaucrats, will soon result in our being forbidden to drive to certain places, at certain times, because such freedom of movement will be considered to be 'unnecessary', and of course, the great catch-all, environmentally damaging. If I ever get the chance to tell grandchildren that I used to ride and drive anywhere I chose, whenever I liked, they probably won't believe me.

I have enjoyed enormous freedom. I've never had to serve in the armed forces, I'm allowed to marry and divorce whom I like, and I can have as many children as I please. Over 70% of us own property, we can complain openly about our Government and for over sixty years, the rise of technology, the spread of English as the global language, the power of democracy, the influential spread of our music, film, fashion and now internet technology, our escalating wealth and the reach and sophistication of our fabulous travelling machines, has made the world our oyster.

But now, the end of cheap money, environmental degradation, global terrorism and - at last - the dawning realisation that every resource is finite, is bringing it all to an end, just as huge numbers of Eastern populations rush to emulate the West. Vast populations are reprising our utterly pointless accumulation of possessions and wealth that has brought earth's biosystems to the point of collapse, in the face of entrenched moral belief and religious teaching. Supplies of rare earths, which languish in their own row beneath the main periodic table are predicted to be exhausted by 2050. Incredibly, in 2010, only 1% of the world's hi-technology electronic devices that rely on these little known elements are recycled. Computers, telecommunication equipment, fibre optics, photography, compact discs, hybrid cars, lasers, nuclear reactor rods, catalytic converters, the most sophisticated weaponry - the list is endless - will become impossible to manufacture by mid-21st century.

The future prospect of our society having to dig up and sift through every 'waste' landfill site to recover its precious contents, will be the most damning inditement of the 20th century's 'dig it up and dump it' industrial model.

Freddie Laker, pioneer of no-frills air travel, became a folk hero to the British people and all his customers, even more so when the established corporate carriers connived and contrived his transatlantic Skytrain's demise. He eventually got his revenge, through the Courts and a sword on his shoulder too, from Queen Elizabeth II.

Following the storm, the morning air was still heavy with moisture close to the coast, the breeze refreshingly cool across my cheeks as I started the Honda. The bike was sticky with salt spray as I eased the throttle open to nurse some warmth into the engine, before pointing the old twin up the hill and away from the harbour. A brightly coloured flycatcher plied her trade, swooping among the night time insects still caught in the fateful glare of an arc light, guiding traffic to the harbour entrance. The crumbling Honda's exhausts, ever louder, bounced their sound from the powdery facades of the plastered stone houses lining the road. I glimpsed snatches of life through windows, doors, down alleys and on porches. A woman washed her face and neck over a white porcelain bowl. Two dogs were locked in a tug of war battle over a disputed bone on brown earth a young mother swept clean; a young child by her feet rolled a coconut with a stick. An old man grinned as he held a laughing naked baby high over his head, ancient and new were all as one at the beginning of this, another, whole, wonderful day, the Gods' gift to mankind.

Struggling to get comfortable on the ragged saddle oozing cold Indian Ocean into the seat of my jeans, I wondered how many million miles I'd travelled so far in my own lifetime. Settling into what turned out to be my penultimate journey on the big blue Honda, three more thoughts occurred to me. One, for the first time in my life, I'd met someone with whom I wanted to have a family. Second, that we will never see such freedoms, nor such a golden age as the second half of the 20th century again. And third, that if my silent prayer in Kandy was granted, my great grandchildren would look back at this period of our history and say,

"My God! Those two were lucky, they were Elizabethans!"

15

The journey north to Colombo became progressively easier as the effects of the tsunami diminished with every mile. In fact, the last twenty miles ended up as a bit of a breeze in the cab of a big Tata truck, hauling a massive load of coconuts to market in the city.

So my extended journey north, which began on two wheels before I was rudely interrupted, way back down the coast, ended on six. My shotgun seat was surprisingly comfortable and I could eat as many coconuts as I wanted. I seemed to reach a natural limit at two and a half. Under my feet, wrapped up in a small shoulder bag was the first personal possession I'd acquired for what seemed like a lifetime. The driver didn't speak any English, but we got on fine with my smattering of Singhalese, sign language and swapping songs. We stopped at a big roadside café / baker's amongst Colombo's southern sprawl, for strong black tea and wonderful pastry hotdogs.

Both my new chum's hands were missing their second and third fingers, it didn't seem to affect his driving too much, and I didn't want to be nosy, but I wondered if it had been an accident, or if he was ex-military - an explosion maybe. Bombs were so regular in Colombo that working parents used separate routes to commute into the city, so their family would have a chance of one parent surviving.

It was hot, mid-afternoon, and the lunchtime rush was over. A waitress on a break who spoke English sat down at a neighbouring table, and as I defended the food and the sugar bowl from the omnipresent flies, she asked the question I couldn't, and the driver spoke with eloquence, honesty and pain.

He loved his truck, it was his living, and his home for days on end. It worked hard for his family, but it was the Bank's, not really his, and had regular inspections by them. On the rare days he got to drive it home, he spent a couple of hours maintaining, and cleaning it. On this occasion, he'd arrived unexpectedly to find his children alone, while his wife, as he'd long suspected, was spending the afternoon with another man. While he waited, in fury, for her return, he worked on his truck, then began to wash it. He was carrying his bucket for a refill from the well, when he caught his four-year-old son on the other side of the truck, scratching at the paintwork with a rock. He lost his temper, grabbed his son by the wrist, and smashed his fingers with the rock.

After the Police charged, then released him, he went straight to see his little boy, who smiled at his father and asked him, from his hospital bed, when his fingers would grow back?

When he got back to his truck, and studied the scratches on the side, he smashed the same fingers on both his own hands, that his son's surgeon hadn't been able to save, with the same rock his little boy had used to write,

'I love my Daddy.' in the dark maroon paintwork.

****

Riding a bike is so much better than sitting behind a windscreen, where you're separated from the journey, watching it like a television, through glass. On a bike, you travel through your surroundings as a part of the landscape, and all your senses are involved. But the truck's doors and a hatch in the roof had been removed to let at least some of the heat out, and we could smell rain ahead, the flowers, farms we passed, vegetables in the markets, the pungent citrus from roadside fruit stalls, cashews roasting, felt the changes in air temperature as we passed unseen lakes and rivers, the heat of the sun, and the gritty taste of the dust in our mouths from the fertile earth of the verdant island.

I try to avoid placing my life in other drivers' hands, particularly if they only have four fingers and two thumbs, but I'd seen he'd looked after his truck and its tyres before I'd got in and he was a competent, safe driver. He planned ahead and wasn't hurried, but made good, constant progress through the thickening traffic heading towards the city, smooth enough for me to close my eyes and not sleep, but get very close to it, my mind wandering.

They say you don't miss your water until your well runs dry, or maybe just fills up with seawater. The silhouette of the strange grey ship I'd seen two days before, cutting towards us from the horizon, had grown increasingly malevolent, the closer it had come to the coast. It had moored about a mile out to sea, low in the water, brooding and threatening, but she hadn't brought her battle group with her on this occasion, that was with the USS Abraham Lincoln off the coast of Indonesia. She was on her own, and like a bitch shaking off its fleas, around a dozen helicopters had sprung from the decks of the giant American carrier. The Cavalry hadn't arrived just yet, but drinking water had.

The choppers came in low over the beach, gently dropping big black plastic tanks the shape of giant Daleks, full of fresh drinking water the warship was desalinating, at a rate of 90,000 gallons (US) a day. The shock and awe wasn't quite as intense as if we'd been under its fire, but the power, reach and sheer presence of the ship was far more than impressive. What had arrived was an immensely powerful weapon of war, capable of destroying cities, armies, aircraft and airports. I remembered some useless statistic I'd read once, that moored in the English Channel in 1940, the ship could have finished world war two in under a month, and I could believe it.

Had the USA taken sides and chosen to fight the LTTE, one of the most feared, and committed rebel armies ever, it is open to conjecture how quickly the carrier could have ended Asia's bloodiest and longest civil war. Unknowingly, an unforeseen effect of the USA's and the West's benign support following the tsunami, was to tilt the balance in favour of the Government forces in the war, then over a quarter of a century old. Colombo quickly became the funnel for what was to become aid of very substantial levels, denied to the Northern districts controlled by the LTTE; the north western coast within its control was badly hit by the tsunami. Tamil villages like Pandirupu, Karaithivu, Thambiluvil and Thirukovil were all completely destroyed, along with the crucial boat landing and unloading facilities the LTTE relied upon for armaments and supplies. The tsunami had left them few alternatives other than to allocate already limited funds purely to survival, which in its own way fundamentally changed the course of the civil war. Though rare, events of such magnitude in the middle of campaigns are often decisive; ultimately, success is determined by the resourcefulness, intelligence and ability of a fighting force to adapt its operational approach to a changed environment.

155

Thirty-three months after the tsunami's monstrous waters receded, they finally washed away the blood of very nearly thirty years of civil war. Until the LTTE's final defeat in May 2009, completely sealed off from the world's media, their backs to the sea, in a cataclysmic, bloody final stand behind civilian shields at Mullivaikal, their fight for independence cost over seventy thousand lives, fifty percent of which, unforgivably, were children.

Heavily outnumbered, in twenty-two fierce battles fought two thousand one hundred and seventy years before, the Singhalese national liberation army raised, trained and led by Dutugemunu, finally defeated the warlord Elara's occupying Tamil forces. The victor became King, and saved Sri Lanka from becoming an unimportant, southern Indian colony. He stamped out the corruption and exploitation of the country's resources that had been endemic amongst the rich and the ruling classes, many of whom had colluded with the Tamil invaders. He restored the traditional ruling system based on Theravada principles, and prosperity returned to the island. Schools, universities and hospitals were built every ten miles, children got access to education, and migration of the cleverest graduates spread Singhalese learning, engineering, expertise and culture across India, Afghanistan and China. During this period Dutugemunu also began construction of the astonishing buildings and monuments that survive to this day.

At its apogee, the LTTE controlled a third of Sri Lanka; apart from its military, capable of demonic violence and self-sacrifice, it had its own police force, Judiciary and Government, although its chief, Velupillai Prabhakaran was often described as a dictator. Every life on the island was affected by the conflict; the military budget caused financial deprivation throughout the fabric of Sri Lankan society, which lived in genuine, constant fear of terrorist attacks.

Everyone who has contributed to China's commercial resurgence has also helped in the LTTE's final defeat. The link is tenuous, but real. Sri Lanka turned its back on the finger-wagging West and embraced a new courtier in the East; it was largely Chinese weaponry, (including, some witnesses allege, chemical weapons) and the terms on which it was supplied that enabled Sri Lanka's Government forces to deliver the final victory, promised by Prime Minister Rajapakse during his election campaign. We can only hope Sri Lanka's incumbent rulers show the same magnanimity and philosophy of acceptance for all peoples in victory as Dutugemunu, and return the country to a new and open, second golden age.

China's return for its generosity is the development of a 700-acre site in the bay of Colombo, Dubai style, reclaimed from the Indian Ocean. 'Colombo City' will be overlooked by a massive new 7-star hotel, built by the Shanghai Hotel Corporation on the site of the disbanded Army camp that existed for years on the Galle face, in the centre of the city.

One of the final pieces of China's energy supply jigsaw is the new development of a massive commercial port funded 85% by China, 15% by the Sri Lankan Port Authority on the southern coast of the island, overlooking the main Asian - European shipping lanes at Hambantota, a small market town devastated in the tsunami, one of its strategic, 'Pearls of the Indian Ocean'.

The tsunami just accelerated decades of planning by Beijing to make it more difficult to cut off their oil supply. China imports the vast majority of its oil and gas via the narrow Strait of Malacca, between Malaysia and Indonesia. At the mouth of the strait sits India's Andaman and Nicobar Islands' naval base, and the USA has a large naval presence in the area. The Chinese have always feared a blockade. Its 'string of Pearls' strategy is a chain of bases across the Indian Ocean to protect its tankers in emergency, or war.

The same technique of military support has been used in China's concurrent courtship of Burma's military junta, supplying £800 million of tanks, fighter jets and weaponry to its southern neighbour in 2010 alone. The prize has been the agreement of a 'golden bridge of friendship', to let China develop facilities at the deep sea Burmese port of Kyauk Phyu, where oil and gas from Chinese tankers will be pumped through a brand new 500 mile pipeline to its Yunnan province.

As China flexes its financial muscles, expanding its economic influence across the region, using profits from the goods it sells to the West, an eventual Chinese military presence at both new ports is inevitable.

Perhaps the LTTE's most significant bequest to the rest of the world is the suicide bomber, invented as the only sure way they could get close enough to Rajith Ghandhi to kill him in 1991, retribution for what they saw as his collusion with Colombo's Government, and the fated imposition of an Indian Army peacekeeping force in the north of the island.

But, as with just about every recent major natural disaster, it was America that steamed to Sri Lanka's immediate aid. Along with the aircraft carrier's capacity to destroy runways, and therefore control the air, it also began demonstrating its ability to clear and repair them afterwards. Earth moving equipment, bulldozers and machinery I can't even describe was

157

airlifted ashore, beginning the job of opening up the disaster zone to the outside world by starting to clear the arterial main coast road, patching up or replacing its bridges with temporary military structures. I hoped it wouldn't be long before the aid agencies brought their own unique, sometimes obscene, blend of help, coercion and corruption to the island, along with the innate incompetence and monumental waste they demonstrate with predictable regularity.

Sure enough, being flown into a major rice producing and exporting country, ton after ton of unneeded rice would soon begin disgorging from their chartered planes landing at Colombo airport, branded with the charities' logos, in the knee jerk knowledge that press photographs and television images would be beamed around the world, boosting donors' morale, and encouraging others to give. The rice flooded the island, destroying agricultural production as surely as if the tsunami had reached the inland rice farms themselves. The influx spawned a new black market all of its own, depressed prices to the point of collapse and compromised the businesses of honest, hard-working farmers and merchants.

I was running out of songs to exchange with the truck driver who seemed to have a never ending supply, having to really scrape the barrel with a medley of *The Battle Hymn of the Republic*, *Born Free* and *The Sheik of Araby*, each one blending into the other as I ran out of lyrics. I think that was enough for both us, we fell into silence and I went over the day I'd spent sitting next to Samanda's hospital bed, he'd recounted the journey north with Marian, and explained why she hadn't travelled back down south with him. When she'd unpacked, she'd found the old '78 record I'd hidden away, broken clean in half. The case must have been dropped, or hit somewhere in transit, and the fragile old record cracked in half, delivering the exact opposite of the message I thought I was leaving her to find. Falling in love again, never wanted to. And now broken. Off. The best laid plans......

There had been no cell phone signal in the north of the island. I thought it was odd she hadn't found a landline in three weeks, but now I knew the real reason for her silence, the reason she'd thrown herself into her assignment, working hard, taking risks, and the reason she didn't board the Queen of the Sea with Samanda, early on the morning of December 26th. The hand of fate made a long dead German singer reach out from the grave, and saved her.

Dusk was beginning to fall quickly across the city as I picked up the bag containing Samanda's beautiful silver shell that had miraculously survived the train wreck. I felt I was nearly at the end of what seemed like the longest road I'd ever travelled. Gently nursing a fiery hip joint, I watched the truck's back lights until they were swallowed by the heaving morass of Colombo's predatory evening traffic, hunting for gaps, hungry for progress. I'd left the remnants of my footwear on the floor of the truck and bedraggled, filthy, dressed in rags, black, bloodied and blue, I limped on bare feet into the hotel, and stood at the front desk like an errant school-boy sent to explain his behaviour to the headmaster.

The receptionist asked me if I needed a doctor.

Ten minutes later, I was standing on the balcony of a beautiful, teak panelled room, overlooking an unruffled Indian Ocean. The water was darkening under a twilight sky bruised with purple cloud, as the rim of the day's giant tropical sun melted into a dazzling orange horizon.

With the modern conveniences of working phones, and the internet we take so easily for granted, all it took was three phone calls, an email, and an indiscreet picture editor in Antwerp to find out the biggest news story to hit the region in living memory had of course, kept her in the country.

Looking back now, it's easy to see how close I was to a total breakdown, constantly on the edge of tears, and no matter how desperate I was to see her, I wasn't physically capable of retracing my steps; it would have been impossible to find her anyway. I needed to try and calm the emotions churning inside me. And rest, and sleep, and not remember my dreams upon waking, and try not to feel guilty when I ate. I consumed far more time than was necessary making the arrangements for Samanda's transfer to the best hospital in Colombo. It was a useful displacement activity, among many others I was able to invent.

I began preparing in my mind to go back, but knew I wasn't ready; we must have been very close, we may unknowingly even have passed each other, travelling in different directions, but I'd found out she'd been stay-ing in a hotel just a short tuk-tuk ride from my own, and figured I'd get myself together and wait for her to come back there.

I let some people know I was OK, some of whom, I'm quite sure, were disappointed. The phone calls home and abroad generated substantial promises of cash for the work that needed to be done - there was to be no escape from the direction my life was destined to take. There were even moments of normalcy. I looked at some emails, mostly serious, pitifully banal under the circumstances. One contained an extract from one of Sir Laurence Olivier's last interviews. he'd been asked whom he believed would be the world's greatest actor after his own death, unhesitatingly naming Jackie Chan, disclosing he found it very difficult to leave his house, without watching the final nine minutes of *Drunken Warrior*.

The sound of a stranger's laughter in the hotel lobby made me swing round in the swivel chair to look, only to see a big empty space, but in many ways it was a stranger's. I'd checked him out earlier though, in the depths of the beautiful old mercury mirror in my suite's dressing room, meeting his eyes for the first time in quite a while, and was surprised to see something worth keeping there. And hope.

I wanted to see her first, before she saw me. I knew it would give me a chance to get used to the idea of being close to her again, assemble all the things I wanted to say in some sort of order, and be calmer when I said them, without the rush of emotion I knew could overwhelm me otherwise. So I decided to hang out by her hotel pool; she loved the water and a swim is hard to resist after a long, hot journey.

So I found a shady table, tucked away in a corner, with a view over the immense, green-blue, sparkling pool, and a backdrop of coconut palm amongst immaculate lawns and bright borders, being manicured by an army of smartly uniformed gardeners. It was totally surreal. Obscene, and impossible to believe that while I sipped golden, broken orange pekoe from porcelain, delivered on a silver tray while I sat next to grass being cut with unnecessary precision, only a short distance north and south lay total devastation and unimaginable horror. But it only confirmed what I'd known all along, I'd just been fooling myself trying to get here, and the fact that Colombo was functioning normally, was in fact, vitally important. Without this, it would have been so much more difficult to go back and help dress the wounds of this most beautiful island, to begin a healing process from which it would eventually emerge, scarred but stronger, more stable, forgiving, and richer in every way.

It was blisteringly hot, but cooler in the shade by the water of the hotel's kidney- shaped pool, and the background noise of Colombo's traffic had faded to a distant, early afternoon whisper. Nobody was swimming, the smattering of guests lounging away lazy lunches, or putting off what they were supposed to be doing to finish a chapter, a cigarette, a drink, a dream. The sound of the eight whirring wings of two dragonflies, fearsomely handsome, bounced off the unruffled surface of the water and woke me from my own reverie. They darted and hovered, darted and hovered above the perfect flat glass of the pool, catching insects inbound to the harvest of nectar on offer from the cascade of bright crimson bougainvillea, tumbling down the side of the hotel's whitewashed walls.

I'd checked in, and waited, every day, for five days in a row, moving to the lobby in the evenings, until I'd made friends with each shift of the hotel's staff. The growing number of envelopes next to the key to her room with my messages on the hotel notepaper, remained unopened in their little pigeonhole. She never did return. Overseen by an assistant porter on his final shift before moving to a new job the next day, her bags had been collected from the hotel by the same taxi that eventually took her to the airport. The envelopes remained behind, forgotten.

Her mobile number rang, and rang, and rang, with no answer, or answer phone service. I didn't know what I was going to do next, where I was going to start, or even where to go.

I never found out who had tucked the agency's business card, with Marian's name on it, under my change in one of the folding leather wallets the waiting staff used to present the hotel's bills. It was only by chance I'd opened my final one, as an afterthought, just to swap the small denomination notes for a couple of dollar bills. I left a hundred instead.

To whomever it was, thank you, from the bottom of my heart.

16

It was one of the furthest flung conquests of the Empire, a malarial posting largely despised by its military and administrators alike, and a very long way from their power base in Rome. Legionnaires suffered constant attack from disparate and feral warring tribes across the lengthy and vague borders of the region. The most ferocious and bloody were launched on their northernmost garrisons by war-painted men, fighting in animal skins and skirts. They launched attacks at random, appearing from nowhere, then melted away into the rugged terrain. It was brutal, crude warfare that forced the Empire to invest heavily in defending its fortified military emplacements.

The Romans introduced currency in coinage to the backward, backwater barter economy they inherited, then collected it back in taxes to help offset the high price of their occupation and rule. But it was far outweighed by the riches of the province's mineral wealth, and its fertile agricultural land that fed the Empire's insatiable appetite for food, wine, and the natural resources it needed to survive.

The land remained coveted and ravaged by war for more than 1,500 years after Rome's departure, but its capital city I now found myself in, had not only survived the Italian and subsequent French occupations, but every other raid and invasion by its warring neighbours, steadfastly straddling the snaking river that had carried its trade for thousands of years. It had endured pandemics of the most terrible diseases, fires that razed huge swathes of the tightly packed wooden buildings, aerial bombing raids by aircraft, much feared pilot-less drones, and bombs planted in crowded buildings by shadowy paramilitary forces. Yet the spirit and humour of its ecumenic citizenry continued to surmount it all.

There was a strong smell of stale urine from the stygian gloom of the narrow alleyways that cut between the tall, century-old oven-baked clay buildings lining both sides of the choking street, where East was meeting West in cacophony. Fumes from the heavy traffic swirled around a stoned junkie beggar, slumped in the rubbish-strewn doorway of a deserted shop on the far side of the street. Its crooked windows were boarded with cheap wood, covered in posters advertising musical concerts, places to eat and stay and political meetings, all surrounded by strange shapes painted in primary colours.

Decay and resurgent life bustled for supremacy all around me. A tall thin Sikh, with the handsome, fierce features of a sub-Himalayan Pathan, framed by a magnificent, long black beard, tossed a thick, dull gold coin into the beggar's plastic cup. The mournful eyes that looked up in recognition of the contribution to the next bag of smack didn't belong to the junkie - hers remained closed in opiate dreamland - but to a young brown and white mongrel, tied to it's mistress's wrist by some cheap, frayed string.

To the left of the derelict shop was a unisex hairdresser's. I'd never seen a man with jewels in his hair before, and it drew me to the scene inside. Nimble, skilful fingers worked glittering jewellery and beads into delicate braided patterns on a row of heads. A separate team of experts painted nails in exotic colours and designs, while their immaculately dressed customers sat under big brown conical driers, baking the braids. The meticulous pride in their appearance shamed the way Plaistow Patricia and I were both dressed.

'Rabwah Greens' was the bright yellow painted Halal butchers and Arab greengrocers to the right. 'Goat Meat', 'Oxen Tale & Darling Spices' were advertised in crude black handwritten letters on the walls. From my vantage point sitting outside the market food stall where I waited, I listened to the multiple languages being spoken around me, and watched all the comings and goings from my high stool. The elderly Mongolian, or maybe Tibetan gentleman next to me I'd tried to engage in conversation either couldn't speak, couldn't speak English, couldn't be bothered, or didn't want to interrupt his fried Ghanaian Tilapia fish, red beans and rice.

I took a sip of my coffee, another nibble of cranberry and pistachio nougat, and turned towards him in persistence, only to find he'd slipped away while my eyes were surveying the scene across the road. His seat had been taken by the peroxide-blond West African taking a breather from selling cassava, snake gourds, watermelon and thin green drumsticks from his fruit and vegetable stall opposite the little cafe. My waitress appeared with a huge grin featuring magnificent, flawless teeth, and an oval plate of food. Her thumb was drowning in a garishly coloured pool of pulses swamping two chickens' eggs, a bright juicy red fruit cut in half, full of green and yellow seeds, minced offal in a tube and black fungi, delicate gills flecked with garlic, next to a thin, crispy oval patty of mixed vegetables.

A small brown and black bird nesting above me on a steel truss supporting the high glass roof of the market pottered around under my seat, pecking at the crumbs left by my predecessors. I ate too, picking at the platter and the Urdu patter of a man of the street, hawking an alleged cheap mobile phone service from the cracked pavement at the entrance to the market. He had a sideline of English language-school fliers he was foisting on unlikely looking prospects.

The olive skinned girl who stepped off the bus, elegant in her emerald green headscarf, wasn't what I was expecting, nor were her heavy Dr. Martin shoes, peeping incongruously from the long black, Muslim outfit. She stepped off the bus in the famous air soles onto the street, which was covered with so many patterns and stripes, criss-crosses, zigzags and circles painted in blue, red, white and yellow, you could hardly see the patched grey tarmac beneath. A bunch of keys appeared from a side pocket of the shapeless gown, she swung the office door of the photographic agency open for business and ten minutes later I'd followed her up the stairs to the black leather, glass and matt grey walls of the office. And she was asking me a question.

"How can I help you Sir?"

"Well, I've been beyond help since about 1984, but I was wondering if you could put me in touch with this photographer?" I said, pushing the primrose yellow card across her thick glass reception desk.

"Ah, yes, Marian's one our best freelancers. Let me take a few details - what's the assignment please?"

"It's a wedding."

"I'm sorry sir, I don't think that's something Marian would undertake - not her sort of assignment at all, she tends to work rather further afield. We have two or three specialists in the agency who I'd recommend for that sort of event. Let me look." she said, glancing at the screen of a neat little laptop.

"Who are the happy couple?"

"It's Marian. And me."

She peddled the party line of course, data protection,

"I'm sure you understand that I can't give out personal details like that - you could be anybody. Why don't you just ring her - look, her mobile's on the card?"

It wasn't a bad question, but she was good enough to keep her sense of humour, give up her lunch hour and listen to a précis of this story over vegetable curry, puri and sweet lassi. She knew no one could have ever made it all up and ended up telling me so many things about Marian of which I had no idea, it made me realise how little I really knew about her.

She trusted me enough to promise me not to let her know I was searching for her, but not enough to give me an address. I paid the bill at the counter, and she was already standing, hands resting on the back of her chair when I got back to the table. She thanked me for the meal and answered my final question before I'd asked it, holding one index finger against pursed lips. She looked down with her almond eyes, drawing my gaze to her other index finger, gently tapping Marian's card.

Dodging through the crowds, I followed the thick, cloying perfume of tiger lilies straight back to the Frangipani tree and the little blind girl's cold, scared hand, and around a corner to a flower seller's stall. Seas of stark colour flanked a head-high marble plinth, on which towered a regal Roselieb statue of a twentieth century king, looking down upon his people in magnificent regalia, clasping a vicious looking sabre under a flowing bronze cape.

I slid past an open fronted shop in the wide train station entrance selling hooker pipes, batteries, cigarette papers, pan scourers, cheap jewellery and bottled water, everything you need for a train ride really. I was still enjoying the flavours of my full English breakfast as I queued for a ticket behind a tall, upright African gentleman wearing a brightly patterned cotton skullcap and a silver jacket, which glowed in the diminishing light as we descended to the platforms of Tooting Bec undergound station.

It was only a few minutes' ride from here to where London's latest bombings were carried out by misguided religious zealots taking their own, and fifty seven innocent lives, on a bus, and tube trains. The low down electric torque of this one thrust us into the shadows of the northbound tunnel with a familiar whine, as I wondered about the rucksack bombers' grasp of history. What had they hoped to achieve with their home made nail bombs where Bubonic plague, Adolf Hitler and Hermann Goering's

Luftwaffe, William of Orange and his band of Normans, the Vikings, Hadrian Caeser and the Roman Empire, the Great Fire, the Saxons and the IRA, inter alia, had all failed?

Now then, a doodlebug - those little bastards were really scary.

I'd waited until I'd found a seat under the wide, curved glass of the train's windows. Heart in my mouth, surrounded by the lilting songs of a gaggle of excited Japanese students, like a gambler lifting the corner of a crucial final card from the baize, I turned over the worn yellow rectangle. And there she was, in the palm of my hand, still out of reach, just; one final journey.

One of the students' iPods was leaking *Fool on the Hill*. The Beatles may have been from Liverpool, but it was here in London they made their name, and recorded the songs that inhabit the mental iPods of billions of people around the world. The art form they perfected was the most important of the twentieth century, far outweighing any other, including literature, and film. They rescued the dying embers of rock and roll, and triggered an explosion of creativity that continues to this day, and not only in music, in one of the greatest triumphs of British culture.

It wasn't the first time I'd thought I must be crazy, and I'm sure it wasn't going to be the last. I was wondering if I was going to be able to swing my leg over the bike at all; I still couldn't lift my arm above my shoulder, and one-handed, I was really struggling to break the whippy little branch off the tree that had grown across the door. I guess that's why they make walking sticks and hammer handles out of ash. In the end I let it have its way and tied it back with some strapping nylon I found in a builder's skip. I only needed one door anyway, and walked through it, into the dust and gloom of a life I hardly recognised. I apologised to the big house spider I made homeless, knocking her off the foot pump, and lifted up the green canvas cover. After I'd got them to the right pressures, I lowered the tyres off the stands to the ground, bolted on a battery, tested the brakes and gave the old girl a drink. She was thirsty.

I hadn't felt this cold for so long it was practically fun. The sun had followed me across the world and finally showed its face, but the travelling had watered it down to a mere shadow of its tropical self. It only had the strength to jab low carat fingers of light through the dark, stark silhouettes of a line of winter's leafless trees. They flanked a cathedral, brooding high on a green hill, not so far away from the broad Tarmac ribbon of an ant-free A3.

The RC45 was pleased to remind me why she'd been a kept woman all this time, flashing her long legs at me, trying to provoke me into slipping her leash. Once we'd both got used to each other's company after so long apart, I didn't exactly give her her head, just allowed her to nod it in the right direction for a moment, but the vicious stab of pain it provoked in my shoulder was enough of a reminder that we'd have to keep going steady for a while, before repeating any serious vows.

Heading southwest out of London, she tugged and growled about her restraints on the long, low climb across the flowing beauty of Surrey's ancient hills. I looked hard right across my shoulder for the view I knew was there over the vast basin that contains London, but the only clue that the city even existed under the low blanket of fog, were the jets stacking high in their queue for Heathrow's runways. We curved hard right around a narrow rim of road through tendrils of mist rising from the eddying, shrouded depths of the vast crater before Hindhead, known as the Devil's Punchbowl. The close proximity to its neighbour, Gibbet Hill, must have filled the condemned souls that were hanged there, with terrible dread. Well, the guilty and the unsure at least, I guess.

The light strengthened, picking out signs to ancient hunting villages. 'Grayshott', * with its lakes of Waggoners' Wells, an immemorial watering hole for horses and travellers between Portsmouth, on England's South coast, and London. 'Welcome to Hampshire - Jane Austen Country' said another. Then, 'Bramshott' , with its immaculate Canadian military cemetery, for those brave men who never made it home from the slaughter of twentieth century wars. Or, with cruel irony, the last great influenza pandemic that followed, which took so many survivors' lives. Here they'll stay for evermore, among the tens of thousands of acres of one of the most beautiful landscapes in the world.

The journey was broken by traffic lights at a crossroads. I sat upright, tucked my gloves inside the fairing, searching for heat from the motor and inspiration, watching early commuter traffic give a wide berth to a solitary horse and rider, ambling lazily across the junction. I double-checked as usual, making sure it wasn't John Bingham ** riding Shergar. Pathetic. Particularly compared to the thoughts greater minds than mine have had, sitting at traffic lights. Leo Szilard for example, conceived the idea of a nuclear chain reaction, not at Hindhead, but not too far away, while staring at a red light in London's Southampton Row. I dwelled on the pro-

---

* A 'shott' is a funnel shaped, fenced area into which herds of deer were driven, then trapped at the narrowest point, where animals were more easily captured and slaughtered.

** John Bingham latterly became better, and subsequently, notoriously known as Lord Alfred 'Lucky' Lucan.

found effect one person can have upon humanity, and the connection between traffic lights and the end of the world. As a student, before he'd fled the Third Reich, he stopped a lecture in Berlin by Albert Einstein with a stiff rebuke.

"But Herr Einstein, what you have just said is nonsense." And he was right.

On a hot day in Long Island in July 1939, arguing with his driver, (the future Nobel Laureate winner Eugene Wigner), with or without the inspirational effect of traffic lights, Szilard finally found where Einstein was living, and explained to the twentieth century's greatest scientist how nuclear chain reactions could be achieved.

"Daran habe ich gar nicht gedacht." * he said.

Einstein's subsequent letter to Roosevelt triggered the Manhattan Project.

I paddled with one foot, slipping the clutch for the tall first gear, and started singing along inside my helmet to Eddie Cochrane's *Three Steps to Heaven*. It doesn't mention Gibbet Hill.

At this time of year in northern Europe, the sun was never going to reach too high for the sky. But as we descended towards England's southern coastal plain, it was blunting some of the cold teeth of the biting wind that had probed every nook and cranny of my leathers, in a relentless search for flesh. Shadows on the verges under the thick high hedges bordering the fields remained white with a stiff hoar frost; three rabbits grazed on the succulent shoots of winter barley in sunlit patches. Two crows played chicken with the traffic flashing over the corpse of a young fox in the nearside lane, a victim of the night. A pair of kestrels circled overhead, weighing up the odds below.

Even though I knew exactly where it was going to be, and promised myself not to let it get to me, my eyes locked onto the horizon as soon as the dark, steel blue grey of the English Channel appeared. I was still nowhere near bolting the door onto what I was suppressing; in fact, I'd only just got it closed and was leaning with my back against it, frantically searching my pockets for a key, still panting with all the trauma, and the effort. There was, of course, no malevolent tsunami in the distance, and the Honda beneath me this time, rode calmly on the short run along the coast. But I relived those moments when the tsunami devoured me, and was still shaking so much at the check-in booth, I couldn't even grip the ignition key to switch off the engine. A member of the crew had to do it for me, and embarrassingly, even open a zip pocket for my documents. I

---

* "I hadn't thought of that."

168

apologised and lied, told them it was the cold.

The big grey catamaran sat low in the dockside water, more predatory insect than feline. I gulped at a huge, unforgivably, cold, Cognac on board, served by a surprised barman, and the tremors of the turbines spinning up beneath me, took over from my own. A dozen or so gulls that had been patiently awaiting our departure on a railing suddenly disembarked, wheeled into the air above us, and screeching, dived like Stukas, searching for seabed bounty, tumbling inside the churning wake we left between the bristling, grey, anchored gunships of the Royal Navy.

As the harbour speed limit disappeared behind us, darker, bottle green shades signified deeper water below. The gulls were reduced to squabbling with each other, and the skipper gave the turbines free rein, pointed his insect towards northern France and she rose up from the water, on sleek twin hulls, to become the graceful feline Seacat she was designed to be.

Travel gives us time to while away, or use to our advantage. J. P. Donleavy's *Ginger Man* had boarded with me, to retell his tragic tale of innocent love and I dwelled upon this most mysterious emotion, so much of which we learn from fiction, so little from those best placed to tell us. I stared at the white caps without noticing their passing, thinking the very first thing most of us are lucky enough to experience is the pure and selfless embrace of parental love; we absorb it, quite naturally, for it is one of nature's great protective driving forces. The love of friends is often undervalued, but natural, particularly when young, the love of siblings seemingly impossible to resist, through shared emotion, experience and in the security of the lee wind of family life.

But navigating through the straits of adult, sexual romantic love, often with the prospect of a lifelong domestic partnership is fraught with every imaginable difficulty, yet is the most sought after facet of our lives. Passionate monogamy is celebrated as the highest achievement in my culture, in film, music, poetry and fiction. It's eagerly promoted by Government through taxation and welfare as a social regulator, and blessed by the Christian church as a Holy union. Nobody would dream of making such an enormous decision based on any other emotion - rage, jealously, envy, greed, misery - it would be absolute lunacy, yet here I was, following a girl around half the world after a chance encounter in a foreign land that lasted only a few short days. Yet my whole body and soul was aching to see her again, the need to be with her, all consuming, my stomach so knotted up with the possibility of her not wanting to see me, I wouldn't even try to call her mobile phone in case she told me so, before I had a last chance to be with her. I'd never have left Kildare to die in Ireland without me. What hubris, what self regard? Why better to have, and lost, than never? Why such madness?

Because love's unfolding emotion enables us to rise above the pain and brevity of our lives, where we find the only true human happiness, sharing so much with our other, he or she becomes ourself, and vice versa. This transforms our lives and their bathetic endings into something far greater, timeless, uplifting our souls to transcend the mundane futility of our existence into a lifelong journey of fulfilment and wonder, our unions perpetuated into eternity through our descendants. And I'd known Marian was my other from the moment I looked down on her, from my perch in the Banyan tree by the bank in Tangalle, and I was ever closer.

With every mile, southwest towards the Atlantic, through Normandy's fallow fertile patchwork of fields and hills to the ancient abbey of Mont St. Michel, the late sky cleared to just tiny patches of alto-cirrus, which glowed orange with the promise of a perfect day to follow. I hunched further forward, stamped down a gear and the cold wind tugged at my helmet, as the V4 howled at the rising moon. There was no time to lose.

I'd slept quickly, and heavily with the fatigue of the journey, waking just before first light. A plume of thick steam cascaded through the open window of my cliff top bathroom. The showerhead delivered its heaviest flow and the water as hot as I could stand on my aching neck and shoulders, as I watched the first shadows of the day race across the grazing polders in the distance towards the Abbey's majestic towers, on the granite island rising from the middle of the vast estuary. The tide was out, the river Couesnon, a silvered snake slithering its silt into the obscurity of the ocean.

Avranches drapes itself over the high cliffs that overlook the final stretch of the river, gripping the rock it's built on like candle wax, melted from the high spire of its church. Legend has it Archangel Gabriel appeared to its Bishop, St. Aubert, in 708, and instructed him to build a church on the small granite island that the tidal waters of the estuary had exposed over thousands of years, by slowly eroding the softer rocks surrounding it. It was neatly written in pencil on the back of Marian's card, her latest assignment, and my final destination.

Photo-shoot. Slated February 3rd-5th.
Mont St. Michel, Normandy
Client: Calavados Tourist Board

Out of courtesy to the other guests, I ran the Honda down the hill in neutral, flipped the kill switch to live, waited for the fuel injection pumps to prime up and bump started her into a lazy burble. I knew Marian would want to play around with lenses in the early light, and I wanted to try and get there before her. I needed that time to compose myself, get as much of the emotion out of me before we were face to face, so I didn't behave like a total arse when we finally met. I ran the bike gently through the wakening town; two lovers sat on three stone steps in front of a single white door, starting early, or finishing late? It was hard to tell. I thought they were smoking untipped cigarettes, but they both bit pieces off the thin white sticks in their hands at the same time.

Maybe I was still dreaming? I could still reach the images of the only one I was pleased to remember from the night, drifting back to sleep after short moments awake, luxuriating in the crisp, cool, thick linen sheets of an enormous bed. My white swan of the night was now fully grown to young adulthood, regal, powerful and proud, gliding her gentle descent, in bright sunshine, to the surface of a long, thin lake to land by her mate, waiting for her on the water. Caressing, nuzzling necks entwined under a majestic willow, bristling in a breeze, fingering the whitest tips of their feathers, stark against the soft, vibrant greens of summer, reflected on the surface of the lake.

Shutters were being raised on shops, joining the boulangers' whose lights had been burning while I was still dreaming. I could just make out the faint melody of *Good Vibrations*, floating through a doorway, following a waiter outside serving a hardy early customer Café au Lait, a croissant scattered with almonds and a shot glass of Calvados, the local apple brandy. I coveted all three, but swallowed some miles on the auto route instead, being a Beach Boy, harmonising with Brian Wilson's reflections,

"Close my eyes, she's somehow closer now,"

The N175 was fast, but I peeled off early to savour the soft light flooding the low coastal farmland. A crudely painted sign surrounded by the crimson remains of Virginia creeper, advertised another of autumn's legacies, the sweet local cider. Two broad, stocky farmers stopped and stared. The man, full beard, red cider nose and blouson, was herding brown and white milking cows through a gate, his wife straddled a roadside ditch in a floral dress, cardigan and rubber yard boots, attacking weeds with a billhook. Behind her, beyond a dormant orchard, a field full of lithe, chestnut

171

horses with neat winter coats, grazed, ignoring all of us.

Huge balls of mistletoe hung from the maple, sycamore and poplar lining the roads, displaying the purity of the Atlantic winds.

"I hear the sound of a gentle word,
On the wind that lifts her perfume on the air."

The locals have conspired to presage one of Europe's most beautiful monuments with plastic advertising, cheap, tacky buildings and shops full of hideous, tourist tat. But the gaudiness of the crude little out of season hamlet only accentuated Mont St. Michel's timeless beauty. I'd stopped as soon as it appeared, suddenly, around a bend, stunned by the enormity and perfection of the pre-medieval Abbey, perching above the twisting narrow streets, walkways and staircases of the granite island that supports it. I was the only vehicle on its causeway, unless you count the bicycle, ridden by a nun sporting a white, Maria von Trapp wimple, eggshell blue habit billowing behind her, coming towards me. She was young, mid-twenties and serene, didn't give me a glance, lost in her world, or prayer, or meditation, or maybe the sound of a Beach Boys harmony too.

"Softly smile, I know she must be kind".

It was a perfect, breezeless, mid-winter's day in northern Europe, weather that can sneak up out of North Africa on a southerly wind, and surprise you with its heat. If there's a few of them in a row, we call it an Indian summer. I've never known why. It was cooler by the water where the incoming tide was galloping through the bay, dragging the flow of the Couesnon back with it. Sea birds squatted on the current for a free ride back to the mudflats and wild banks where they'd hang out until the Atlantic retreated later on, then feast on whatever the ocean had scoured from the bed of the estuary, and left behind.

I'd climbed the steep, winding walkways from the ancient miniature town's (pop. 41) narrow street to the ramparts that fringe the Abbey halfway up, and swept the edge of the bay, with binoculars, looking east. I figured she'd want the rising sun behind her, to bank some safe distance shots to begin with, but I quickly realised she could have been anywhere along several miles of coastline and the only pictures she'd want to take would be the most difficult. I nursed a coffee and turned the yellow card over and over in my hand; I knew the number by heart anyway. I resisted the temptation.

I climbed higher to the next level, on a narrow staircase past a small, neat graveyard, cursing the flat soles of my Alpine Stars. I looked down on the small wooden tiles that roof many of the buildings clinging to the Abbey's skirts, and squinted at a million diamonds flashing from the surface of the tide, ripping past the island.

A small inflatable skipped diagonally across them - it took me a few seconds to pick it up with the binoculars, but suddenly, unmistakably, there she was, kneeling down in the skittish rubber boat, one hand on a grab handle, the other protecting an aluminium camera case from the buffeting and the spray.

The boat disappeared from view on the seaward side of the island and had slowed to a crawl by the time it reappeared at the little concrete landing ramp near the island's main entrance, a couple of hundred feet below me. There was a flash of glistening grey and crimson wetsuit as her pretty bare feet gripped the side of the boat, pushed and laughing, Marian disappeared into the freezing ocean waters, diving away from me, shimmering under fragmented glass, for a frighteningly long time. I held my breath too, but she won by miles, cruising to the surface a hundred yards away with languid ease, before an expert turn towards me. She cut across the current in a powerful, lazy crawl, copper hair streaming in languid water as she found the ramp beneath her and stopped, standing up, waist deep, sweeping her hair back, then hands held together, fingers meshed behind her head, breathing hard, refilling her lungs.

She'd lost weight, her breasts were flattened, neat beneath her taut wetsuit, wrapping feminine curves. A gold chain sparkled around her neck, her face dusted by new freckles; I watched the muscles in her gently sculptured arms tense as she scooped her hair back behind her ears. She was natural, no makeup, standing there gazing up at the great granite edifice, planning her next shot.

Life, and honesty, and care and humility shone from her face as I watched her prepare for her next pictures, tripod, lighting, cameras, meters, all arrived from the back of a neat blue and silver motor home parked close by. I retraced my stone steps down each staircase, until I was just inside the portcullis and drawbridge, behind the main entrance. The Hasselblad on the tripod was pointing straight towards me. Marian stooped behind it, making some adjustments. I guessed she was waiting for just the right number of tourists to be walking through the entrance with its ancient backdrop to make the shot, but not too many to make it seem crowded. I moved out of the shadows, walked quickly then stood, stock still, foreground centre shot, facing her in the bright sunshine where I knew I'd be out of focus.

She straightened up from behind the camera, and turned away to reach for something behind her.

"Marian, it's me. I've missed you so much."

She froze for a few seconds, then turned slowly to face me.

"Here, I've brought you something." I said, and held up Samanda's fabulous shell, glittering silver in the bright winter sunshine.

"I don't know where, but she takes me there.
Oh! My! My! What a sensation!
Oh! My! My! What elations!"

The End